THE ANCIENT OF DAYS

AN EPIC FOR ALL TIMES!

The roots of the story of Ronstrom are very old. Some lie hidden in the dreams of ancient man and some herald the quests of modern peoples. THE ANCIENT OF DAYS, however, is its own kind of book, told with excitement, vision, and the full scope of a greatly gifted storyteller. Though Ronstrom's message is an ancient one, it speaks to today's mysteries and our search for a way of life.

THE
ANCIENT
OF DAYS

IRVING A. GREENFIELD

THE ANCIENT OF DAYS is an original publication of
Avon Books. This work has never before appeared in any form.

AVON BOOKS
A division of
The Hearst Corporation
959 Eighth Avenue
New York, New York 10019

First Avon Printing, June, 1973.

Designed by Lila M. Culhane

AVON TRADEMARK REG. U.S. PAT. OFF. AND
FOREIGN COUNTRIES, REGISTERED TRADEMARK—
MARCA REGISTRADA, HECHO EN CHICAGO, U.S.A.

Printed in the U.S.A.

TO ANITA, RICK AND NAT FOR BEING THERE
WHEN I WAS WITH RONSTROM. . . .

THE
ANCIENT
OF DAYS

I

The sky is a dappled gray of swiftly moving clouds; the scent of snow is heavy on the air; and the wind, though it moans like a ravaged woman as it blows across the flat open land, rips at my face and hands like the teeth of a wolf.

I move at an even pace, keeping well behind the bear but never letting him get too far in front of me. I have been tracking him since the gray sky was several shades lighter than it now is.

I first saw him in the forest, many miles away on the side of the world where the sun disappears at the end of its journey across the sky. Twice I loosed my arrows at him, but each time the hand of the wind brushed my arrow aside. The second arrow struck the earth so close to him that he turned, reared up, and looked at me.

I stopped! Perhaps that was a mistake? Perhaps I should have rushed him and driven my spear deep into his belly, opening it to free his spirit with the gush of his blood? But I did not do that. I looked at him as he looked at me.

Standing on his hind legs, he was enormous. With his black lips parted in a grin, he nodded his head several times and then, just before he dropped down on all fours again, he waved his right paw at me, beckoning me to follow . . . .

I know that if I am to kill him, I must do it soon or I will lose him as the gray light deepens and becomes darkness. I will kill him to stop the angry growl in my stomach. Though I am a hunter, I have eaten no more than roots and rat meat for a long time. And there are those of my people who have not even had the meat of the rat. But I do not think of their empty stomachs. Even when I am in the circle of their huts, I shut my ears to the wailing of the old men and the cries of the children. I have heard the wailing of the old ones and the cries of the children all my life. I do not know why my people do not have enough food. Some old men say that a curse was put upon us, while others claim we have offended The Giver of Life. I listen, say nothing, and let them argue. They are foolish old men as they waste their time trying to explain why they go hungry. The least they could do is help the hunters catch more rats, squirrels, or even a rabbit. But squirrels and rabbits are very scarce . . . when I kill the bear I will have enough meat to keep my stomach filled, while the old men will still be talking.

The bear is still in front of me. The forest is well behind us. The land all around is flat, though off to the side, where the sun never travels, I see the dark smudge of some hills. But I do not like it here . . . it is a place where the spirits of men stay after they leave this world. The old people say it is holy ground.

Though I am not afraid, I am uneasy. The clouds have lost their shading and are now one continuous dark gray, like the color of slate where the Rock People live. I quicken my pace, drawing closer to my quarry. I can almost taste its meat and feel its warm blood ooze from between my lips. My stomach growls angrily for real meat.

Suddenly the bear pauses; I stop. My chest is heaving from the long hours spent trotting after him. I swallow huge gulps of air. The bite of the wind is even sharper than before. My body is wet with sweat.

The bear sniffs the air; I do the same. He has caught the scent of another animal. I, too, pick up the smell. It is not the reeky stink of a wolf, or the fetid odor of a rat.

In the fast failing light I look around. My eyes are better than the bear's. The scent is strongest to the right of the bear. I strain my eyes in that direction. The gloom is too deep for me to see anything. I slide off to the right. The odor becomes stronger, muskier . . . I know it is a man. But I still cannot see him. I move in closer. The bear has not moved. He stands where he stopped and moves his head from side to side.

I wonder if another hunter has been tracking the bear. If that has happened, we will kill the bear together and then we will fight for the carcass. One of us will die. The one who lives will have the bear and his stomach will be filled for a long time. That is the way of our people.

Of all the hunters among my people, the only one beside myself strong enough to kill the bear is Rigga. From childhood, when we fought over the first rat we killed, I knew that someday I would have to fight him again. It would then be for his life. Rigga knows this, too. I see it in his cold blue eyes every time he looks at me.

I move closer to the source of the scent until

I can see the man. It is not Rigga. This man is old, too old to flee . . . I stop!

From where I stand I can see him quite clearly. He is very old. The skins he wears are in tatters. He is facing the bear. Perhaps he has fallen asleep? My first impulse is to cry out a warning. As I begin to shout, I clench my jaws. His presence is a boon, not to be tossed away.

The bear has become more interested in him than he was in me, or perhaps the brute mistakes him for me. Regardless of the reason, the bear is confused. Killing him will now be easier. The old man is my bait.

I quickly circle to the right.

The bear detects my scent, and he begins to growl.

I move near the old man. He remains motionless. I see that he has a cowl of goatskin over his head.

The bear is now very angry. He rears up on his hind legs and, roaring out his challenge, he waves his huge forepaws in front of the old man.

The man does not stir.

I move closer. I place an arrow against the string of my bow, draw it and, sucking in my breath, I wait. The old man stinks.

The bear drops down on all fours and begins to run toward the old man. He growls angrily. Then suddenly, when he is very close, he rears up on his hind legs again.

I loose the arrow. The twang of the bowstring lives longer than the swooshing sound of the arrow as it rushes through the air. I nock another arrow and let it fly!

The first arrow has lodged in the throat of the bear. His last growl is more like a scream. The second arrow strikes him in the chest. He dances on his hind legs and vainly tries to tear the piercing agony out of his body. He falls forward, runs to one side, and again rears up.

I am still not sure that I have killed him. I leap up from behind the old man, and with my spear in my hand I run toward the stricken animal shouting: "I, Ronstrom, have killed you; Ronstrom the hunter . . . I, Ronstrom, have opened your body to free your spirit!"

I plunge my spear into his thick black-hair coat. When I pull it free, blood follows in a steaming gush. The bear struggles to his feet, turns on me, and tries to swat me with his right front paw. I laugh, dart to the left, and thrust my red-tipped spear into his chest, close to where one arrow is already lodged. The animal drops to his knees. His once ferocious growl is a pitiful bleat.

I pull my spear free. A stream of blood as thick as my arm pours out of him. He rolls on his side. He is dead or dying. I drop my spear and with my knife I quickly slit open his belly. To lessen the bite of the wind I rub his hot blood on my body. Even as I skin the animal, his heart is still beating. But by the time I have wrapped the hot bloody skin around me, his heart has stopped.

I stand up. The first few flakes of snow fall into the steaming pool of blood at my feet.

I gather a few twigs and pieces of dried grass to start a fire. There is little in the way of good wood on the flat land. So I rip up several large bushes.

Once the fire is well lit, I cut away two large chunks of meat from the hind quarter of the bear's carcass and throw them on the fire. The dripping fat makes the fire sputter and hiss. The meat is still red and dripping with blood when I take one of the pieces from the fire and begin to eat it.

The old man is seated in front of me. He has not moved nor said a word. But he has been watching me. In the red glow of the wavering firelight his eyes shine like bits of black rock. When I take the meat from the fire his eyes follow my movements, and when I swallow I can see the muscles in his scrawny neck work though he has chewed nothing.

I finish eating the first chunk of meat and skewer the second on the tip of my knife.

"Part of that is mine," the old man says. His voice squeaks like a boy's or a woman's. He bobs his head up and down under his cowl as though he is agreeing with himself.

"No," I answer. I lift the meat to my mouth and bite into it. The blood leaps up and runs into my dark beard.

The old man lifts his thin hand and points to the meat on the end of my knife. "Part of it," he says, "belongs to me."

I laugh and continue to eat. The old man has lowered his hand, but I do not like the way he is looking at me. There is something in his glowing black eyes that makes me uneasy. "Why are you here, old man?" I ask.

His lips draw back in a grin. Except for a few rotted stumps of teeth, his gums are toothless. "I have come here to die," he says.

I look around me. The snow is falling faster now, and the sound of the wind has changed from a moan to a howl. The bloody carcass of the bear is already white. I face the old man again. Drawing the skin of the bear more securely around me, I ask, "How are you called?"

"Gendy," he answers. "Gendy, the priest."

"The priest?" I ask. I do not know the meaning of that word, though I remember having heard it when I was a boy.

"In the service," he says, "of The Giver of Life. But that was long before you came out of your mother's body."

"That must have been many winters ago." I laugh. "The woman who was my mother has been dead for many summers."

"Will you share your meat with me?" he asks.

I shake my head. "It was I, Ronstrom, who killed the bear," I answer.

Gendy nods and in a voice just above the snap and crackle of the fire, he says, "Yes, it was you who killed him, but it was I who helped you."

I do not answer him. I eat the last piece of meat on my knife, leave the fire, and cut several more pieces of meat from the hind quarter of the bear. I take them back to the fire and put two of them into it. Then I sit down, look at Gendy, and say, "Tell me what you did."

He cocks his head to one side, but his eyes never leave my face. "I did nothing," he answers. "It was you who did the killing."

"Then what right have you to ask for meat?"

"The right of a hungry old man."

"All of the old men are hungry," I answer. "If you would stop talking and catch rats——"

"The right of a man who has been used by another," Gendy says.

I pretend not to understand.

"What would have happened if I ran away?" Gendy asks.

"I still would have killed the bear," I tell him.

Gendy shrugs his narrow shoulders. "Perhaps," he says, "if The Giver of Life had willed it."

15

It is pointless to argue with him or, for that matter, with any man who believes that The Giver of Life has anything to do with my killing the bear. Old men have peculiar ideas. I glance back toward the carcass of the bear. I have enough meat for a while. Besides, if I feed him, I could use him again. Good bait is as scarce as good game. I throw another piece of meat into the fire. "That one is for you," I tell him.

He nods and lifts his face toward the falling snow. His lips tremble and he makes low, throaty sounds.

"What are you doing?" I ask.

"I am praying," he says.

I laugh and stab the first piece of meat with my knife. I bite into it and tear off a good-size chunk with my teeth. It is juicy and when I chew on it my mouth fills with the taste of blood. My stomach stops growling.

I pass my knife over the fire to Gendy.

With it he removes the meat from the fire.

I watch him eat. His bites are small and he chews each piece of meat, sucking the juice out of it before he spits what is left into the fire. As I look at him, I wonder how long it will take him to die. I remember that he had said he had come here to die. Even though we are seated close to the fire, I cannot be sure there is death in his face. Perhaps it is because his wispy goatlike beard hides what I am looking for?

Gendy sucks his way through another piece of meat. I have had my fill and lean close to the fire to feel its warmth. The blood on the bearskin has begun to harden in the cold. It is still snowing and the wind is building a mound of it over the carcass of the bear.

"It was good to taste meat again," he says, licking his fingers.

"It is always good to eat meat," I answer.

Gendy nods and, looking straight at me with his shiny black eyes, he tells me that I am a fine hunter.

"The best!" I reply.

He chuckles and asks if there is none better.

"None," I reply, "though Rigga boasts to being my better."

He pulls at his goatlike beard and comments, "There is always one who boasts that he is better than another."

I do not know whether he has spoken for or against me, but I say, "I am strong, I am swift and the flight of my arrows and spear is true . . . I have taught myself the ways of the forest. . . ." My voice trails off. I think of nothing else to tell him.

"And Rigga," he asks, "has he not done the same?"

In truth, he has, and I nod.

"Then what makes you the better hunter?"

His question makes me shift my position. I have always known that Rigga is a good hunter, but I have always known that I am a better one. I look at Gendy and try to think of the words to explain why I am a better hunter than Rigga.

Gendy chortles and says, "And which of you has taken more women?"

Again I shift uneasily. Rigga's appetite for women is greater than mine. His reputation as a despoiler of virgins is greater than mine and no man's woman is safe if for some reason she has caught Rigga's eyes. As for myself, I too have used my manthing on both virgins and the women of other men. I have never used force, unless I took a woman as a prize of war in a raid on another people's camp.

Gendy waves his hand in front of him.

I take that for a sign that our conversation is over. I am glad that I do not have to answer his last question.

We are silent. I look into the fire and Gendy is staring at me. I think about the bear and compliment myself on having killed it.

"Once," Gendy says, "there were many bears in the forest."

His words make me feel as if he can see those words I speak inside my skull. I look up at him.

"There were moose, deer, and all types of birds. The people were happy. The children laughed and the old people were cared for by their sons and daughters."

I know he is talking nonsense. Old men and children always talk nonsense.

"The people worshipped The Giver of Life."

The fire is dying, and I get up and fetch more bushes and twigs for it. When I sit down again, I am cold and I pull the bearskin tightly around me. I wonder why Gendy, who is dressed in tatters worse than my own, does not feel the cold. Perhaps he is so old that he has no feeling? I know that when a man lives for many winters and his hair becomes white and his voice becomes like a child's or a woman's, his manthing fails him, and he feels no need to mount a woman. Gendy is that old, maybe even older.

"Those were good days," Gendy sighs, after I have settled myself at the fire.

"If the people had their bellies filled with meat," I say, "they must have been good days."

"No one went hungry."

I nod, though I do not believe him. For as long as I can remember, the children, as soon as they were able, and old people were left to hunt on their own. Those who found food lived. Those who could not hunt or scratch for roots and insect grubs died. I watched the woman who was called my mother die with the belly that swells up when it is empty, while I chewed on the neck of a rabbit.

Gendy bends his frail body closer to the fire. His black eyes are still on me and he says: "They made a wager——"

"They?"

"The Giver of Life and The Keeper of Darkness," he answers.

I am immediately sorry I asked.

"If The Keeper of Darkness won, then The Giver of Life would forfeit our people. We would then worship The Keeper of Darkness."

"And has he won?" I ask, hoping to hear the end of his nonsense.

Gendy pulls at his wispy beard. "No," he says, "not yet, even though he has smote our people with fire, flood, and famine. He still has not won. . . ." There is a kind of wild exaltation in the sound of his voice.

I do not like it; it makes me uneasy. Even his eyes seem to glow brighter.

Once more Gendy waves his skinny hand in front of him. He sighs deeply and bends closely to the fire. Snow has capped both of his skinny shoulders and topped his cowl. That he was once a priest—though I am still not sure what a priest did in the service of The Giver of Life—seems impossible, but it is even more impossible for me to imagine that he was once young.

The wind is howling and swirling all around us. I can no longer see where the carcass of the bear lies. And yet, where we sit there is only enough of the wind and snow to make us know that winter controls the land.

It is something to think about and I look into the fire. My thoughts do not take purchase of anything and I let the red image of the wavering flames fill my skull. The fire hisses, a twig crackles, and turns to white ashes. My stomach is filled and I am growing sleepy.

"There is a place," Gendy mumbles, "a place where the Rock People live, where the sun never crosses the sky——"

I stand up and shake my legs. I do not want to hear more old man stories.

Gendy rolls his eyes up to me. "I will tell you——" he starts to say.

"I do not want to know," I tell him sharply and I sit down again. "I am tired."

"There is a talisman in this place I speak of."

I put the last of the bushes on the fire. The flames leap at it, and it becomes flames too. I look through the fire at Gendy. He has not moved. When the flames fall below the level of our eyes, I see him nod.

"In a cave," he says, "halfway up a mountain with twin peaks that jut up toward the sky like the nipples on a woman's breasts when she is in her moment of passion. . . . Deep in this cave you will find it."

"A talisman," I sneer.

"It will make you stronger than you are, braver than your enemies, wiser than you ever thought you would be."

"Will it put meat in my belly when I am hungry?" I ask angrily. His jabbering about a talisman annoys me. I know what a talisman is. Some of the old people still wear them on their thin arms or around their scrawny necks. I even killed a man who had one.

Two summers ago I chanced on a strange man hunting close to the forest of my people. My arrow struck him in the leg and when I went to him I found him clutching a small blue rock. I ran my spear through him and then brought his head back to where my people were camped. His talisman did not help him.

"This is no small blue rock or bit of red metal," Gendy says.

His words startle me. I am sure he sees into my skull. Perhaps he is not a man? Perhaps he is a spirit? Such a thought sends waves of prickles up and down my back. It is one thing to fight a man, but how can a man do battle with a spirit? But he has taken food; with my own eyes I saw him suck the juices of the meat. That way he was no different from any other old man. I gather my courage and ask him why he has told me about the talisman. "Why, if it is as powerful as you say," I ask, "do you not go to the cave and take it for yourself?"

"I am too old," Gendy replies.

"But you were young once."

He shakes his head. When he moves the cowl remains in the same place as his face swings from side to side. "I am not the one," he says in a low voice.

I do not know what to say. I remain silent. I do not want or need his talisman. I have what I need, and my hand reaches out to touch my bow and spear.

"Remember," Gendy intones, "the twin peaks that look like the nipples of a woman's breasts when she is in her time of passion."

I still do not speak.

Gendy raises his face toward the black sky. Snow falls on his cheeks and quickly makes white smudges of his eyebrows.

Though I cannot hear him, I see his lips are moving. I know he is praying to The Giver of Life. Lest he start talking to me about some other nonsense, I stretch out close to the fire and, drawing the bearskin over me, I pretend to sleep.

How can I sleep after listening to Gendy's foolishness? His first story about how my people lived before the wager between The Giver of Life and The Keeper of Darkness would have been enough to keep me awake. To live without hunger is not to be alive. I shake my head, turn away from the fire, and close my eyes.

Again I try to sleep, but cannot. I am thinking about the cave and the talisman that is in it. If it is as powerful as Gendy says it is, then I would never again go hungry; I would always have meat in my belly. I know it is nothing more than an old man's nonsense. I roll toward the fire again and look at Gendy. He has stretched out. His face has snow on it. I do not know whether he is asleep or dead. If he is dead, he found what he came for.

I sit up. The fire is nothing more than glowing embers now. I do not understand why I am doing it, but I take the bearskin off my shoulders and throw it over Gendy.

He stirs, but does not wake.

I pick up my bow and arrows and spear. I take another look at Gendy and wonder if in some strange way he is using me for bait as I had used him? I silently slip into the dark abyss of howling wind and swirling snow.

II

I am engulfed by the falling snow and shrieking wind, and I quickly begin to regret what I have done. Had I been wiser, I would have waited until morning or, if I had to leave, I would have taken the bearskin. It was foolish of me to leave it with Gendy. Now even if I want to return to where the old man is, I cannot. The snow has obscured everything.

I move in the direction of the mountains, toward that portion of the sky where the sun never travels. But it is night, and because of the storm I cannot even see the fixed star to guide me on my way.

I keep my head bent, as though I am butting it against the raging wind, but it is the wind that is butting against me. I wonder if the talisman is worth the pain I feel?

Now and then I must pause to regain my strength. The mist of my breath forms strands of ice on my beard. Sometimes I shout my name above the sound of the howling wind. This is truly the land of the spirits, for I am sure I can see them move when the curtain of snow suddenly parts. I do not know if they are following me, but I sense another presence beside my own—something larger than myself. I feel it glide over me the way a huge bird swoops and turns in the air without ever moving its wings. To catch sight of it, I turn my eyes upward. Almost at once the falling snow forces me to close them.

The night passes and with the coming of the first light the wind and snow diminish and then cease. Just before the sun rises the gray clouds are streaked with reds, greens, and then yellow. The clouds scud across the sky and when the fullness of the sun moves above the rim of the earth the sky is a brilliant blue.

I look toward the mountains as I stop and rest. They are still a smudge on the blue sky. It will take me many days to reach them, and then I will have to find the mountain with the cave. I breathe deeply and continue my journey.

The brilliance of the sun on the snow hurts my eyes so that I am forced to keep them closed. But the hard whiteness seems to burn its way through my lids. My eyes throb with pain. Circles of reds, yellows, and oranges drift inside of them. It is still bitter cold.

By the time my shadow is very small on the white snow, I look toward the mountains. They are no nearer than they were at daybreak. I continue to move toward them and wait impatiently for the coming of night so that the light from the snow will not hurt my eyes.

The sun swings across the sky and finally dies in a red sky. A silver half-moon casts a soft light over the snow. I pause and wait until the fixed star shows itself before I continue my journey.

Though I have not eaten anything all day, my stomach does not growl. I do not feel hunger. I am eager to reach my goal; nothing else matters. I travel throughout the night, pausing only once to pass water. Steaming in the cold air, it rushes out of my manthing and stains the white snow yellow.

The night passes . . . another day is born and dies. Night comes again . . . it ends when a new day begins . . . the alternation of days and nights are strung together like white and black beads on the thread of my journey.

The mountains are no longer smudges against the sky. I can see them quite clearly. Some have caps of snow; others are just stony wind-swept summits.

By now what Gendy told me about the cave is branded into my skull. I think of nothing except the talisman. I wonder what shape it will have and whether it is made of red metal or yellow. Perhaps it is wood or some oddly shaped rock.

The mountains grow in size. I can see their ridges.

For some time I have been in the land of the Rock People. I have seen signs of their camps and several times I have seen a band of their hunters, but they have never seen me, even when I pass within a few paces of them. They are not truly great hunters.

I reach the base of the mountains late in the day, when the clouds cover the face of the sun. I stop. There are many more mountains than I thought there would be. I do not know which way to go to find the one with a cave halfway to its summit.

As I look up, I feel a brooding presence nearby. Something inside of me tells me to go to the left. I do, and quickly find myself in a narrow passageway. I follow it. I move through the twisting channel until I emerge on the other side of the mountain and in front of me is another mountain with twin peaks that look like a woman's nipples when she is in her moment of passion.

I break into a run, reach the mountain, and scramble up its flank. With goatlike agility, I leap from ledge to ledge. My heart is racing faster than my feet are moving.

As I climb higher, the wind becomes stronger. Powerful gusts hammer at my bloody hands, but I cling tenaciously to the side of the mountain, pressing myself against it as though it were the body of a living woman. My body is wet with sweat, and I feel more excited than I have ever felt while hunting or on the body of a woman.

Finally I see the cave! It is halfway to the top just as Gendy said it would be. The last few feet are the hardest. The rock face is very steep. My hands are bleeding. My face is cut, even my legs are badly bruised. I do not care because I am too close to my goal to stop for a mere cut or bruise.

I raise my bloody hands, gain a good strong hold on the ledge above, and with an enormous burst of strength I lift myself on to it. I stop. The cave is directly in front of me!

The beat of my heart is the beat of a drum. I stand up, take a deep breath, expel the air with a loud sigh, and commence to walk toward the entrance of the cave. I pause between each step, savoring the moment, enjoying the expectation of what I will find.

The opening to the cave is narrow, like a pair of lips, or a woman's slit. I must stoop to enter. Inside, the blackness is deep, and I see nothing. But I hear the frantic scurrying of small animals. And I hear the sound of the wind as passes across the narrow opening. I can also hear a pounding in my ears.

Slowly the blackness thins, and I see that the cave goes deep into the mountain, perhaps to its very heart. Off to the right is a large rock and on it is a stout piece of wood about the length of my arm and almost as thick as my wrist. I take the wood, cut some chips from it, and set fire to them. When they are burning, I place one end of the wood into the flames. In a short time I have a firebrand, and I begin to move deeper into the cave.

The passageway is narrow, and several times I am forced to bend my knees in order to pass beneath a rib of the mountain. I hold the torch in my right hand, and as I walk I look at the walls, hoping to catch sight of something that I might recognize. I know it is a foolish thought.

The quavering voice of the wind reaches back into the cave. Though I am out of the wind, I feel colder than when I was climbing up the side of the mountain. I am cold, and I am still sweating.

Without warning the tunnel widens and I find myself in an enormous gallery. The wavering light from my torch fails to reveal either its top or its sides. I follow a slope down to a lower level and not more than ten paces in front of me I see a huge circular rock. Certain that the talisman is on that rock, I quicken my pace. Suddenly that peculiar brooding presence is with me again, but I am too close to my goal to think about anything else.

I reach the circular rock and hold the torch over it.

There is nothing there . . . nothing . . . nothing is there except a few bits and pieces of rock . . . a circle of stones!

"The talisman!" I shout. "Where is the talisman?" The echo of my voice mocks me.

Tears come to my eyes. I have not cried since I was a child, and now I stand and weep. There is no red metal, no yellow metal, and nothing of wood.

"I found the cave," I sob. "I found the cave."

Through the blur of my tears I look at the stones. Some are arranged in a pattern of three: two support a third. A round flat stone is in the center of the total arrangement. It catches the light from the torch on its smooth surface and throws it under the archway of——

Suddenly what I see seems familiar. Only the arrangement of the stones is strange, but everything else is not. The top of the huge circular stone has been worked to resemble the place where I left Gendy. I back away. The old man has tricked me! He has cast some sort of an evil spell on me. I begin to tremble.

Then I turn and start to run, but my legs fail me. I slip to the floor of the cave. My torch dies. I am in total darkness. I hear myself whimper. I look up at the circular rock and above it hovers a faint white light, a kind of mist. I rub my eyes, but it does not go away. I struggle to move but cannot.

"Ronstrom!"

I hear my name, and I am weak with fear.

"Ronstrom you have found the cave and you must do what must be done."

My throat and lips are dry. I try to speak but only make ugly sounds. I cough and force myself to cry out: "I do not understand."

"In time you will," the voice replies. "You must gather the people to you . . . if they are to survive, Ronstrom, and become greater than they once were, they must follow you . . . tell them that you spoke to The Giver of Life; tell them that, Ronstrom."

I shake my head. This is like the pictures that fill my skull when I am asleep. But I know I am not asleep. The light above the circular rock flickers.

"Stand, Ronstrom," the voice says.

"I cannot," I answer.

"Stand," The Giver of Life commands.

I get to my feet.

"Come close to the altar."

I obey.

"Remember well what you see, Ronstrom . . . Remember it!"

"I came here for a talisman," I shout.

"That is your talisman," The Giver of Life answers me. "It is yours and you will give it to your people."

"I do not understand," I cry.

"Build what you see. Build it for The Giver of Life. It is the goal of your people, Ronstrom."

"I am not a builder," I shout. "I am Ronstrom, the hunter."

"You will obey!" The Giver of Life roars. "You will obey!"

"My people will not believe me—they will not follow me. Give me a sign, something to prove to them that You have charged me with the task——"

The Giver of Life laughs, and the sound of his laughter echoes and re-echoes in the depths of the cave until the very walls begin to shake.

I drop to my knees. His laughter scourges me!

"You have your sign, Ronstrom," The Giver of Life tells me. "You have your sign!"

The light above the rock dims. I am wrenched from the floor and flung into the tunnel, and I feel

29

myself tumbling toward the entrance. I shout, but the words remain caught in my throat.

In a matter of moments, I am on the ledge outside the cave. It is covered with snow and the wind is howling. I look toward the entrance: it is no longer there.

III

I work my way down the side of the mountain, pausing only to collect my weapons. I do not know how long I was in the cave. But when I reach the base of the mountain the sun is shining. It is warm. The snow is gone and everywhere I look I see the light green of new grass.

I do not think about what happened in the cave. I am not sure that I was in a cave and I do not want to believe that I spoke with The Giver of Life. If I am sure of anything, it is that Gendy cast an evil spell over me.

I journey homeward to the forest of my people.

Each day the sun lingers in the sky longer than it did the previous day. The air is warm and buds begin to appear on the branches of the trees.

Now and then I kill a rabbit or bring down a bird. My stomach is not empty, but neither is it full.

I do not travel at night. Usually I find a niche between two or more rocks and sleep. At the end of a day's travel, I am very tired. My sleep is always disturbed by visions and voices, but when I wake I have no memory of what they were.

One day when the sun is almost at the end of

its journey across the sky, I pause for a moment to look back at the mountains. Though I can see them with great clarity, I can no longer make out their details. The ridges and escarpments have all melded into the gray mass. The farther away I get from them the more foolish I feel for having gone to them to find a cave.

I turn and am about to continue when a sudden breeze brings the scent of smoke to my nostrils. I sniff at the air. It is strongest to my left. I turn toward it. The glare of the sun is gone and against the blue sky I see a thin white wisp of smoke. The breeze has bent it like a twisted sapling.

I am still in the country of the Rock People, but the smoke carries with it the smell of food. His meat is more substantial than what I have been eating. My stomach growls. I crouch low and move swiftly toward the place from where the smoke is coming.

As I draw near, the smell of meat becomes very strong. The growling in my stomach is louder. I climb a huge boulder and look down. My eyes first go to the fire pit. I see the haunch of a deer. Water fills my mouth and I swallow it.

I move my eyes from the roasting haunch to the hut. It is small and, like those constructed by my own people, made from the bark of trees set over a frame of saplings.

I move my eyes again. This time I see a man. He is about my size. To get the meat, I will have to kill him.

I search the rest of the clearing for signs of other men. I see none.

Suddenly the breeze shifts! The man raises his head and looks toward me. I flatten myself against the rock. I hear him say something. Though I do not understand his tongue, I know that there is someone else with him. Perhaps another man? My chances for killing the both of them are not very good. But then I hear the sound of a woman's voice. The possibility of getting the meat is still mine!

Slowly I lift my head over the rock. The man has moved away from the hut. I think he has caught my scent but cannot tell where it comes from; the Rock People are not good hunters.

I nock an arrow to the string of my bow and even as I draw the arrow back I leap to my feet. I loose the arrow, and it flies at him with a swooshing sound. He hears it, turns, and screams with pain as the flinthead buries itself in his shoulder.

His cry brings a brown-haired woman out of the hut.

The man pulls the arrow from his shoulder. He sees me. Grabbing hold of his spear, he scrambles up the rocks toward me.

There is no time for me to run or fit another arrow. I must fight him as he will fight me, with a spear.

He leaps on the rock where I stand. As soon as he sees me he stops. There is a look of surprise in his eyes and his jaw is slack. But the moment I start to move he clenches his jaws and meets my first thrust with a swift sideward movement that almost breaks my hold on my spear.

We jab at each other. The movement of one is countered by the movement of the other. My heart bangs inside my chest. I am sweating. . . .

We circle each other, thrust and block, and thrust again.

My opponent has a red beard and his eyes are green.

The longer we fight the angrier each of us becomes. The blood from his shoulder drips on the rock. Once he almost loses his footing and I hear a cry of anguish from the woman below.

Even as we fight, I catch sight of the sun. More than half of it has already died, and its death has stained the clouds red and yellow.

I sense he is tiring. I, too, am tired but there is no way to call a halt to what we are about. I have already drawn his blood, and he must try to draw mine.

The wooden shafts of our weapons make a sharp smacking noise whenever they are knocked together. Sometimes there are two, three, or even four smacks in quick succession, but more often there are long pauses between them, as each tries to gain the advantage over the other.

The woman shouts something to the man.

He is too winded to answer.

She shouts again.

This time he answers.

A few moments later the woman climbs on to the rock. She is carrying a club and begins to move toward me with it.

The man drops one hand from his spear and with it he pushes her back.

In that instant, he cannot defend himself. I risk all and pulling my arm back I hurl my spear at his stomach. It finds its mark!

He screams and tries to pull himself off my spear. He drops to his knees. . . .

I run forward and, grabbing the spear, pull it free, only to plunge it into his heaving chest. His bones splinter under the force of my thrust. His stomach is torn open and his guts float in blood. He makes a loud wheezing sound when he breathes.

I pull my spear out of his chest and drive it into

his throat. A plume of blood spurts up and then falls to a stream. His eyes are wide open and glazed.

I leave him where he fell and turn my attention to the woman.

The club she held now lies on the rock. The back of her hand is in her mouth. Her amber eyes are wide open.

Suddenly her body begins to tremble and tears stream from her eyes.

I do not understand what is happening to her.

I gather my weapons and with my foot push the body of the man over the other side of the rock. The woman tries to stop me, but I throw her down. When the body is gone I pull the woman to her feet and motion toward the fire pit. I can see from the expression on her face that she understands I want food.

As soon as I reach the fire pit, I pull the haunch from it. Quickly I cut myself a good-size piece of meat. I devour it. I take another piece of meat from the haunch, but this one I eat more slowly. I even take time to look at the weeping woman. I cut some meat and toss it at her.

She does not reach for it. I shrug. She will eat when she is hungry.

Sitting back and chewing on a third piece of meat, I watch the darkness spread over the sky. The stars begin to show themselves, and from the way the crescent moon hangs in the sky I know it will rain before morning.

I lick my fingers. In the dim light of the fire I look at the woman again. For a moment I remember how the man tried to protect her, but I do not understand why he did it. Had he let her join him, he might have killed me. He must have had a reason for doing what he did. Whatever it was it cost him his life.

The woman has stopped weeping. She is comely looking. Perhaps she is seventeen or eighteen summers. Her left breast is bare. She knows I am looking at her, but her eyes avoid mine.

I stretch and feel another kind of hunger. I have not been with a woman for a long time. My manthing begins to stir and grows hard. I stand up and go to the woman.

She does not move. I reach down to touch her face.

She draws away.

I do not speak her tongue, but I know she understands what I want. I bare my hard manthing.

She shrinks away.

I shake my head, throw her down.

She fights me . . . she screams . . . she beats on my chest. . . .

I force her thighs open and push my body between them.

Her breasts rise and fall as though she was running hard. She tries to roll me off her.

I pin her hands under mine and then I shove my manthing into her.

She screams . . . her cries become whimpers.

There are tears on her face and her lips tremble as I begin to move my manthing in the tunnel of her womanhood. I feel her wetness and it is good.

Soon she begins to move, too. Her whimpers have stopped and her lips are parted. Her eyelids have made slits of her eyes. She moans and sighs.

I release her hands. Her body is supple and her belly is soft and warm under mine. Her breath is sweet and comes in short gasps.

I move more swiftly!

The woman circles my back with her naked thighs.

I feel the pleasure in my loins mount. Soon my fluid will rush out of my manthing. My own breath is fast now.

The woman's head thrashes from side to side. Her body becomes hard under mine. She is in her moment of passion and the nipples of her breasts are erect. She screams! The sound of her cry slashes the dark silence of the night.

When my fluid gushes out of my manthing I shudder and grunt with pleasure. Though my eyes are open I am blinded and with my sightless eyes I see myself flying between the stars and the crescent moon. It is a good feeling!

After a time I roll off the woman and stand up. I offer her my hand. She takes it and when she is on her feet we move into the hut to sleep.

I am awakened by the sound of rain falling on the roof of the hut. The day is just beginning and the sky is filled with gray clouds.

The woman awakes. She makes a fire and the smoke curls up to a hole in the roof. She goes out and brings back the haunch of the deer. She puts it on the fire and after a while we eat.

From what I can see of the things in the hut, the man I killed had many more things than anyone of my people. There are several clay pots and many skins. His weapons are good, too. I take his knife, which is sharper than mine.

The woman watches me.

I go to the door of the hut and push aside the skin. It is still raining. I cannot stay too long. If I were to be found by other men of her people, they would kill me. I turn toward the woman and motion that I am going.

She shakes her head.

Again I motion that I am going to leave.

The woman comes closer. She points to my forehead and with her finger traces a line on it.

I do not understand, and I shake my head.

She points to my knife and then to my forehead.

I put my fingers on my forehead—and then I feel it. There is a scar there. It starts at my hair on the right side and slants down to my eyebrow on the left side.

The woman points to my beard and quickly pulls hair from it.

The hair is white.

She points to it and then to my head.

The hair on my head is white, too. I shake my head and try to explain that I am a young man and not an old one.

She just stands there and looks at me.

I know she does not understand. How could she understand when I do not?

Again I try to tell her that I am a young man. But she just looks at me. Finally I make one more attempt and I bare my manthing.

She misunderstands and, drawing back, she moves close to the fire, where she lies down and offers me her womanhood.

I become aroused and mount her again. But this time when my fluid gushes from my manthing I do not fly between the moon and the stars. Instead, I have a vision of myself in a huge cave and I hear a voice say: "You have your sign . . . Ronstrom, you have your sign!" And even as I grunt with pleasure I understand how I came by the scar and the white beard and hair of an old man. The Giver of Life put his mark on me!

It rains for several days and I stay with the woman. Though there is enough to eat and it is a pleasure to have a woman to mount whenever I want to, I am restless.

My nights are filled with visions and voices. I cry out in my sleep and I am wet with sweat when I wake. I do not want to be anything other than what I am: Ronstrom, the hunter. Yet each time I tell The Giver of Life this, He only laughs at me.

I even think of remaining with the woman, but the first morning that the sun shows itself, I leave and resume my journey home.

IV

After many days of travel I reach the flat open land where the spirits of the dead walk at night. And the next morning I come to the place where I slew the bear and left Gendy the priest. The bones of bear and man are bleaching in the late-afternoon sun. The bearskin is gone.

I turn and look toward the mountains. They are no more than gray smudges in that portion of the sky where the sun never travels. I face the forest of my people. It is not too far ahead of me and I walk slowly toward it.

The signs of game are few. The people look at me and shake their heads. I do not know whether they recognize me or think I am a stranger. But I can see that the woman, children, and old men are too busy grubbing roots out of the ground to concern themselves with me.

I go to my hut. It is empty. The skins I once owned are gone, as are the arrow and spearshafts. I am angry and rush from my hut. But once I am outside in the late-afternoon sun, I realize that whoever took them must have thought I was dead.

Perhaps Gendy's bones were mistaken for mine.

My anger vanishes when I see some of the hunters returning with their meager catch of rabbits.

I step out into the clearing and say: "I am Ronstrom."

The band of men stop.

"I am Ronstrom," I repeat.

The men look at me. Their eyes study my face and then one says: "You are Ronstrom." The others nod and go to their huts.

This is the way I rejoin my people. As the days pass I am told by various men that everyone thought I was killed by a bear. Rigga told them that. He said that he came upon the bear just after the animal killed me and slew it himself. He even took its skin to prove how brave he was.

The story makes me smile but I say nothing, and no one asks what really happened to me. I do not tell them I have gone to the mountains and that I have spoken to The Giver of Life.

When Rigga first sees me he does not know what to say. He is slightly taller than I am. His shoulders are broad. His beard is the color of dark honey and his hair is brown. He looks at me with his cold blue eyes and in them I see that he was the one who took the things from my hut.

"Old man," he asks, "can you still hunt?"

I nod.

He laughs scornfully and says: "I do not mean for rats and rabbits."

I again nod and answer: "Perhaps you have forgotten who I am?"

"You are an old man with a white beard and white hair . . . you are——"

"I am Ronstrom," I tell him.

He feigns surprise.

"Surely," I chide, "you have not forgotten me!"

41

I see that several of the other men have come close to us.

His lips twist into a snarl, and he says: "Ronstrom's bones——"

"They are the bones of Gendy the priest."

"If you are Ronstrom," he challenges, "tell us where you have been. It has been a long time——"

I smile and say: "To the mountains under that portion of the sky where the sun never travels."

"The land of the Rock People?"

I nod and say: "Yes, to the land of the Rock People."

The men who have gathered to listen to us begin to chatter among themselves. No man in their memory has ever gone there and returned.

"That is the talk of a foolish old man," Rigga says with a laugh. He points to the scar on my forehead and says, "Next you will tell us how you fought them and——"

"I fought and killed one," I say. "But he did not put the mark on my forehead or turn my beard and hair white."

"Then tell us——"

With a wave of my hand I silence him and say: "I will tell you when it is time for you to know. Perhaps you will know without my having to tell you."

I return to my hut.

Outside the men are still talking about what I said to them. Rigga's voice is louder than the rest. He tells them that he was sure the dead man he found was Ronstrom. Moment by moment his anger increases until it is so hot that none of the other men dare remain close to him.

I spend my days hunting. My catch is no better

or worse than it ever was. And at night I seldom return to my hut without meat of some kind, even if it is only a rabbit or a squirrel.

When I sleep I am always disturbed by The Giver of Life. He is at me like a gnat. I cannot rid myself of him. He will not listen when I tell Him that I am a hunter.

Sometimes I think about the man I killed. I still do not understand why he risked his life to save the woman's. When I sometimes think of her, my manthing becomes hard.

Then one morning while I am hunting I see Foss, the maker of huts, tracking a rabbit. I watch him stalk the animal until at the very last moment he fails to make the kill.

The incident remains with me all day and when I return to my hut, I still think of it.

A poor hunter will fail to kill his quarry or drive good game away. Still worse, he might wound the animal in such a way that it is able to flee deeper into the forest and, though it eventually dies, the hunter is unable to get its meat.

I stop thinking only long enough to roast a squirrel, but as soon as I begin to eat I also begin to think again. Soon I realize that some men are better hunters than others. And some men are better arrow makers than those who hunt. And there are men who make huts better than either the hunters or the arrow makers.

I drop the rest of the squirrel back into the fire and leap up. This is the first time that I have ever looked at the men of my people in that way. I feel a strange kind of excitement. Prickles rush up and down my back. There is something within my reach if only I can take the next step, if only I can connect all the men and their skills and make them work as one.

If the hunters did nothing but hunt and the makers of arrows did nothing but make arrows and the hut makers did nothing but make huts. . . .

I take a deep breath and with a sigh I let the air out. I am not used to thinking so long and so hard. I am sure that if all of the hunting is left to the men most skilled in this calling then there would be more meat for everyone.

I sit down and pull the charred remains of the squirrel from the fire. The meat is not as bloody as I like it, but nonetheless I eat it.

Somehow I must present my plan to the men. Even though I have the white beard and hair of an old man, I know they will say that I am too young to tell them what to do. I know that if they do not do as I ask, they will continue to go hungry.

That night when I sleep I hear The Giver of Life say, "You have taken the first step . . . you must take many more, Ronstrom."

And in my sleep I cry out, "I am a hunter, not a builder."

But The Giver of Life only laughs. . . .

I bolt up! I tremble and I am wet with sweat. After a while I lie down again. Through the smoke hole in the roof of my hut, I see a patch of black sky filled with stars. Then I sleep.

V

Many days and nights pass. I hunt, eat, and sleep. What I have to say to the men of my people I keep in my skull. I do not know how to begin to tell them what they must be told, but each day I look at the various men and I see things I never saw before. Not only do I know who are the best hunters, but I also discover that many of the arrow makers are fine carvers. I tell nothing to anyone about what I have seen. At night I think and think until my skull aches and when I sleep I am pursued by The Giver of Life.

The only pleasure I have is looking at Alvina, child of Gibben's woman, who died three winters ago. Gibben's hut is not in the same clearing as mine. I must go some distance to get to his hut. Gibben is a short, big-chested man. He is one of the best hunters in the forest. I would talk to him about my plan but I think he would only laugh. When I go near his hut, I go only to see Alvina.

Alvina is a woman of fifteen summers. The top of her head reaches to my nose. She has soft black hair and gray eyes. Her bare breasts reveal nipples of a pale red, the color of a flower. When I see her, my manthing begins to throb. I would like to have her for my woman before some other hunter takes her.

Alvina seems to know when I am nearby. She comes out of the hut and always stands so that I am able to see her. I would like to speak with her, but I do not want to start trouble with Gibben. He has often boasted that Alvina would go to the man he chooses for her. It is a foolish boast and everyone knows that he wants meat—perhaps a deer—in exchange for Alvina. If I kill a deer I would not hesitate to exchange it for her. But there are no deer in our forest. Soon a hunter will take her by force. That is the way the men of my people have always taken their women.

I think of Alvina through the summer when the sun is hot and the nights pleasantly cool. I am so filled with a longing for her that nothing else seems to matter. I spend most of the time looking for signs of game bigger than squirrels, rabbits, and rats. I travel to the ends of the forest and into its depths, but I do not see what I am looking for.

One day when the sun is hidden by thick black clouds and the wind roars angrily over the land, making the forest sigh with pain, I find myself looking out at the flat open land where the spirits of the dead sometimes walk. In the distance the sky is torn apart by flaming arrows and the huge earth drum booms. Wide patches of rain move across the land like giant men. I lower my eyes and look toward the place where I slew the bear and shared my meat with Gendy the priest. Suddenly I leave the shelter of the forest and start to move to where Gendy's bones are. I have in my heart the need to see them, and perhaps to even put them in the earth. I do not try to understand why I feel the way I do.

The arrows continue to burn their way across the sky and the earth drum is louder than before. The huge rain giants are now moving slowly toward the forest.

I do not go very far when I see a child. He belongs to Ansgar, an arrow maker. Not far from the boy is a stake. Between the boy and the stake is a length of rope.

I stop! I have never seen a child tethered to a stake. Something is wrong. I have tethered animals to stakes to catch other animals. Suddenly I remember how I used Gendy for bait.

The wind carries the wailing of the boy to me.

The scent of wolf is in the air.

The sky becomes darker.

I sniff at the air again and catch the scent of man. Someone is using the boy for bait. I run forward. To kill a wolf is a feat worthy of a good hunter. But as I near the boy, I find myself listening to his cries and I know I cannot use him as I used Gendy. If I am to kill the wolf, I must do it without risking the boy's life.

I run toward him. My knife is drawn and I am ready to cut him loose. As I reach him and lift my knife to sever the rope, I hear my name.

I whirl around, expecting to see Gendy's spirit or perhaps the white light of The Giver of Life. But neither one is there. I see Rigga. He is running toward me.

"Let him be!" Rigga shouts.

I turn back to the boy, cut the rope, and tell the boy to run back to the forest.

"Ronstrom!" Rigga shouts.

I face him.

He has stopped a few paces from me. His lips

47

are drawn back in fury. His blue eyes glow with hate.

I drop my spear and unsling my bow and arrows. I hold my knife out in front of me. My heart is beating very fast. My knees are weak and my legs feel like wet grass. The time has come for me to fight Rigga.

He knows it, too. He has dropped his spear and has unslung his bow and arrows. He holds his black obsidian knife in front of him, too.

We begin to circle one another and with each circle the distance between us becomes less and less. The rain giants fall on us.

"I will not let you cheat me of my catch," Rigga snarls.

I do not answer. It is useless to talk. I only want to kill him.

We close. Rigga thrusts at me and I feel the sting of his knife on my arm. I suddenly push free, and backstep out of his reach. My blood spills down my arm. I am wet with sweat, but I begin to circle Rigga again.

"Old man," he taunts, "old man, you are as good as dead!"

I rush him. My knife sticks into his shoulder. I pull it free and try to slash at his stomach.

He growls with anger and brings up his knee against my manthing.

The force of the blow makes me feel as though I have been lifted up and the next moment slammed down on the ground. My stomach rushes to my throat. I am doubled up with pain and I have trouble breathing.

I force myself to keep my eyes open.

Rigga's shoulder gushes blood. He bends low and comes charging down on me.

I roll to one side.

Rigga crashes into the place where I was.

The pain has left me and I spring to my feet.

Rigga also recovers.

We begin to circle each other for a third time. Rigga's face has been scratched in the force of his fall. It is covered with a mixture of blood and mud.

He thrusts his knife at me, but I slam it down with a blow from my knife. The shock splinters both weapons. We are forced to fight with our hands and feet. We stand locked in each other's embrace.

Even as we struggle, each to bring the other down, I have a swift vision of two giants locked in mortal combat. The sky above is filled with flaming arrows, turning the darkness of the sky into a hot whiteness, and the booming of the earth drum makes the ground tremble beneath our feet.

Rigga grunts and pushes against me.

I echo his grunts and push against him.

Rain and blood drench our bodies.

My chest heaves and I try to drink in as much air as I can. My throat is rough and dry. I try to throw him over my right hip. Because of the mud on his body, I cannot get a good hold. Both of us tumble to the ground and as we fall we are released.

"I will kill you!" Rigga cries hoarsely.

I push myself up and hurl myself at him.

He rolls away and I land in the mud.

A moment later, he is on top of me. He has a good hold on my head and is trying to push my face into the mud. I reach behind me and grab his beard. I pull so hard that he roars with pain and lets go of my head. Still holding tightly, to his

49

beard, I push him off me and with a tremendous yank, I pull out a handful of his beard.

He screams in pain.

I roll out of his reach.

We lie in the mud trying to push our bodies to make one last effort to kill the other. Neither has the strength to come. I watch Rigga.

My body is battered and bruised. I ache and my throat feels like rough stone. I turn my face up to the rain and open my mouth. The water feels good and I swallow each mouthful I collect.

I hear Rigga move and look at him.

He is crawling slowly on all fours toward his spear and arrows.

I force myself up and go to mine.

He reaches his weapons and I reach mine. We both stand.

"This is not the end, Ronstrom," he shouts above the whining of the wind. "This is not the end . . . I will kill you."

I expect him to hurl his spear, but he turns away from me and slowly makes his way back to the forest.

For now, it is the end and I lean heavily on my spear. I could not have fought any longer. My strength is gone and I sink wearily down into the mud. I cannot hold my head up and my eyes close. Regardless of the rain and the wind I stretch out and sleep.

I dream. . . .

I am in the place where I now sleep. It is not raining. It is night. The moon is full and its light turns everything white. I am standing where I slew the bear and I look down at Gendy's bones.

The bones begin to move. They join themselves

to each other as they were when Gendy was alive.

I am frightened and I try to run, but I cannot move my feet.

Gendy's bony right arm comes up and he points his finger at me. "Look to the forest," he intones. "Look to the forest; it is all there."

"What is there?" I ask.

He shakes his skull and repeats: "Look to the forest."

Before I can speak Gendy's bones collapse and fall noiselessly at my feet.

I turn and look toward the forest. The sky is blood red; huge columns of black smoke climb up the sky. Animals of all sorts run from the flames. Does, bucks, bears, wolves, and birds are on fire and scream in terror.

I sense I am looking at something that happened in the past. Nonetheless I tremble with terror and in my sleep I cry out: "I do not understand."

Just before I wake, I hear the rolling laughter of The Giver of Life. . . .

VI

The rain giants are still battering the earth when I awaken. In the distance, the earth and sky tremble from their anger. The sky is very dark.

I am wet and I shiver from the cold.

The fight I had with Rigga is locked in my skull. My body aches from the blows he gave it, and I rub my arms and legs to ease the pain in them. Above the sound of the rain I can almost hear him bellow as he left this place and went off into the forest. He will try to kill me as I will try to kill him again. It is the only way left to settle the bad feelings between us. I do not know why I fought him over the boy.

I get to my feet and wince with pain. There is some small pleasure in my knowing that Rigga, too, is suffering from the blows I gave him. It is not easy for me to move as I gather my weapons together and slowly go toward the forest.

One portion of the sky becomes lighter. The blackness changes to the color of mist. Soon all the blackness will be gone and I will be able to see the clouds. I turn from the growing light and begin to trot.

As soon as I reach the shelter of the trees, I make

straight for my hut. When I am safe inside I coax the glowing embers in my fire pit into flames, which I feed several faggots.

The fire soon drives the chill from my body. As I sit and watch the smoke curl up toward the opening in the roof I think of Alvina as an inner fire matches the heat of the one burning in the fire pit.

I do not have to close my eyes to see her naked in my skull. I know that her breasts are full and high, that her stomach is flat, and that her hips are wide . . . I would feel great pleasure putting my manthing inside the sheath of her womanhood . . . perhaps I would be the first to satisfy myself on her body. The possibility that this might be so makes me nod. I lick my lips with anticipation, as though I am about to feast on a good piece of meat. My blood is pounding in my ears and my manthing is a lance.

I shake my head and the pictures of Alvina's naked body slip out of my skull. There I sit with my legs crossed and stare at the column of gray smoke. It is like the trunk of a slender tree that has grown out of the fire pit.

I do not want to remember the way Gendy's bones joined together and danced before me . . . I do not want to remember what he told me . . . I do not want to remember The Giver of Life's deep rolling laughter.

But I do! And not each by itself but all of them come together. Like the waters of a rain-swollen river that swirls over its banks, those terrible memories swirl inside my head. Soon the column of gray smoke blurs and my head throbs with pain.

The hut has suddenly become too warm. I remove one of the burning faggots and with my

53

hands beat out the flames on it, but the hut is still too warm.

I stand up and go outside. The rain has stopped. The sky is a mixture of ragged gray clouds and patches of blue. Here and there the yellow light of the sun streams down. The strong scent of growth fills the air and the leaves on the trees seem to be a deeper green than they were before the rain giants passed over the land.

Several times I fill my lungs with air. The pain in my head becomes dull. Even as I stand outside my hut, the pieces of blue sky fit together until almost all of the gray clouds are gone. The yellow light of the sun enters the clearing near my hut. It washes over me with a delicious warmth that sinks deep, easing the hurt I sustained while fighting Rigga.

I strip off my skins. Naked, I bask in the sun. I hear the whir of a bee's wings as it hovers over a yellow flower. A bird whistles to its mate and is answered.

The ache in my head is still there, just above my nose and between my eyes. It is there because the memory of the dream is still in my head. And though I cannot be absolutely certain, I am almost sure that The Giver of Life put the pain there to remind me of the dream and will probably keep it there until——

I bolt up!

Someone is approaching my hut. I am naked and without weapons.

If it is Rigga he will not give me the chance to fight. He will kill me, take my head, and boast how he came upon me and slew me.

My heart pounds wildly. My chest feels as though

it is bound by stout thongs. If I am to die I am determined to die fighting!

I grab my skins and rush for my hut. In moments my nakedness is covered. Then grabbing my spear and a wooden shield, I run from my hut. From my throat comes the scream of challenge!

Two figures at the far edge of the clearing stop.

Even with my vision clouded with the red of violence I can see that neither of them is Rigga. One is the boy I cut from the tether and the other is his father Ansgar the arrow maker. They stand motionless, not knowing what will happen next. They are drenched with sunlight and behind them the trees of the forest close into a solid wall.

My chest heaves with unspent violence. The blood lust seeps out of me and the red before my eyes falls away like a withered leaf when the cold wind blows. To show them I mean no harm I drop my spear and wooden shield. My breath is easier and I do not hear the pounding of my blood.

Ansgar is a thin man with black hair and black eyes as black as the rock he works with. He raises his hand and calls out across the clearing, "I come in peace, Ronstrom."

Weaponless, I go toward him and he and his son come toward me. When we are very close I motion him to sit down.

He nods and he and his son sit down.

For a while neither of us speaks, but I can tell from the way Ansgar is looking at me that he is trying to see past my face. His eyes probe mine, but I do not look away. Finally he places his hand on the head of his son and says, "The boy told me what you did."

I say nothing.

"He fought Rigga," the boy says.

Ansgar nods and his eyes look at my arm where Rigga's knife opened it.

"Rigga could not kill him," the boy says. "They fought hard and long and I watched them."

"He is my only son," Ansgar tells me.

I nod and answer, "He has grown since last I saw him."

"My other children," Ansgar continues, "a boy, five summers older than this one, and a girl but two summers younger, are gone. Their life spirits fled when the fever came. Many children and old people gave up their life spirit then."

I nod. I do not know whether he is telling me about something that happened while I was here or while I was away.

"You were not here," he says quietly as if he knew what I was thinking.

I remain silent. I do not know why Ansgar has come to speak to me and I glance over my shoulder to where I dropped my spear and shield . . . there is a considerable distance between me and my weapon——

"The boy's name is Garth," Ansgar says.

"Garth," I repeat, looking at the boy. He smiles at me.

Ansgar rubs the palms of his callused hands over his bony knees. "My woman," he says, putting one hand on his son's shoulder, "wants you to take him . . . she—I give him to you."

"What can I do with a boy?" I ask, leaping to my feet.

"He is yours," Ansgar replies stubbornly.

Garth scrambles to his feet. "I want to be a hunter," he tells me.

I look at him. He is skin and bones. His hair is black and his eyes are like his father's. Had I not cut him loose, I would not now be asked to take him. There are times when interfering in someone else's affairs has a way of——

"His life spirit belongs to you," Ansgar says.

"I did what any other man would have done."

Ansgar shakes his head.

It is useless to argue with Ansgar. Arrow makers are like the rock with which they work. To alter the shape of his thoughts, I would have to chip away at it for the passing of too many days and nights.

"He will do everything you tell him," Ansgar says, looking at his son.

The boy nods. "And when I become a great hunter," he tells us, "I will never be hungry again."

Ansgar quickly apologizes for Garth's foolishness. "He is twelve summers," he explains, "but he still chirps like a bird."

Suddenly I understand what is happening. Ansgar and his woman want their son to live. If I take him, I will be the one who provides his meat.

I look at Ansgar. This time it is I who see deep into his eyes. Behind their black hardness there is a pale wavering light such as I have never before seen in the eyes of a man. Such a light might be better kept in the eyes of a captive woman who begs not to be ravished and, if ravished, to be allowed to live.

Ansgar is begging me to take his son!

I want to turn away, to tell him to keep his son, to do anything but look at the pale wavering light in Ansgar's eyes. I do not turn away and with a slight nod I say, "I will take him." I can scarcely believe what I have said.

Ansgar claps me on the shoulder and tells me "You shall never want for arrow- or spearheads."

I look at Garth. He is smiling and I try to remember when last I saw a child smile.

"Someday," Ansgar tells his son, "you will be a great hunter."

Garth suddenly breaks away from us, runs a short distance into the forest, and quickly returns with the few skins for his pallet. He has become mine!

VII

Garth is quick to learn. As the fruit slowly ripens on the trees he snares many rabbits and squirrels. He has a good eye and with a killing stone he can down a bird in flight.

Soon after he comes to live with me I ask Foss the hut maker to build a hut for Garth some distance from my own. I give him as many rabbits as I have fingers. The boy has heard me cry out in my sleep to The Giver of Life and has asked me about Him.

I could not tell the boy about something I do not know. Besides, if I did tell him all that has happened to me he would probably not believe me. And he might speak of it to other members of our tribe. I do not want that to happen. I do not want them to think that I am stranger than they already think I am.

With Garth at my side, I spend long hours in the forest and though I do not speak much to the boy he somehow knows I am pleased. In only one passing of the moon through all its parts, he has filled out and seems to have grown taller.

Life through the summer is easy. Small game is

plentiful and Ansgar, true to his word, keeps me well supplied with arrow- and spearheads.

The time of the heavy fruit and deep green leaf is past. At night the wind already is beginning to howl and bare its sharp teeth. And the brilliant, white moon, that blots out the wandering stars and dims the others, swings low over the earth, drenching it with its light so that even though it is night the dark masses of the mountains, where the Rock People live, are clearly visible.

If I dream at night, by the time I wake I do not remember what I have dreamt. I almost begin to believe that The Giver of Life has decided to let me be what I am, a hunter. Late in the afternoon one day, I find myself thinking about the old man, Gendy. I remember how his bones came together and the words that came out of his fleshless lips.

Garth senses something and asks, "Is anything wrong?"

With a shake of my head I deny that anything is amiss and then tell him: "I was thinking about a dream I had."

He does not speak for a while but then he says, "My father's woman would always go to the old ones to ask them the meaning of her dreams."

"The old ones?" I question.

Garth waves toward where the sky is the color of blood. "Some of the old ones," he explains, "know about such things."

I shrug. I do not know if he is right. No doubt his father's woman told him that and who can believe what a woman will tell a boy?

We move one behind the other over the trail that will take us back to my encampment. For a while I lead and then I fall back and the boy moves out in front. In the lead, he applies himself to the task of looking for signs of game. Though we have killed several rabbits, a little more practice cannot hurt the boy.

As I follow Garth, I give myself over to thinking about the old ones.

Most of them are as old as Gendy was when I first met him. Perhaps some are even older. They live on roots, nuts, and berries. Now and then they might catch fish in the river or snare a few mice. Toothless and often almost blind, they are old beyond the reckoning of age by the passage of men, summers or winters.

That one of them might be able to help me understand my dream has never occurred to me. I have heard of a woman going to them for advice, a special potion—they are skilled in the use of herbs—and to bring on, or stop, the flow of blood from their bodies that some say is caused by the movement of the moon. Never have I heard of a man going to the old ones for anything.

I do not know if I want to put my dream before them.

Suddenly Garth holds up his right hand.

I stop!

The boy stands motionless in front of me.

I move my eyes along the trail. From what I see I know we are very close to my encampment. I search for signs of game. There are none. Then I hear sounds. They come from the clearing where we live.

The light in the forest is very dim and the big leafy tops of the trees blot out most of the darkening sky.

Garth has his face turned toward me. I motion him to drop to the earth. Noiselessly he falls down.

I do the same and on my belly I work my way to him.

"Rigga?" he questions in a whisper.

"I do not know," I answer.

"What should we do?"

"Nothing until the earth is covered with darkness." And so, flat on our stomachs, we wait.

Night comes swiftly. The wind moans through the trees, and the leaves, as they move, sound like rushing water. It is cold enough to make me wish I had another skin over me. Two fires suddenly blaze up in the clearing and I say to Garth, "I do not think Rigga would light fires."

He agrees.

I get to my feet. Garth stands, too. Holding my spear at the ready, I move up the trail at a trot. As soon as I break into the clearing I see Garth's father, Ansgar, and several other men from our tribe.

Garth enters the clearing and stops at my side.

The flames from the two fires bend to the will of the wind, making their light leap over the faces and bodies of those standing between them. A piece of wood is chewed through by the flames and falls into the fire with a soft sigh.

Ansgar is looking at the many rabbits that I and Garth have taken during the day's hunt. Even though it is night there is enough light coming from the fires to let me see his eyes. They burn with envy, with hunger!

I still have not moved, but I have taken the measure of the other men with Ansgar. Two are hunters and one is a maker of clay pots. The two hunters are holding spears, but not in a throwing position. The maker of clay pots is not armed.

"I have come to talk," Ansgar says.

"Then talk," I answer.

He hesitates, looks at those who are with him, and finally finding his tongue again, he says, "Meat is very scarce."

"It has been the way since I can remember," I tell him. "And even before that, if what I have been told is true."

"It is true," the maker of clay pots says in a reedy voice that matches his thin body.

"But you," one of the hunters complains, stepping forward, "always have meat, more meat than anyone else."

I move and point my spear at him. Should I have to hurl it at him I would not miss. His life spirit would leave his body through the opening I would make in his chest.

Ansgar speaks again. "My son too stalks and kills game," he says.

"He has learned what I have taught."

Again there is a long silence, interrupted only by the sound of the wind and the popping and crackling of the burning faggots.

"The boy," Ansgar says, "is by his birth my son."

"And mine," I remind him, "because I saved his life spirit."

The hunter who has not moved says, "All of us here have blood ties to Ansgar and through him thus to the boy."

"I am not a hunter," Ansgar says.

"Nor am I," the maker of clay pots squeaks.

"Part of your kill," the hunter, who stepped forward, says, "belongs——"

Anger flashes through me. "I will give you nothing," I tell him. "The boy is free to go back to his father. But the meat I kill I keep. That has how it has always been and how it will always be. If you," I say to the hunters, "are not skilled enough to make your own kills then let Ansgar teach you how to make arrowheads or let the other one teach you how to make clay pots."

He begins to move.

I do not hesitate. My spear makes a swooshing, higher-pitched sound than the moan of the wind.

He screams as the stone tip lodges deep in his chest. He tries to pull it out and pitches forward.

The second hunter comes bounding at me. His howls slash the darkness!

I wrench Garth's spear from his hand and go to meet my attacker.

Ansgar and the maker of clay pots have scurried out of our way and are cowering in the shadows, close to Garth's hut.

The man comes charging at me, hoping to impale me on his spear. I leap off to one side. The second hunter cannot stop his charge and it carries him well past me.

Even as I wheel around, I hear Garth scream. It is a death scream. The spear that was meant for me has lodged itself in the boy.

I hurl my spear at the man's back. He shrieks in agony, lets go of his spear, and staggers around.

I race to Garth. The spearhead is lodged in his belly. The skins he wears are soaked with blood and blood seeps out of his mouth. I ease the spear out of his belly, but the pain makes the boy scream.

Behind me the second hunter falls to the ground with a thud.

I know Garth's life spirit will soon leave him. I lift the boy into my arms.

Slowly I walk toward the fire and I shout, "Ansgar, come look at what you have done. Ansgar, come look at your son!"

He moves out of the shadows. Behind him is the maker of pots.

"I fed him," I say. "I taught him to hunt. He would have been a mighty hunter, Ansgar."

He remains silent.

The boy gasps and goes limp in my arms!

I do not understand what is happening to me. My vision blurs and water seeps out of my eyes. There is an ache in my throat that does not go away when I swallow.

Without speaking to Ansgar again I lower Garth's body into the fire and let the flames do their work. It is better that his flesh be consumed that way than by the crows or rats.

All night I sit by the fire and when it burns low I give it more wood.

All night I sit and watch the smoke of the boy's body taken by the wind and spread over the moon-drenched trees.

My body is numb and though I can straighten my back it feels bent. The night grows gray and dawn comes. The wind drops off and the yellow fingers of the sun push through the trees.

Nothing remains of Garth's body. The flames consumed his flesh, leaving only the bones. I will wait until the ashes cool and then I will gather his bones together and in some glen deep in the forest I will place them in the earth.

I cast my eyes about for Ansgar and the maker of clay pots. They are gone and so are the bodies of the two hunters I slew.

I stand and look about me.

The grass in the clearing is stained with blood. I shake my head and cry aloud, "And all for meat, for meat!"

My voice sounds hollow and quickly dies in the

crisp morning air. And then I notice that the kill of yesterday's hunt is missing. In the end Ansgar and the maker of clay pots got what they came for.

I glance back at the fire pit, where Garth's bones show white against the gray ash and, dropping to my knees, my body shakes as unfamiliar sounds come from my lips and water flows from my eyes.

VIII

For the passing of many days and many nights, I feel nothing. Not hunger. Not even the stirring of desire when I chance upon Alvina.

I move my hut from that bloodstained clearing to one deeper in the forest. I burn Garth's hut.

The members of the tribe I meet either look away when they see me or hurry off in a different direction. I do not know what Ansgar or the maker of clay pots told the others of the tribe about me, but whatever it was it has made them even more afraid of me than they were when I first returned from the mountains of the Rock People.

Even Alvina does not look at me any more.

At night I sit and stare into the flames of the fire. Often I can see Garth's body in them. Sometimes I think about the man I killed after I left the cave in the mountain.

I remember how he used his body to shield that of his woman.

If I had had the opportunity would I have done the same to protect Garth?

I cannot answer my own question. My mouth fills with a bitter taste. I will never know.

My sleep is restless and filled with dreams. But

when I wake I have no memory of what the dream was about. All that remains is a strange feeling of uneasiness.

Days of not eating drives me to hunt again and I spend most of the morning stalking several rabbits, all of which at the last moment escape the sureness of my arrows. By afternoon I am wet with sweat and very thirsty. I am not far from the river and go to it without pausing to do any more hunting.

I reach the river, drop my weapons, and fling myself into the water, taking huge gulps of it into my mouth. When my thirst is satisfied and my body cool, I climb back on to the bank and stretch out in the warmth of the sun.

The sky is blue. The clouds, looking like great beasts, move slowly across it. A lone kestrel hangs motionless in the air.

I lower my line of sight. The leaves on the tops of the trees, and those facing the part of the earth where the sun never travels, are already changing from green to yellow. Some of the yellow ones are beginning to turn red and brown on their edges.

I think of the long dark days that lie ahead, of the biting cold and the swirling snow, and scramble to my feet. As soon as I am erect, I look upstream. And I see the huts of the old ones. They are clustered on the bank of the river a short distance from me.

I shake my head, start for the forest, and stop.

I still remember the dream I had after I fought Rigga. I shrug. It no longer matters to me if the others in the tribe think me strange. I turn and go along the bank to the encampment of the old ones, who might tell me the meaning of the dream.

The hut I sit in has a foul smell, more like the lair of bear or a wolf than the dwelling place of a man or a woman. In the dim light I cannot tell whether the old one on the other side of the fire pit is a man or woman. Some people are neither one nor the other and their bodies possess breasts and a manthing or the slit of a woman and the chest and beard of a man, but I do not understand how that could be.

The old one who faces me has long gray stringy hair and a face like the inside of a dried cracked skin. He is almost sightless and when he moves about he probes his way with a staff cut from an oak. He is frail, but I am almost certain that when he was younger he was tall, broad, and very strong. Or, if he is not a man, as I think he is, then he must have been a wonderful woman to look at, full-breasted and wide-hipped. The kind of woman to make the blood of any man race with lust.

But it is easier for me to think of him as a man rather than a woman. His arms are very thin, the skin dark with those long blue lines that spout blood when cut. His fingers are long and bony. And his hand trembles like a leaf touched by a breeze.

I am still in the hut until the yellow light of the sun leaves the riverbank and hangs only in the tops of the tallest trees. The old one's name is Corb as I was told by another of his kind who first led me to him. He said that Corb would tell me the meaning of my dream.

The light outside turns gray and I grow restless. Corb has not spoken since I entered the hut, except to tell me to sit down. And now and then he has mumbled something, but the sound of his voice has been much like the sound made when one rock has been scraped against another. I could not understand anything he was saying—if he was saying anything—since old people often sigh, wheeze, and make grunting noises that can easily be mistaken for speech.

Corb reaches behind him and, taking a handful of dried twigs, leaves, and grass, feeds them to the fire. The flames leap up and cast our shadows darkly on the walls of the hut.

The old man coughs. Spittle runs out from the corners of his thin blue lips and drips slowly into tufts of hair sticking out from the side of his face like pine needles.

My legs are numb and filled with the prickly feeling that comes when a portion of the body has been kept idle too long. I want to move but do not. I look toward the hut's entrance.

The sunlight is no longer on the tops of the trees and soon darkness will settle over everything. My stomach growls with hunger and makes me remember that I have not eaten for the space of several sunrises and sunsets.

Corb moves again. This time he uses his other hand, and taking some dried leaves and bits of flowers in his bony fingers he salts the fire with them. The flames do not leap higher but thin columns of bluish smoke push their way toward the low roof of the hut and then crawl to the small opening in the center.

The sour stink in the hut changes to something more fragrant, almost like a flower with a sweet unidentifiable secret.

The numbness leaves my legs and I decide to wait no longer for Corb to speak and ask, "Are you skilled in giving the dreamer the meaning of his dream?"

Corb nods and his long stringy hair flows over his face. He does not attempt to push it back to where it was.

I take a deep breath and when I let the air loose, I announce, "I am Ronstrom."

"Ronstrom," he croaks. "Ronstrom, the hunter."

His voice does sound like rocks that are ground against each other, but in it there is also a definite croaking.

Corb repeats my name and more spittle leaks from between his lips.

"Then you know who I am?" I ask, proud that my skill as a hunter is often spoken about.

"I know," he says.

The wind increases and moans as it passes through the forest.

"There is none equal to my skill as a hunter," I tell him.

"But today," he answers, "all your arrows missed their mark."

A sudden heat invades my body and my cheeks burn. "A shift of the wind at the last moment," I explain.

Corb's laughter erupts. He sputters, coughs, and wheezes. Now he is laughing at me and I know from the sounds I previously heard that he has laughed at me several times since I entered the hut.

Angry now for having let an old man make a fool of me, I say, "I have come——"

"Ronstrom, the hunter," Corb says, still sputtering, "Ronstrom, whose hands are bloodied with the blood of other men. Oh, how well I know you, how well I see you!" As he speaks, the timbre of his voice changes. It becomes high-pitched, like the shrill squeak of a bird of prey.

My skin crawls and flecks with bumps. I doubt that Corb is a man. I clear my throat and say, "I have killed only those who would have killed me."

Corb's lips part in a toothless smile and he sprinkles more herbs and flowers into the fire. The columns of smoke rise out of the fire, come together just above the orange tips of the flames and twist together like forest vines into one thick trunk of ascending smoke, around which the hut begins to slowly move.

"Your dream, Ronstrom," Corb grates. "Tell me your dream."

I tell him about Gendy's bones, how they joined together, what Gendy's spirit said to me, and how The Giver of Life laughed. Even as I speak Corb vanishes behind a pall of smoke.

My vision dims. When the smoke lifts, I see Corb is on his feet.

He is very tall and very gaunt. His arms are outstretched. The tattered skins he wears hang from his limbs like the wings of a bat.

I look up at him. The inside of my head feels soft and white as if it is filled with the morning mist.

Corb begins to sway from side to side. Now and then he moves his arms in front of him. A strange new sound comes from his throat. First it swells and then contracts. I do not understand what he is doing. But I soon realize he is using words. I hear my name and I listen.

Ronstrom . . . Ronstrom, he who has come to speak his dream of stones and bones.

Ronstrom, Ronstrom, the mightiest hunter of them all, is rattle-tattle blind. . . .

Ronstrom, Ronstrom, it is not for you to choose or say.

Ronstrom, Ronstrom, what woulds't thou do, run from He who has given you legs?

Ronstrom, Ronstrom, the dream you dreamt is not for me to divine. Ronstrom, Ronstrom, young as you are, your beard is gray and your face marked . . . Ronstrom, Ronstrom the blood of several colors your hands, the blood of many more will add their stains to what is already there.

Ronstrom, Ronstrom, the mightiest hunter of them all, is rattle-tattle blind. . . .

Ronstrom, Ronstrom, the mightiest hunter of them all, is rattle-tattle blind.

Ronstrom . . . Ronstrom . . . Ronstrom . . .

Corb suddenly staggers and I realize that he has been whirling around, that the hut, too, has been whirling around. . . .

I pass my hand over my eyes.

"Ronstrom, Ronstrom," Corb wheezes as he labors to breathe, "Ronstrom, the hunter, will pass . . . Ronstrom, the builder, will——" He falters.

My head throbs.

"Ronstrom, the builder!" Corb shouts.

The words swell out and repeat themselves over and over again. "Ronstrom, the builder . . . Ronstrom, the builder . . . Ronstrom, the builder. . . ."

They swing back and forth in my brain like the alternation of day with night. Now from one side of the sky, now from the other. And out of the chant of "Ronstrom the builder" comes the words, "Look to the forest . . . Look to the forest. . . ." Somehow the spirit of Gendy has entered the hut.

73

Corb's voice grows weaker. He falls to his knees.

Even though my vision is blurred and my head throbs, I see that Corb's thin bony hand is holding onto the column of smoke. It is the column of smoke that prevents him from toppling into the fire.

I do not believe what I see, and again I pass my own hand over my eyes.

Corb is still holding onto the column of smoke.

And I am still being called "Ronstrom the builder. . . ."

And Gendy is telling me over and over again to "Look to the forest. . . ."

"No!" I shout. "No . . . I am a hunter . . . I am Ronstrom the hunter!"

"Ronstrom the builder . . . Ronstrom the builder . . . Ronstrom the builder. . . ."

"Look to the forest . . . Look to the forest . . . Look to the forest. . . ."

"I am Ronstrom the hunter!" I shout, using all my energy to leap to my feet. "I am Ronstrom the hunter. . . ."

Corb pulls himself up, hand over hand; he uses the column of smoke to gain his full height and when he stands erect he chants, "Ronstrom, mightiest hunter of them all is rattle-tattle blind. . . ."

A deep, dark laughter rolls across the sky and shakes the earth.

And then like a great dark bird Corb flutters to the ground.

The hut stops spinning. The column of smoke is wafted to one side by a stray breeze that enters the hut.

My vision begins to clear. The voices are silent.

I am trembling and as I bring my eyes into focus I look across the fire pit at Corb. His eyelids are open. The whites of his eyes stare at me. Without having to touch him I know he is dead. The flames in the fire pit die, too. The hut is plunged into darkness.

I crawl through the opening and feel as though I am leaving the world of the dead and once more entering the world of the living.

The night is crisp and clean-scented. I take several deep breaths and, as I walk slowly away from Corb's hut, I look up at the sky.

It is filled with small bits of flickering light. My eyes seek the one around which all others seem to swing. It hangs in that portion of the sky where during the day the sun never goes.

As I plunge into the forest I wonder whether Corb was a man or a woman.

Whether he was one or the other, or even if he was part of each, no longer matters now that he is dead. As I hurry back to my hut, I try not to think about what happened. Corb never did tell me what my dream meant; he probably did not know.

IX

The rain giants walk hand in hand with the wind over the land. Day after day the face of the sun is hidden by dark-gray clouds.

The people of my tribe shiver in their huts and huddle close to the fire pit in order to keep warm. They are fearful of what will happen when there will be more night than day, when the wind will change partners and travel with the snow, and when the terrible cold will dig into their bodies like a skinning knife.

They stare into the flames of the fire and dream of meat. But most of all they are frightened even as I am frightened that the long darkness, and all the misery that it brings, will remain with us; that the sun will never find its way back to us, that the darkness will become even longer, and there will never again be day.

These are terrible thoughts to think, even for me.

No matter if the rain giants and the wind are about, I hunt. The forest always offers me something. If it is not a rabbit or a squirrel to fill my belly with, it is something to gratify me in other ways—a grassy glen where I can find shelter from the wind and the rain, or a bush ripe with red berries that are good to eat.

There are many thing to think about, but most of all there is the feeling that I am as tall as the tallest tree, as fleet as a deer, and stronger by far than any bear. This feeling makes me aware of myself as a man, as a hunter, and as creature of the forest.

When the rain giants and the wind leave, the clouds quickly follow, and the sunlight once more pours over the land.

Other hunters come into the forest, but none stop to speak with me. I am shunned by everyone. They are afraid of me.

One morning I find myself close to Gibben's encampment, and without any hesitation I go to see Alvina. Since Garth was slain I have not thought about Alvina. To keep her in mind would not have been possible. She is like a lovely doe, soft and full of life. My thoughts have been too dark to live side by side with thoughts of her. But now those dark thoughts are gone and I want very much to see her.

She is sitting outside the hut. Her face is turned toward the sun. Her eyes are closed. Her long black hair is tied tightly behind her head with a piece of rabbitskin. And her bare breasts rise and fall with her slow breathing.

I move closer.

She stirs and opens her eyes, sees me, and stifles a cry with her hand.

I move still closer and Alvina indicates that her father is in the hut.

"It is time we spoke," I say in a low voice.

She looks toward the hut and then at me.

I wonder how she sees me. Does the gray of

77

my beard make her think I am an old man? Does the scar on my forehead frighten her?

Suddenly she says, "Others say there is the wolf in you."

I have never heard her speak before. Her voice sounds like the soft rush of water when it flows swiftly between the river rocks. I would like to hear that sound in my hut. I would like to hear it in the dark of the night when my manthing seeks the slit in her body.

"They say," she continues, "that you are more wolf than man, that some strong magic made you that way when you went into the mountains."

I shake my head.

"Ansgar says you become a wolf when you hunt."

"He is a foolish man," I answer. "I am a man like any other man."

"But you always have meat, more meat than anyone else," she counters.

"That is because I am a better hunter than anyone else."

Alvina is silent. Her hand goes to her hair.

I watch her, enjoying the upward movement of her breasts, and I wonder if her nipples would, like those of other women I have lain with, swell and become hard if my manthing was in her body.

"Why did you go to the mountains?" she asks, dropping her hand to her side and flushing under my stare.

I shrug. How could I explain it to her, a child of fifteen summers? A woman who knows nothing of what a man must do?

If I told her about Gendy she would not believe me. If I told her of the cave she would not believe me. If I told her about The Giver of Life she would be frightened. And if I told her all that I must do she would mock me for my foolishness.

"Why did you go?" she asks again.

"To hunt——" I say.

"Hunt what?" Gibben asks, pushing his way out of the hut. There is anger in his eyes when he looks at me.

I do not know what to answer. "There is less game there," Gibben growls, "than there is here. The Rock People are eaters of birds' eggs and roots."

I say nothing. I do not want to make him angrier.

"I have heard," he says, looking hard at me, "that Corb, one of the old ones, is dead."

I remain silent.

"It is said by others," Gibben continues, "that you went to see him."

"And what else is said by the others?" I ask, holding my anger close to me lest it free itself and make me hurl my spear.

"You came to him with a dream," he answers and adds with mockery in his voice, "like a woman."

My fingers tighten around the shaft of my spear.

"Is that so?" Gibben asks.

I nod.

He glances meaningfully at Alvina. Then he says, "I have been told that strange sounds came from the hut. That all of the old ones were so frightened that they fled from their encampment."

"We talked long into the night," I tell him.

"And in the morning when you left his hut——"

"Corb gave up his life spirit——"

"No," Gibben says, "you took it from him because you did not like what he told you."

"And you have heard all this?" I ask in a voice honed with anger.

"There is more," Gibben says. "But I for one do not believe that you become a wolf."

"Perhaps," I answer playfully, "that is the only true thing you have heard."

Gibben gives me a strange look and Alvina grows pale.

"Perhaps," I say, "all that you have heard has no more substance than the morning mist?"

Gibben waves what I said aside. "You are not like the rest of us," he says.

"Where am I different?"

"You are a young man," he replies, "but you are an old man. There is a scar——"

"Many men have scars."

"But not like that one," Gibben says. "That scar was not made by a knife or spear. It was burned into your skin, but not by fire. I know what the skin looks like after it has been eaten by fire. That scar did not come from the fire. And your eyes are filled with what you have seen. They are too deep for any man to understand. Yes," he continues, nodding his head, "I do not think you belong here any more Ronstrom; I think you should go back to the mountains."

Alvina gasps.

Gibben admonishes her with a stern look and to me he says, "Rigga has seen her and wants her for his woman."

A sudden heat flashes through my body. "And what does he offer?" I ask, trembling with anger.

"To fill my hut with meat."

"And if I offer to do the same?" I ask.

Gibben shakes his head. "She has never had a manthing inside of her," he says.

I know he wants to bargain. I look at Alvina. She is standing very still. Her bare breasts are thrust forward and if she were not afraid of her father I am certain she would remove the skins covering her slit to spur me to better Rigga's offer. I want Alvina for my woman, but I will not pit myself against Rigga to win her.

"Twice as much," Gibben says, "and she is yours."

"And if Rigga offers to fill three huts with meat," I ask, "then what will happen?"

"She is certainly worth whatever a man is willing to give," he says, and taking hold of Alvina's hand he exhibits her to me. "She will do all that a woman must do for a man."

I shake my head.

Gibben scowls and Alvina looks questioningly at me.

"I cannot spend my days filling your huts with meat," I tell him. "I would fill two, Rigga would fill three and I four. There would be no end to it. That is not a game for a man to play, Gibben, even if the prize you dangle before him is your daughter."

Alvina's face is flushed and the color spreads over her bare breasts. Her eyes glow with anger.

"I give you fair warning, Gibben," I tell him, "when the time comes I will come and take her for my woman."

He scowls and then, boasting, he answers, "By then she will be Rigga's woman and the spirit of life will be swollen within her."

"If Rigga fills your hut with meat," I say, "you must abide by your word. But if he fails to fill your hut with meat and you give her to him I will still claim her for my woman."

"Rigga will kill you!"

"He has already tried and failed," I say.

81

"If you take her from me by force," Gibben warns, "I will kill you."

"It is hard to kill a wolf," I tell him, "very hard." And hefting my spear I turn and walk toward the forest.

"Ronstrom," Gibben shouts, "I warn you not to think you can take her by force! I am not afraid of you. You will bleed just like any other man. Ronstrom, take heed of what I am telling you."

His words like arrows pursue me into the forest, but they are soon blunted by the wall of trees that comes between us.

Gibben for all his bluster and swagger is afraid of me as are the others of the tribe.

X

Many times the sun crosses the sky and is followed by the black cloak of night.

I keep to myself, avoiding those of my tribe, even as they shun me. I hunt and my belly does not growl with hunger. Often I think of Alvina and my manthing grows hard with lust. Because there is bad feeling between me and her father Gibben, I wonder if she will ever be my woman.

At night when the wind comes up and makes the tree bend, I sit close to the fire pit in my hut and think if, as Gibben said, I am different from the other men in the tribe. If I am, it was Gendy's doing, for it was he who sent me to the cave in the mountains.

If I am different from the others it was The Giver of Life who marked me, who turned my hair and beard white.

But I cannot escape from my own foolishness, for it was I who asked The Giver of Life for a sign that the people could see, and he marked me and gave me the white hair and beard of an old man.

I stir the fire with a stick and put several more faggots on it before settling down to stare at the flames again.

My people are afraid of me and will, rather than follow, run from me. I cannot gather them together, as The Giver of Life commanded me. Even if I succeed in convincing a few to follow me, where would I lead them and what could I promise them?

These thoughts lean heavily upon me as a heavy mantle of skins lies across my shoulders. Such a cloak gives no warmth. As I stretch out close to the fire pit, I wonder if Gibben spoke with greater wisdom than he knew when he told me to leave my people and return to the mountains. There at least I could live without having to carry out the word of The Giver of Life.

My eyelids grow heavy and I slip easily into the deep darkness of sleep. I dream again and what I see makes me cry out!

I wake with a start and grab my spear. The flames in the fire pit are gone; only the red glow of embers remains. The inside of the hut is as black as my dream. I wonder if I am still asleep, but the hard feel of the spear's shaft is enough to reassure me that I am awake. I move into a crouch. I sense something by sniffing at the air, but cannot determine its scent. Perhaps it is upwind from me. My heart is beating very fast. I am ready to hurl the spear should anyone or any animal come through the entrance.

I wait. Nothing happens.

I suck in my breath and as I slowly let it out it makes a low whistling sound. I reach for my knife, thrust it securely into my girdle and, taking my skin shield, I crawl outside the hut.

The night has gone, but it is not yet dawn. The sky is gray and only a few of the brightest stars are still visible and one of those between the others is brighter than all the others. Soon the sun will come up over the rim of the sky and everything but the pale shadows of the moon will be driven away.

The forest is filled with swirling mists. It is the time when the spirits of the dead return to their graves. My skin prickles and I shrug my shoulders to cast off thoughts about dead men.

I take several steps, stop, and glance over my shoulder at the hut. I would like to return to it, build up the fire, and warm myself until the sun's light comes in long shafts through the trees. I do not go back. Instead, I take several more steps and then through the gloom of the swirling mists I see a huge, dark shape.

I stop!

I do not know what I am looking at. The mists are too thick and too many. But whatever it is, I know it is very big. I also know its presence woke me from my dream.

A sudden breeze parts the swirling mists and I catch a glimpse of dark-brown hide. It is not a bear. The mists close again and breathing deeply I move closer. I am no longer fearful. It is some kind of an animal.

Even as I move toward it it moves away from me.

I follow!

The sun is above the edge of the earth. Its long yellow fingers push the mists away and I see the animal for the first time.

It is a stag, a huge stag with a great set of antlers. Its hide is brown but when it passes through the light of the sun it becomes almost reddish.

I try to get closer, but as soon as I am within

killing distance the beast lifts its magnificent head
and moves off at a trot.

I make several attempts to close in on it and
each fails.

Now and then it turns its head toward me and
gives me the feeling that it is taking my measure.
I do not like this feeling.

The sun is above the rim of the earth, but has
not yet reached its highest point in the sky. The
stag is still in front of me and I have not yet hurled
my spear at it. Though the sun is shining the day is
clear and crisp. I am wet with sweat from the
chase, but I am determined to kill the stag. I will
keep at him until he is too weary to continue and
then I will make my kill!

The thought of having all that meat makes my
stomach growl and my mouth water. I even think
that I might bring part of a haunch to Gibben.
Perhaps such a gift from me will change his feelings toward me.

The stag moves again and I am close behind him.

The beast does not stop. He goes deeper and
deeper into the forest.

I am hot and thirsty. The animal looks back at
me and I shout, "I am here. I will not stop until I
have you!"

He crashes through the thick undergrowth, making a path that two big men walking side by side
could easily use. He is larger than any animal
I have ever seen!

If I kill him it will take several trips to bring
the meat back to my hut. Perhaps it would be
better for me to skin him where he falls and——

He has stopped!

I slow my pace. The wind is right. He cannot
get my scent. I am almost close enough to hurl

my spear. The thud of my heart is very loud and my blood sings in my ears.

The beast shakes his head and the tips of his antlers flash yellow in the sun. His forefeet paw the soft earth.

I am very close.

He turns his huge head toward me. His muzzle is very black and wet. His huge nostrils quiver and there are flakes of white foam along his dark lips. His chest heaves as he struggles to fill his lungs with air. The spear in my hand feels wonderfully light. I lift it, pull my arm back, and then send it hurtling through the air at the exposed portion of his neck.

The sudden swoosh of my spear startles him. He rears up on his hind legs, blotting out the sky.

I feel as though he is going to strike me down and I drop to the ground. I see the flash of my polished spearhead as it pierces a shaft of sunlight. It hangs in the air and then drops to the earth.

Where the stag was is nothing. The beast has gone!

I beat the soft earth with my fist. To have not made the kill enrages me. Had I brought him down I would have something to boast about, something that not even Rigga could deny or equal. I retrieve my spear and look for signs that I might follow, but there are none!

I do not understand how such a huge animal could move without leaving a track.

I look back. His marks are everywhere, in the thick undergrowth and along the sides of the tree, where his pointed antlers grazed the bark.

I shake my head and notice that even the trees in this part of the forest are different from those that grow where I usually hunt, or those near my hut.

These trees are taller, straighter, and only a very strong wind would make them bend. And their leaves are a deeper green than I have ever before seen.

Everything is different, even the flowers seem to be more brilliantly colored than others I have seen.

I suddenly wonder where I am.

Every hunter knows there are enchanted places in the forest, places that a man might find his way into but never out of. And there are animals, phantoms of animals that will lead a hunter on and on until he has left the world he knows and finds himself in——

I break into a cold sweat and with a weak feeling in my knees I start back over the trail made by the stag, as he crashed through the forest. I gather my courage and quicken my pace. And then I begin to run, expecting my way to be suddenly blocked by some evil spirit. Nothing comes before me except my own sweat, which falls in great drops from my brow and dims my vision.

I cannot keep running. My legs are too tired to continue and my chest feels as though it is about to split open. I come to a small stream and, gasping, I drop down next to it. I fill my parched mouth with water and immediately begin to cough. When I stop coughing the ache in my chest has gone and I drink again.

Too weary to stand up, I roll on to the bank and look up at the clear blue sky that shows through the branches of the trees. Many birds fly past; some of them I do not recognize.

After a while I am able to stand and even though my legs are still shaky I start to walk.

The forest is filled with signs of game. Deer tracks and those of the boar are everywhere. Fruit, nuts, and berries grow in profusion.

I am overwhelmed by the signs of food. It does not seem possible that this is the same forest where men are happy to grub roots and kill a rat or a rabbit.

Soon I am back into the part of the forest I know. Here the trees are stunted, their leaves already mottled brown and yellow from the sting of the night's cold. Here there are only signs of rats, squirrels, and rabbits.

I pause to kill a rabbit and then hurry back to my hut. By the time I reach it, night has filled the sky. But clouds hide the stars and the moon. The wind's sharp teeth nip at my arms and legs.

I sit near my fire pit with the smell of rabbit in my nostrils, while outside I can hear the mournful wailing of the wind.

I am hungry and eat the rabbit very quickly. Then I crush its bones with my teeth and suck out the insides.

I close my eyes and think of how wonderful deer meat would taste, or how much pleasure I would have munching on the juicy bones of a boar. And opening my eyes, I say aloud, "And it's all there in the forest. All the signs are there!"

Then somewhere deep in my own skull I hear Gendy say, "Look to the forest Ronstrom . . . look to the forest . . . it is all there!"

I leap to my feet and toss the rabbit bones into the fire, where they sizzle and snap.

The hut seems too small for me. I am even bigger than my tremendous shadow.

"It is in the forest," I repeat. "It is in the forest!"

89

I can no longer stay in the hut. I must go outside.

"It is in the forest!" I shout into the night. "It is in the forest!" And I know that The Giver of Life has given me a sign.

I fall to my knees and look up.

The clouds open and I see a fragment of the night sky. The sound of the wind becomes louder and in its voice is the voice of another.

"Ronstrom," it calls, "the time grows late . . . Ronstrom the builder, the time grows late . . . gather the people to you . . . they are yours to command for your command is but mine and mine is the law. . . ."

The voice rolls out of the dark star-filled sky and shakes the ground on which I kneel. I cannot look up. The blackness is more intense than any light I have ever known. But I must answer Him and I say, "I am Ronstrom the hunter. I am loved by none and despised by all. I cannot do what you ask!"

"Gather the people to you," The Giver of Life thunders. "Gather them to you and build me what I have shown you must be built . . . I have given you a sign . . . use it . . . gather the people to you . . . they need not love you . . . And if they fear you, turn that fear into your own purpose, into my purpose."

"I am a hunter!" I cry. "Choose a worthier man than myself. I am a hunter."

The clouds rush across the open patch of sky and I hear the deep booming laughter of The Giver of Life. . . .

I remain on my knees. Though I shake my head,

I know there is no escape from The Giver of Life. To do what he wants me to do is more than——

Suddenly the night is pierced with the cries of many men and from the forest they come running toward me. Like a man who has just satisfied himself with a woman, my strength is spent. I cannot move.

I am surrounded!

"You saw him!" a voice I recognize as belonging to Ansgar, the arrow maker shouts. "You saw him, baying at the moon like a wolf!"

My eyes find the faces of those who encircle me. The maker of clay pots is there and so is Gibben. And there are some I do not know, who are probably with the others for the pleasure of the kill.

"Say something!" Ansgar yells. "Tell us——"

Before any of them can move I spring to my feet! Startled, they fall back.

"Leave our forest," one of them warns. "Leave our forest and we will not harm you."

My answer is a short harsh laugh.

"He has the bark of a wolf," Gibben says and he rushes at me, flailing the air with his club.

I am able to side-step his rush, but then someone else comes at me from the other side. The blow smashes against my leg and sends me sprawling to the ground.

My attackers scream with delight and close in on me. By rolling myself into a ball I try to protect myself. But their blows fall so furiously on my body that I quickly lose my hold on the world and slip into a deep dark void.

I have no idea how long I have been in the void, but soon the blackness becomes red and I feel pain in every part of my body. It takes all my effort to open my eyes and then everything I see is blurred.

I try to move and soon discover I am bound, trussed up on a pole like an animal.

My back smashes against the earth and I realize that I am being carried somewhere.

The red boils in my eyes, but it is not the sun that does this. It is only the pain. Again I force my lids open. It is still night. I feel the sting of the wind on my battered limbs. There is the taste of blood in my mouth and blood drips from my nose. I cannot see the men who are carrying me, but I hear Gibben urging them to quicken their pace.

These are the men The Giver of Life wants me to lead; these are the men I should gather to me; these are the men who are to build——

"Never!" I croak, spitting blood. "Never!"

"What does he say?" the man at my foot asks.

"Nothing," his companion answers. "He is just moaning."

"I tell you," Ansgar says, "we should kill him while we have the chance."

"I agreed to this," Gibben answers, "but not to killing. He will not come back."

I close my eyes and try to pull myself up on the pole. But the effort is wasted and the movement causes me a great deal of pain. If I am not going to be killed I wonder what they intend to do with me?

Once more I slip off into the black void. When the red fills my skull and eyes again I awaken. I open my eyelids. The yellow of the sun is so bright that I quickly close my eyes. When I open them again I know that I am alone. I have been tethered to a stake on the plain where I used Gendy for bait and where I freed Garth when Rigga tried to use the boy the same way.

Now it is my turn!

I wonder who the hunter is or if there is a hunter?

I shake my head. Gibben would not kill me, but he would leave me naked and defenseless to let the killing be done by a wolf or a bear. It would have been better if he had killed me. I close my eyes and calmly wait for my death.

XI

The death I wait for does not come. But I am so bruised and battered that I want to die.

All through that first day I sink and rise in the black void. My eyelids are too swollen for me to keep them open and my head throbs with pain.

Night comes. The wind is bitter cold and each gust slashes like a well-honed knife at my naked body. My teeth chatter and I cannot stop myself from trembling. I open my eyelids and perceive a portion of the sky.

Water flows from my eyes and I cry out "Giver of Life, where are you? Why have you let them do this to me?"

The words are clear in my skull, but the sounds that come from my lips are as different from what is in my head as what I am to what I was. No words come forth and I hear only the tormented groaning of a wounded animal.

Naked, I remain on the ground and shiver the night away.

The sun comes and warms me.

Night follows and I whimper from the bite of the wind.

The sun comes again and night returns.

A cold rain lashes my nakedness and I lay in the mud, huddled into a ball.

The rain ceases and I sink into the dark void again.

One morning I feel the warmth of the sun on my body and I move. There is less pain in my body and when I open my eyelids I can see everything clearly. I slowly get on my feet. The effort causes me to wince and it takes all my strength to climb up the pole bit by bit until I stand erect!

And when I am on my feet I see what has been done to me. I am not only tethered to a stout pole, but I am on view to everyone in my tribe. The ground where I stand is littered with rocks and offal that has been thrown at me. And even as I stand I am gaped at by those who have been watching me.

I understand what Gibben meant when he told Ansgar, "He will not come back."

Not only am I tethered but I am also guarded. The man who guards me stands beyond the limit of my tether. I look at the people in front of me.

One of them throws a rock. It strikes my shoulder, but I do not feel it.

Suddenly I hear laughter. My eyes move off to the left where the laughter comes from. Rigga is there.

My anger flares, but dies just as quickly. It is senseless for me to waste my strength. I am like a man whose manthing does not respond to the sight of a woman.

"There," Rigga bellows, pointing to me, "is the great hunter Ronstrom—there he is!" He stops, his words choked off by his laughter. "That one there," he tells the others, "threatened to kill me. I do not think he will threaten anyone again. There is the

95

man you feared. He does not look so frightening now."

Someone throws another rock. It strikes me on the side of the head. I fall to my knees. Blood trickles down. I do not even bother to wipe it away. I wait until the haze leaves my eyes and then I pull myself up again. . . .

"No more rocks." Rigga laughs. "One might crack his skull and free his life spirit."

The others agree that it is better to keep me alive a while longer. "At least," one of the men says, "he makes us forget we are hungry."

"Besides," another comments, "he will die when the first snow comes."

The crowd moves away, but Rigga remains. He stands and looks at me for a long time.

I let my eyes say the words I cannot speak.

"Still you challenge me?" he growls.

I say nothing.

"Next time," he says, "I will let them throw their stones."

I remain silent.

He gathers a mouthful of spit and lets it fly at me. But I am too far away from him for it to reach me.

He growls an insult and then more clearly he says, "Alvina will be my woman. She has seen you here and does not think you will be able to do what must be done to a woman by a man." He laughs, turns, and lopes away.

His mention of Alvina makes my throat ache. For her to have seen me the way I am is almost too much for me to bear and I slowly shake my head from side to side. I am unable to keep myself from moaning and sinking down to the ground. I wrap my arms around the pole and moan the afternoon away.

At night I gather pieces of offal that litter the ground and eat them. Then I look at the guard who sits close to a roaring fire. He is not the one who watches over me by day.

Even as the sun's light alternates with darkness my strength returns. It surges through my body. When night comes I no longer feel the sting of the wind. The raw offal I devour fills my body with vigor and when the people of the tribe come to torment me I stand erect, proud, and silent.

After a while Rigga no longer comes, nor does Gibben.

When I am strong enough I begin to watch the guard. I keep my eyes on him night after night. He knows that I am watching him.

When he can no longer stand my stare he cries out, "Look somewhere else Ronstrom, or I swear by the food in my stomach I will blind you!"

I do not answer, and I continue to watch. Sometimes the leap of the red flames in the darkness and the shadow of the man slip from sight and my eyes are filled with the image of Gibben and Rigga.

I want to kill them and the thought of killing them fills my body with a heat as intense as heat I feel when I possess a woman. I will kill them slowly, hacking off their limbs one by one until they beg me to free the life spirit from their bodies. Such thoughts are more meaningful to me than food.

I feel nothing but anger toward the people of my tribe. They are fools and deserve no more than they are getting from the forest.

But even as I think these thoughts, others enter my head. They are not very clear and I do not understand them. I know that no matter what my feelings are toward Gibben and Rigga, I will not kill them. I will let them live, and I will gather the people of my tribe to me.

I will do these things because I can not undo what The Giver of Life has done to me. . . .

The guard suddenly leaps to his feet. "I warned you, Ronstrom!" he shouts, rushing at me.

I am on my feet. The beat of my heart has quickened. I stand ready and waiting.

The man comes at me with his spear!

I can only use the length of my tether.

He thrusts at me with the spear.

I draw back, putting the pole between us.

He curses and tries to stab at my face.

I leap from one side to the other and back again.

He follows my movement with his spear, but I am always quicker than he.

"Ronstrom!" he shouts. "I will——" He never finishes telling me what he will do.

I whip part of my tether around his spear and he is thrown off-balance. I leap on him, driving my heel against the broad of his back. The blow stuns him. I slip the knife from his girdle and cut myself free. He struggles to free himself, but he is no match for me.

Quickly I bind him where I was a short while before bound.

He pleads for his life, telling me, "It was all Rigga's doing. His and Gibben's. Oh, please," he whines, "I had nothing to do with your capture."

I take his clothing and his weapons.

"Tell them," I say to him, "that I will be back. Tell the people that I, Ronstrom, will be back. Tell Rigga and Gibben that I give them their lives even as I give you yours. Tell them I do not walk alone, that I do not run alone, and that I do not stand alone. Tell them all what I have said."

I plunge into the depths of the forest, where I lost the trail of the stag. I hunt, rest, and search for the stag.

It is good to be free again. I eat well and have a comfortable shelter in a cave not far from the bank of a river.

The sun's journey in the sky is shorter and shorter each time it comes up over the edge of the earth, and the days are almost as cold as the nights. The wind is blustery. The reds and yellows of the leaves make the forest look as though it is in flames.

When I am not hunting or looking for the stag, I sit at the entrance to my cave and think about what I must do. The thoughts do not come easily. And when they come they are not in order. I must string them together the way a woman strings beads. After many days and nights of thinking and stringing the thoughts together I know what must be done and how I must do it.

Once the thoughts are strung I hang them in the back of my head and spend all of my time looking for the stag.

The day that I find him the sky is covered with dark-gray clouds. A cold wind blows down from the mountains where the Rock People live and there is the scent of snow in the air.

I see the animal standing on the bank of the river, not far from my cave. He is looking straight at me. His breath steams in the cold air. He has my scent but does not flee.

I move closer!

He turns directly toward me. His antlers are

huge. He bobs his head up and down and paws the soft earth with his right front paw.

I lift my spear and just as I am about to hurl it I pause. There is something about the stag that fills me with feelings I never before experienced. I want him to bolt and run. I do not want to separate his life spirit from his body. But to do what I must do I cannot let him live.

The spear leaves my arm and cuts the air with its swooshing sound.

The stag leaps up!

The spear drives into his huge brown chest and cuts his heart in two. A torrent of blood gushes like a great red waterfall down his dark skin. His feet give out from under him, and he rolls over on his side. His breath no longer steams in the cold air. He is dead!

I stand over him and as I pull my spear out of his body the first snow swirls down from the gray sky. I take the animal's skin and the top of his head, but I cannot bring myself to eat the flesh of his body. I build over it a huge fire and let the flames do what I could not.

XII

The leaves are pulled from the trees by the teeth of the wind. Many of the days are sunless. Snow dusts the trees.

Soon I will go back to my tribe and gather them to me. Now I must wait until there is more night than day, until I know my people are numb with fear.

On a day when the world is filled with swirling snow and the wind howls like a prowling wolf, I mount the top of the stag's head on my own, place his dark skin across my shoulders, and slowly make my way out of the depths of the forest.

I do not attempt hiding. I told them I was coming back and that is what I am doing.

I walk slowly along the trails of the forest where I know I will be seen. I say nothing. With a quick sideward movement of my eyes I often see the people cower, afraid of what I might do.

I go from encampment to encampment and say nothing to the people there.

I see Gibben, but remain silent.

I do not even speak to Rigga when I come upon him.

Only when I see Alvina do I stop and say "Do not be afraid."

She nods, but cannot hide the fear in her eyes.

I would reach out to touch her face so that she might know that I am still a man and not a spirit from the forest, but I cannot do that. I am walking a different path now. Perhaps later I can think of her as a woman and act like a man.

It does not take long for the people to follow me. And when there are enough of them I stop and turn.

They fall back.

I wave my hands.

Some drop to the ground.

"Who are you?" one of the men shouts.

"Ronstrom the hunter," I answer.

They shrink back even more.

"Why are you here?" Rigga questions, coming forward with his spear ready.

"I gave you your life," I say, shaking my huge antlers at him, "and now I have come to give you all life."

Gibben pushes his way out of the group. "Do you take us for fools, Ronstrom?" he questions, coming closer than Rigga had dared.

I brandish my spear at him and say, "I have given you your life, Gibben. Do not be foolish enough to make me take it from you."

He hesitates and moves back. His face is twisted by anger.

I glance around me, not to look at anything in particular, but to think of what I will next say. But I see that the sky is a mixture of light and dark grays. The snow has stopped falling and the wind has dropped off.

"Why are we standing here like fools?" Gibben

questions. "That one there," he says, pointing to me with his spear, "has come to mock us, to shame us——"

"He should have been killed!" Ansgar the arrow maker shouts from the crowd. "I told you he should have been killed!"

A loud murmur of approval comes from those who stand in front of me.

"Kill him now!" a man yells. "Kill him now!"

A spear swooshes through the air.

I stand absolutely motionless. If I am to die there is nothing I can do to prevent my life spirit from leaving my body. Should I run, the air would suddenly be filled with more spears than I could possibly escape. I strangely am not afraid!

The spear strikes the snow with a thud in front of me. Another spear quickly follows the first and then another follows. None come near enough to do me harm.

The people are mystified, and in their faces I see a mounting fear. Increasing their apprehension even more, I say, "As long as I wear this robe and this stag crown your spears, your arrows, even your warclubs, are usless against me."

An anxious murmur fills the cold air.

And then Gibben asks "Why have you come back, Ronstrom?"

"To bring the people life," I answer.

"But they are alive," Rigga says, waving his hand back toward the others. "Even with your magic robe and crown of antlers you should be able to see that the people are alive."

His words and tone have enough mockery in them to make some of the bolder men in the tribe snicker.

I ignore Rigga's bid to make a fool out of me

103

and I say, "Do my bidding, and I will give you meat."

My words startle them and though there is snow on the ground, the cold air is suddenly filled with a loud beelike buzz. Few of them believe what I have said and one man calls out, "Tell us again what you will do, Ronstrom."

"I will give you meat," I repeat.

The buzz from them grows louder and more excited. Their breaths steam in the cold air and look like puffs of smoke.

Gibben faces them. He waves them silent. "Let Ronstrom tell us more," he says. "Let him tell us how he, for all the gray of his hair and beard, is still a youth of twenty summers and can do what we older and more experienced men can not do."

He does not turn to me when he finishes speaking, and I know it is his way of showing the others how little he thinks of my words. As for myself I did not realize it would be so difficult to speak to my people. I move and the crunch of the snow beneath my feet makes a loud sound.

Gibben swivels his head toward me and says, "I do not think you can tell us, Ronstrom. I think that you have come here to make fools of us. I do not think your robe and stag head are magic, and I do not think that we should do your bidding."

The best hunters in the tribe immediately agree with him.

"You have come to us out of the forest," Gibben says, "to try our patience. I told you once and I will tell you again in front of all of the men of our tribe: you are not one of us. You are different——"

"Gibben!" I shout, making my voice deep to give it a rolling quality. "Gibben, you are a foolish man and those who heed your words are even more foolish."

He whirls around. With all his might he hurls his spear at me.

I do not move and Gibben's spear joins the others in the snow before me.

The people begin to buzz again.

"Listen," I tell them, "it is in my power to keep meat from your bellies or to give it to you, as I see fit."

The buzz stops and deep silence falls over the people. They do not know if I hold such power, and they are afraid.

"I can give you meat," I say, "if you do my bidding."

"What would you have us do?" a man questions.

"Only the best hunters will hunt and they will hunt for all. Everyone will do——"

"I will not hunt for another!" one of the hunters shouts.

"Nor will I!" another one cries.

"The meat I take is my own," Rigga growls.

"He is the foolish one!" Gibben shouts, pointing to me. "To think that men will hunt to fill another's belly!"

"You have been dying," I tell them, "for more winters than any of us can remember——"

"And if I give my meat to another," a hunter yells, "he will live and I will die!"

I try to tell them how the work will be divided, but they are too angry to listen. Those who are hunters are determined to keep what they kill, and those who feed mainly on roots and insects are more than willing to claim a share of anyone's meat. Arguments spring up like summer weeds.

Gibben knows what is happening, and there is

laughter in his eyes. Of all the hunters' voices Rigga's is the loudest. "I will kill any man who tries to take my meat," he proclaims.

Once more I call for silence. Gradually the din of angry voices grows less and when there is silence I say, "There was more meat in this forest than ten tribes could eat. Then the children played and grew fat and the fat melted away and they become strong men and women. No one went hungry. The winter did not see the old ones or the children give up their life spirit. The hand of death did not come until a man or woman was weary of this world and eager to leave their bodies here and let their spirits find a new place."

The words tumble out of my mouth like the rush of water over a falls. I do not believe I am speaking. But the sound of the voice is mine. Some of what I say was told to me by Gendy the night I gave him the meat of the bear. Other things spring to life from I know not where but my tongue finds them, and I say, "I do not speak of rat meat or the meat of a rabbit or a squirrel. The meat I will give you is that of a deer, of a boar, of a bear, and of birds that I cannot name. And from this meat will come children who will not cry because their bellies are swollen with hunger. And from this meat will come nourishment for the old ones. And from this meat will come——"

"It cannot be!" Gibben shouts.

But the people hardly hear him. They are entranced by what I have told them.

"It cannot be!" Gibben cries. "He has clouded your minds and dimmed your eyes with the flow of his sweet words. If there was such game in the forest surely other hunters would have seen it. Why have none but you, Ronstrom, seen the deer, the boar, and the birds you can not even begin to name?"

I shake my head. I do not know how or what to answer Gibben.

"I have not seen the animals and the birds you tell us about!" he shouts. "And Rigga has not seen them——"

The other hunters shout that they have seen nothing of the game I said I saw.

"And who," Rigga wants to know, "told you about things none of us remember?"

"Gendy," I answer. "Gendy, the priest."

"And where is this Gendy?" Gibben questions, but he does not wait for an answer. He says to the people, "Ronstrom is not telling all. How can he give you meat? Only by taking from those who——"

"Gibben," I thunder before he damages too much with his words, "it is you who are a fool!"

My words strike him silent. A sudden silence drops over the people of my tribe. It is not a silence given with respect, nor is it the silence of nature in all of its various seasons. This silence is taut, stretched like the cords in Gibben's neck. It seethes with blood, and though not a sound is heard the shriek of death is in the icy air.

I wait for my tongue to find the words. My heart begins to race. I sweat, and then I take several deep breaths.

Gibben growls and grabbing Rigga's spear, he shouts, "This time I will not miss!"

Even as he raises his hand to hurl the spear, I answer his shout with a wordless one of my own. The sound of my voice stays his hand, and when he lowers the spear I say, "I do not stand here alone; I do not walk alone and I do not hunt alone.

The gray of hair, the gray of beard and mark on my forehead, is a sign for you to———"

The words fail me and once more my movement in the snow makes loud crunching sounds.

"My words," I tell them after a pause, "come from The Giver of Life. It is He who stands here with me, who walks with me, and who hunts with me. It is He who protected me when I was tethered to the pole and it is He who will give you meat. . . ."

"I thought you would give us meat," Gibben challenges.

I stammer and try to explain, but Gibben will not let me.

"Who and what is this Giver of Life?" he demands to know.

Soon everyone is shouting the same question.

I can not quiet them, but Gibben does. When there is silence he turns to me and says, "Tell us what manner of man is The Giver of Life?"

I hesitate, but he presses me for an answer. "He is not a man," I finally say.

The people murmur among themselves.

"A spirit then?" Gibben says.

"More than that."

"What does he look like?" Rigga challenges.

I remain silent.

"Surely you have seen him?" Gibben taunts.

"He is a light," I explain. "A very bright light and a voice, a voice———"

"A very bright light and a voice." Gibben laughs. "That only you can see and hear—is that what you expect us to follow? I have heard of your Giver of Life and others here have also heard of him. The old ones talk of Him. He was once a god but gods, like men, do not always remain where they are.

108

He is no longer a god. He is hardly a memory. . . ."

The people smile and then snicker.

I grow angry. "The Giver of Life," I shout, "will give you all meat!"

"And what would The Giver of Life ask in return for the meat he gives us?" one of the men questions. "If he gives us meat what will he have for himself? Gods, too, grow hungry."

"Answer the man!" Rigga laughs.

"He has need of our hands to build——"

"Build!" a hunter cries. "I am a hunter, not a maker of huts. I do not know what it means to build."

"What is it He wants built?" Gibben asks.

I remain silent. To say more would serve no purpose. My words have fallen on deaf ears. I cannot tell Gibben or anyone else what The Giver of Life wants the people of my tribe to build. I myself do not know what it is. I cannot name it.

"I doubt that you know," Gibben mocks.

"Do not anger me," I warn.

"You see how much I am frightened by you," he says and immediately feigns shaking with fear.

I stride quickly to where Gibben stands and grab hold of him. Lifting him high above my head, I fling him into a mound of snow.

"All of you have until the next sundown to make up your minds," I say, looking straight at them. "Those who follow me will have meat. Those who choose to remain as they are now will know the pangs of hunger and feel the hand of death."

Without waiting for anyone else to speak, I gather my cloak about me and walk into the forest. The crowd opens its ranks to let me pass.

"Ronstrom!" Gibben shouts after me. "Ronstrom,

I am not someone you pick up and hurl into the snow."

I do not stop or look back. As soon as I reach the trees it begins to snow again and a swirling white veil drops between me and my people. The wind howls wildly through the trees.

I am angry with myself for doing what had to be done so badly. I said the wrong words at the wrong time and let Gibben make a fool out of me. Had I listened to someone speak as I spoke to my people, I too would have laughed at what I had heard.

It takes more than a cloak of skin or a crown of antlers to make a man a leader of other men.

XIII

I go to the hut where I lived before I was taken captive by Gibben and the others. I do not light a fire because I fear it would reveal my presence to those who are against me. I sit and stare at the empty fire pit. My thick robe keeps me warm and protects me from the gusts of wind that blow through the large chinks in the hut's wall.

I am restive. My encounter with the people of my tribe makes me doubt I ever will be able to do what The Giver of Life demands I do.

I am not yet old enough to command the respect of men whose gray hair came not, like mine, from a sudden experience but through living many, many summers. My words to those whose lives stretched out beyond mine were like a child's prattle.

I am weary, but unable to find a place in the hut that will accept my body and allow me to sleep.

I cast my eyes toward the opening. The snow is still falling, and I can hear the howling of the wind as it threads its way through the trees.

I stand up and leave the hut. The snow is falling so fast that it turns the brown of the stag skin into a white mantle. I hurry through the forest.

The wind sounds like a pack of ravenous wolves

and each flake of snow that strikes my face and hands feels like the sudden prick of a fishbone needle. Overhead the sky is filled with dark rushing clouds. I quicken my pace.

Soon I am out of the forest and I walk on the plain where Gendy's bones lie buried. The earth is covered with snow. The wind here is even more savage than it is in the forest. After a while I stop walking and, gathering my great robe about me, I sit down on the snow-covered earth.

I do not have to see the naked ground to know that I am sitting in front of Gendy's grave. The weariness in my body seeps out. Soon I remember that it was on a night like this that I shared meat with Gendy and he told me about the cave in the mountains where the sun never travels. I shake my head. It seems almost as though it never happened.

I close my eyes and think of what I would say to the old man if he were sitting in front of me as he had so long ago. The words would not come easily to me, but I would tell him that The Giver of Life has made a poor choice by choosing me to do his bidding.

Perhaps I want Gendy's spirit to rise up and talk to me as it has so often done in my dreams?

But I see nothing but the swirling snow and hear nothing but the howling wind. And yet I feel strangely contented. A soft inner glow fills me.

I stand up and without thinking I say aloud, "I will come again, Gendy. I will come again."

I cannot help laughing at myself and, gathering my robe more securely around me, I walk slowly back to the forest. The night is almost spent and despite the snow the sky is touched with gray when the sun opens the day.

Before I reach the glen where my hut is I see

footprints in the snow. I have had visitors, and I sense danger. It is near, very near. This time I will not let them take me captive, and even as I suck in my breath I know that my visit to Gendy's grave probably saved my life. Silently I thank him as I stalk those who stalk me.

The marks in the snow tell me there are three men hunting me. I wonder if Gibben or Rigga are with them.

My blood grows hot and my breath steams in the cold air. The snow has stopped falling, but the wind is still blowing it around in one direction and then another.

The tracks I follow are deep and well made. Sometimes they become less visible than a spider's web in the full glare of sunlight.

Those I stalk are soon so close I hear their voices. Gibben and Rigga are not with them. I do not recognize any of the men by the sound of their voices. But I know that if they capture or kill me they will become important men amongst my people. No doubt they are as many summers old as myself. I shake my head. If I could talk to them I might convince them to hunt a different quarry, but I am sure they would not listen to what I say.

Though in the gray light they are dark shadows I am close enough to see them. They stand close together. They do not know what to do.

The tallest one says, "He must be close. We have seen his tracks."

"I think he has turned into a wolf," another says.

"He will turn back into a man," the third affirms, "as soon as he feels the sting of our spears or arrows."

There is no doubt that they will hunt me until they find me and the day is still young. The sun

113

IRVING A. GREENFIELD

has yet to journey across the sky before it drops below the edge of the world.

It is they who are hunting me. I do not want to run from my pursuers. I clench my teeth together. If I do not kill them they will try to kill me.

I set my spear against a tree and, notching an arrow in my bow, I draw it back against the string. The arrow suddenly sings through the air. The bowstring makes a twanging sound.

The tall one screams, clutches his bloody breast, and drops to the snow, his life spirit gone.

Another arrow sings its death song in the cold morning air. A second hunter cries out and is quickly silenced as the sharp point opens his throat.

The third hunter runs. I do not follow him. Let him tell the others of my wrath and my vengeance. There is no need for me to boast of it.

I take my spear and, slinging my bow, I walk to where the two young men lie. The tall one is face-down in the snow and, spreading out from under him like the flow of water when it runs from a cracked vessel, his warm blood seeps into the cold snow. I go to the other. He is sprawled on his back. His legs are twisted away from each other. He is still alive and the life spirit that is still in him steams in the cold air. His eyes are open. They are blue, the color of a light sky or a robin's egg. He makes strange gurgling sounds deep in his throat. There is a question in his blue eyes. I know all too well what he is asking, and I answer, "It was you who wanted to kill me."

His face twitches with pain and a soft moan comes from his lips. More blood flows from the wound in his throat. He shakes his head. His lips turn purple and there is a film in his eyes. His

114

breath no longer steams in the cold air. His life spirit has left his body.

I lean on my spear and look at the two bodies. I wonder if I should take the heads of both and carry them back to the tribe. I do not act on the thought and I turn away, leaving the two hunters where I slew them. The wolves and rats will find them soon. I go deep into the forest and wait until the sun is low in the sky before I return to the place of my people.

Some of them are already waiting. I pass before them and mount the small rise where I stood the previous day. Several more join those who are there.

Gibben comes and I can see from the look on his face that he has heard about the two hunters I slew.

Ansgar and the maker of clay pots come.

Rigga arrives and immediately he and Gibben turn their backs on me and talk to each other. Now and then one of them glances over his shoulder to look at me.

When all are assembled and the sky is filled with the color of sunset I say, "I have come for your answer."

Before anyone can speak Gibben shouts, "The blood of young men freshly slain stains your hands! Leave us, Ronstrom, before it is too late and your blood stains——"

"I came for an answer!" I shout.

"None will follow you!" Rigga answers hotly.

"Let them speak for themselves."

"I will not let——" Gibben starts to say.

Even before he finishes, his words are in my ears and my arm is pulled back. My spear is up and I am ready to hurl it at Gibben's heart. There

115

is another change. And out of the corners of my eyes I can see that I am framed by a black sky. I feel taller than I am . . . taller than those to whom I speak . . . taller than the trees that ring the snow-covered clearing.

Gibben falters.

"I will not let you stop what must be done!" I shout.

He is bewildered and draws back.

"Who will follow me?" I ask.

Except for the sound of blowing snow, there is silence.

"Where I go," I tell them, "there is meat."

Still no one moves.

"Where I go the belly will not growl for food."

Rigga begins to snicker.

Then suddenly a voice says, "I will go Ronstrom. I will go with you."

I look toward the edge of the group. A small, wiry man with hair the color of slate pushes his way to me. "Let him pass," I say and a path is opened for him.

"My name is Shute," he tells me.

I nod.

"I will go, too," another man calls.

My eyes find him. He is tall, thin, and hollow-cheeked.

"How are you called?" I ask as he steps away from the rest of my people.

"Thorp," he answers.

Two more come forward. One is a young man with hair the color of the sun's light. His name is Clegg. The other is older by far than any of the others. His back is bent and his gums toothless. His name is Ogg.

116

Not as many come to answer my call as there are fingers on one of my hands.

Then another man announces that he wants to go with me. This one is broad-boned and if he had the food to eat might even be given to being fat, but as he stands he looks even hungrier than the others. His name is Dargen.

The last man to call out is Nesbitt, a hunter. He is tall, slender, dark-haired, and dark-eyed. He is not a very good hunter.

None other chooses to follow me!

"Get your families together," I tell the men. "We will leave at once."

"But it is night," Dargen says. "It will be easier if we wait until morning."

"We leave immediately," I answer sharply. I do not want to tarry lest any of the men doubt the wisdom of their actions and change their minds.

"Why so rapid a departure?" Gibben asks, all too lightly. "You and your followers are welcome to remain——"

"We will depart," I tell him. And to those who choose to follow me I say, "No time is to be wasted. Gather your families and your——"

"They will take nothing other than the clothes they wear and the weapons they carry," Gibben says. "Everything else will be left behind to be divided among those of us who remain behind."

Instantly Gibben's words bring forth protests from the men who stand with me. I am able to see his plan and I respond, "They will leave only with the clothes they wear and the weapons they carry." But when my band of followers turn to me, I tell them, "It is better to leave that way than not to leave at all. You will not lack for anything. I promise you."

117

"And those who leave our tribe and our part of the forest," Rigga says, "will not be able to return."

"Is that the way it will be?" Ogg asks.

I shrug. I do not know whether Rigga and the others intend to keep me and those with me out of this part of the forest. If they do, it will mean an endless series of fights and many deaths.

"Tell them," Ogg insists, "that they do not have the right to do that."

"Their numbers give them the power, and from that power they have taken the right."

Ogg shakes his head. He does not understand, but he does not say that he will not go with me.

I wait until my followers bring their families. Together we are a pitifully small group. I nod and, leaving the mound on which I stand, I begin to walk into the forest.

Those who follow form a column and I hear their footsteps crunch in the snow.

The shouts and jeers of the others stay in our ears until there is a considerable distance between the encampment of our tribe and where we are.

In the forest it is very dark and the wind bites cruelly at our faces and hands. The people soon tire, but I do not let them rest. I am fearful that Gibben or Rigga might be on our trail. I know all too well courage is a poor commodity among those who follow in my footsteps.

Gibben knows this and so does Rigga. I do not want to give them the opportunity to gain strength from our weakness.

XIV

I do not permit anyone to stop. Several times I change the direction of our march, because I fear that Rigga or Gibben might harass us.

The women whimper from the cold. They are too weak to maintain a rapid pace. Children cry and are harshly silenced by their fathers.

I try to be everywhere at the same time. Even as I lead the column I drop back to urge those who straggle to quicken their step.

The faces of those men who chose to follow me are set with hardness. I do not know whether they are angry with themselves or with me. If they are angry with themselves that anger could easily inflame me. If they are angry with me, that anger could be turned against me.

After traveling in a straight line for a while I swing off to one side. Like the wail of a forest spirit a low moan of despair rises behind me, but I do not even look over my shoulder. I know that we are in danger. The last time I changed directions I saw the telltale evidence of another band of people. I did not stop to examine the tracks. They were mixed with ours. If those who follow us are skilled hunters they cannot be far from us.

There is the crunch of snow behind me. I turn and see Clegg. He trots alongside me to keep my pace.

"Ronstrom," Clegg says, "we are moving like the stars that swing around the one that does not move."

He is right, but I say nothing and wait to hear more.

"I see the same signs," he tells me. "There," he points, "is a flat-topped rock and over there is a dead tree."

I nod.

"But why?" he asks.

"To confuse and tire those who track us."

"But it is we who are tired," he answers, gesturing toward the column behind us. "The women whimper and the children cry. There are those who cannot keep the pace you set."

"I, too, am weary," I answer, "but if I let this weariness guide me I would stop, rest, and fall asleep. If I slept I would not be able to defend myself from the attackers."

He nods, says nothing, and drops back with the column.

I do not know why I bothered to speak to Clegg. He has no reason to know my thoughts. I do what must be done!

The sound of an owl rises above the whine of the wind. Instantly I halt and with my hand signal the column to stop.

I suck in my breath and slowly let it out. It steams in the cold night air. I wait to hear the screech of the owl again. When it comes it is quickly answered by another and then by still another. Each cry comes from a different part of the forest.

The first is in front, the second came from the rear of the column, and the last from the side.

Those who stalk us are nearly all around us. The only way out is through very thick underbrush that is heavy with snow.

I look back at the column. We are in no condition to fight. Those who are around us know our weakness.

Nesbitt comes up to me and says, "I did not think they would come after us."

"They will kill us," I answer, "if we let them."

"Perhaps we could talk——"

"There will be no talk," I tell him.

Then suddenly a voice comes from somewhere in front of the column: "Ronstrom," it calls, "it is you we want."

The voice belongs to Rigga.

"The others can go back," he says, "if you give yourself to us."

"Get the other men," I tell Nesbitt. And in a few moments they are around me. "You have heard Rigga speak. Now you will hear me." And I say to Rigga. "I will not give myself to Rigga and the others who are with him. I will do what I said I would do. I will give you meat, but you must do my bidding."

"Ronstrom," Rigga calls, "you have spoken falsely to those who follow you. There is no game other than rabbits, squirrels, and rats and sometimes a small deer. They are guiltless in the eyes of the tribe. The lure of meat is a great temptation. But you, Ronstrom, you are guilty of claiming to be able to do more than any hunter, more than any man. I speak for all the hunters of our tribe. Your words have made us look like blind men to those

121

who depend on us for meat and for that you must be punished. . . ."

I do not answer them. If any man with me thinks I have spoken falsely, he can leave the column. I will not stop him.

My mind is busy with more important things than finding words to answer Rigga. He will get no answer from me now. When I answer it will be when I give my followers what I promised to give them.

Suddenly I realize that though Rigga and his men are practically all around us, neither he nor those with him know exactly where we are. If they did know, they would have fallen on us.

"Tell the people," I say to the men with me, "to make absolutely no sound and to crawl into the heavy underbrush. If a child cries let his mother give him her breast. Hurry and tell them what I have told you."

Soon all of us are in the heavy underbrush.

"Ronstrom," Rigga calls again, "why do you want your people to suffer even more than they have already suffered this bitter cold night?"

His words make my anger grow hot. I do not want my followers to suffer. I would give them——

A child suddenly bawls and is silenced by the quick thrust of his mother's pap into the babe's mouth. The mother and child are close to me and I can hear the sucking sounds made by the child. I wonder if the mother has any milk. So many women have lost their milk.

"Ronstrom," Clegg whispers, "I think they are coming closer."

From out in the dark forest comes the unmistakable crunch of footsteps. Rigga has with him many more men than I have. They are soon out of the forest and come so close that any one of us could reach out and easily touch one of them.

"They were here!" Rigga shouts. "I know they were here!"

"Perhaps Ronstrom worked some of his magic," one of the men says.

I am surprised that he thinks I can perform magic. It was foolish enough when Ansgar accused me of turning into a wolf, but for anyone to think that I can——

"If it wasn't so dark we could see if Ronstrom went through the underbrush," another man complains.

"Perhaps," Rigga answers, "he did not go through it. Perhaps——" And without warning he hurls his spear at the growth. It flies through the air and lands with a thud at my side.

Other men throw their spears. Some are caught by the tangle of branches. The snow deflects others. But one finds its mark. It enters the body of the child sucking on its mother's breast. The child's life spirit leaves his body and he dies with his mother's breast still in his mouth.

Rigga's men begin to retrieve their spears. Quickly I lean toward the dead child and pull the spear free. I hold the bloody stonehead until the weapon is claimed by the man who threw it. My hand is wet with the blood of the child. The spear is suddenly wrenched from my grasp!

I wait for the man to discover the blood on the head of his spear. I wait to hear his cry of delight, but he makes none.

"He must be here," Rigga tells his men. His voice is full of anger. "Ronstrom and the others must be here. We will wait."

The wind suddenly picks up and with it comes

the snow. A whirling whiteness forces Rigga and his men to abandon their search for us and seek the shelter of the forest.

"Quickly," I order, "everyone, we must continue our march."

"What shall I do with my dead child?" Shute asks.

"Take him with us," I answer. "We must leave nothing to show Rigga where we were."

As we begin to walk again, Shute's woman carries her dead child in her arms.

The wind-driven snow blinds us and the deep drifts make it impossible to move quickly. The fury of the storm is our shield against Rigga.

Night gives way but dawn does not come. The wind is still howling. Snow is everywhere. Where the first light of day should crack the lid of night, the sky is still dark.

We plod through the snow, but each of us looks through the swirl of the snow at that portion of the sky where the sun should be.

The light is very feeble. I am afraid that the sun has lost its way, that it will never again show itself, that we will be living in a place without light and without warmth, and that the earth will always be covered with snow. Even when the leaves are full and green and flowers grow in the forest we are always afraid that when the leaves are on the ground and the flowers in the forest are dead, the sun will leave us forever.

The women are the first to cry, "The sun is gone. It will never come back!"

The children are soon wailing the same words.

The men try to keep silent, but some of them cry out in wordless anguish.

I say nothing about the sun and urge them

on, knowing that if I had a strip of hide in my hand I would whip them to move faster.

All through the day there is darkness. When night comes it is only a deeper-hued blackness than the day that preceded it.

The storm does not lessen until morning. With the first light at the edge of the world the people drop to their knees and weep with joy. Even if I could, I would not stop them. I, too, fall on my knees and, with my heart beating wildly, I watch the first yellow fingers of the sun creep over the edge of the world.

"It is back!" the women shout. "The sun is back!"

The children echo the cry of their mothers, while the men look at each other and silently nod as though they never doubted that it would return.

We take time to bury Shute's child in a shallow grave, over which we place many rocks to stop the wolves from devouring the body.

We begin to walk again and when the sun is high overhead we reach the river. My cave is not far away and I call a halt to tell them that we are close to the end of our journey.

I am greeted with silence.

"Soon," I tell them, "you will have shelter and food."

"This part of the forest," Nesbitt says, "does not look any different from where the rest of our people live."

I nod.

"But you said——" he begins to complain.

"That I will give you meat," I answer quickly. "And I will. The snow covers the earth and all that is on it, but look at the trees."

"They are naked like the trees in the rest of the forest."

"But they are taller," Clegg says, "and their trunks are thick and sturdy."

I nod and waving them on we resume our march. As I walk I think about those who are behind me. It will not be easy to hold them together or to hold them to me. If I am ever to be free of The Giver of Life, I must do what He has demanded of me and when it is done, He will no longer be able to claim me as His own.

Much of the river is covered with ice, though in places near the banks there is open water.

We cross the river on the ice. Directly in front of me a buck leaps out of the forest and slowly walks to open water. He bends his head and drinks.

I halt the column and quickly move forward! My people need the flesh of that deer, and I cover the distance between myself and the animal at a run.

The buck senses something. His head jumps up. His head turns toward me. The wind is right and he has my scent.

I am behind him. He is cut off from the forest. He looks along the bank. Perhaps he sees the column? Suddenly he leaps on the ice. He loses his footing. His legs slide out from under him. He scrambles to regain his footing. But it is too late!

I loose an arrow. It hums through the cold air and, flashing in the sunlight for a moment, it enters the back of his neck. Another arrow goes deep into his haunch and then I am on him. I thrust my spear into the front of his neck. Hot red blood gushes over the white ice.

Seeing the kill and running to me, my followers shout words of praise.

I stand away, while mothers hold their children to the gushing fount of blood as the deer's life spirit slowly leaves his body. When no more blood flows, the women immediately begin the work of skinning and quartering the animal. Soon the air is filled with the scent of roasting meat.

I go to my cave, stretch out, and let sleep claim me.

XV

The snow flies and the wind howls. The sun is still weak and often the clouds are so dark and thick that day is only a lesser darkness than night.

I hunt. Those with me are too weak to do anything more than the simple tasks necessary to prepare the meat I bring for eating. Even the men are drained of their strength. The Giver of Life has held to His word and has given my people meat.

They are covetous of their share of the kill and scowl warningly at their neighbor. As the days pass and the supply of meat does not stop, they do not feel the need to be angry when they see a neighbor looking at their meat.

The children are the first to show signs of change. Their swollen bellies shrink, and they run and play with each other in a manner unfamiliar to me and to those whose children they are.

The women use the skins of the animals I kill for clothing and the men busy themselves digging new fire pits.

At night we all sleep in the cave. We are warm and comfortable while the wind and snow batter at the huge skin that hangs across the cave's entrance.

Each evening when I return from the hunt and

set my kill down I join the other men and tell them of the chase. I tell them where in the forest I first saw the animal and then where I slew it.

Though these men are with me, they are strangers to me and I sense they feel the same way about me. I do not know their strengths or weaknesses. I do not even know their skills or lack of them.

I speak to them. They hear my words. I wonder if they understand them. I speak less and less of my experiences of the chase. After a while I sit in silence, speaking only when I want something done.

And then one evening when I return from the hunt with a good-sized boar I do not join the other men at the fire pit. I sit alone at the back of the cave where I sleep.

When the meat is ready Shute's woman, Dara, brings me a huge chunk and sets it before me.

"It is the best cut," she says in a whisper.

I look at it . . . it is red with blood and smells good. I turn my face up to hers and say, "I do not need the best cut. Give it to the others. A few pieces of meat will be enough for me."

Her eyes go wide, but she does not ask the question that is on her tongue. She picks up the meat and quickly returns with smaller pieces.

The others cast furtive looks at me. A leader is always given the first and best cut of any kill . . . they do not understand why I do not want what is rightfully mine.

I do not understand why either. Perhaps I am no longer as hungry as I once was or perhaps it has something to do with the difference between us because I am not like them.

Gibben was right when he told me that though I lead them I am apart from them. I am alone, even as I sit here in the rear of the cave. They are afraid of me and knowing that they fear me fills my chest with a strange ache, one I never before felt.

When I finish my meat I stand up and leave the cave. Outside the sky is a clear blue and the sun is almost at the far edge of the earth. The wind is still and though heavy snow remains on the ground there is a warmth in the air that foretells the coming of summer.

I stand so the sunlight is on my face and I feel its heat on my forehead and on the bridge of my nose. My eyes are closed, but I open them as soon as I hear someone approach me. I turn and see Ogg, the man with the bent back.

"Ronstrom," he asks, "have we done anything to offend you?"

His question surprises me and I shake my head. I see the others looking at us. They are just beyond the entrance to the cave.

"Then why are you angry?" Ogg asks.

"I am not angry," I tell him.

"You sit alone, you eat alone, you stand alone, and you are not angry?"

I take a deep breath and when I speak, I say, "It must be that way."

He does not understand.

"Tell the others," I say, "that I am not angry."

"I do not think they will believe me," he answers in a low voice.

I shrug.

Ogg turns around and goes back to the cave.

I do not look back over my shoulder. The answer I gave Ogg will not satisfy the others.

As the light of day begins to fade I become lost in my own thoughts. Soon I must call the men together and tell them what must be done. That I must do this lies heavily on my shoulders. I do not know how each of them will respond to what I say.

A child suddenly runs towards me. It stops and looks up at me. Fear fills its face and with a cry it turns and flees back to the cave.

I sigh loudly and walk slowly down to the river to drink. When my thirst is gone I return to the cave and, without speaking to anyone, I make my way to the rear. I stretch out on a bearskin, pull my stag robe over me, close my eyes, and soon feel myself sink into the darkness of sleep.

"Ronstrom?"

I hear my name.

"Ronstrom?"

The voice does not resemble Gendy's croaking.

"Ronstrom?"

It does not sound like The Giver of Life either, whose voice is louder than the boom of thunder.

"Ronstrom?"

The voice is not part of a dream. It has a soft, purring quality to it.

Again it calls my name.

I open my eyes. A dark shadow is bending over me.

"It is Dara," the voice tells me.

I start to sit up.

"No," she says, "let me join you under the robe."

"But why?" I ask.

"I will tell you as soon as I am under the robe."

I move and she slips in beside me . . . her womanly scent fills my nostrils . . . I have not been so close to a woman for—I feel her pressing herself to me.

"It is not good for a man to be without a woman," she tells me.

"Who told you to come to me?" I ask.

"It was spoken about and I said I would go," she answers quietly.

131

Her breasts are against my chest. She opens her bottom covering so the heat of her loins licks at my thighs. Her hand is already on my manthing.

"You are Shute's woman," I say, finding it hard to keep my thoughts straight.

"He is willing to share me," she says.

I have never really looked at Dara but in the darkness of the cave, in the closeness of our embrace, I see something of her. She is a woman with a flat broad face. Her breasts are large and her body is sturdy. But I have no feeling for her.

"This was not a thing to decide without me," I say.

"We do not want you to be angry with us," she answers. "I come to you for the meat you have given us." Her hand is around my manthing.

"I do not——" She has kindled lust in me. But I will not burn with it. I reach down and pull her hand away from my manthing. "Go back to Shute," I growl. "Go before my anger——"

"But you are ready for a woman," she complains.

"Go!" I command.

She scurries out from under the stag's robe and returns to her place beside her husband Shute.

I am sure I hear whispering, but I roll over on my side and despite the fire inside me I soon feel myself slipping into sleep again.

My refusal to use Dara moves me even further away from the people who are with me. For some reason I come to understand that I am to stand alone as they are to stand together. It is the way things must be.

The days grow warmer and the sun lingers in the sky. The ice on the river breaks with loud snapping noises. The ice floes move swiftly downstream. The snow vanishes and the earth is naked, waiting for the grass to come.

When the trees show the first buds I call the men together. I have not spoken to them since before the snow left the earth. We sit around the fire pit. I look at them. They are no longer thin with hunger and they are well rested.

"With the coming of the grass and the summer that follows," I say, "there are many things that must be done."

They nod in unison.

"The work must be done by everyone," I tell them. "Huts must be built, new fire pits dug, spear- and arrowshafts have to be made. Clay pots are needed . . . water gourds have to be made."

"And who will do all this?" Ogg questions.

"Each of you will do a part of it," I answer.

"I am no maker of clay pots," Nesbitt declares. "I will hunt with you, Ronstrom."

The other men look at me, waiting to hear what my response will be, but I do not answer Nesbitt. I do not even look at him. "Each of us must work to do those things that must be done," I say. "Huts for each family must be built first."

The men, with the exception of Nesbitt, look questioningly at each other. Then Thorp says, "None of us know how to make a hut."

"That is true, Ronstrom," Shute affirms.

"The cave has served us well," Ogg comments. "To build huts would——"

"Huts will be built," I say. There is an edge to my voice that they can not fail to hear.

"And what about all the other things you say must be done?" Dargen questions. He is fatter now than he was when I first saw him.

"They, too, will be done!"

"We are not arrow makers," he complains. "And none here know how to make a clay pot."

"It is not right," Ogg says, "to make us work when there is no need for it. Your skill as a hunter is all we need."

Words fly between them like so many wheeling birds. At first I am angry with them, but soon I realize that they are too foolish to understand they are no longer free to say what they will or will not do. I wait until their idle chatter ceases and then I say, "I will hunt no longer for you."

None of them have words to answer that.

"You were to do my bidding," I reminded them, "and I was to give you meat . . . I have given you meat, but you refuse to do my bidding——"

"Nesbitt will give us meat!" Dargen shouts. "He is a hunter, too, and game is plentiful."

I stand up.

"Where are you going?" Ogg asks.

"To my place at the back of the cave," I answer.

"You will not share our meat," Thorp calls after me.

"I did not think I would," I answer. I sit down and lean against the wall. I close my eyes. The men with me were not worth taking. Though they have eyes and see they are blind.

Much later, when the embers in the fire pit glow red and the cave is steeped in darkness, I am still awake. I can not find the black waters of sleep. Restlessly I move from side to side. Something sends prickles over my skin. I reach for my knife and wait.

Suddenly a man leaps out of the darkness and comes hurtling down on me. I roll out from under him. I have the chance to push my knife into his back. I do not take it. Instead, I throw myself on

134

him and twist his arm until his scream of pain flashes throughout the cave.

Everyone is awake. The fire is set to blazing.

The man I hold is Nesbitt. He is desperately trying to free himself from my grasp.

The other men crowd close to where he lies. They shake their heads.

"He was a foolish man," I say, breathing hard.

No one answers.

"I give him his life," I say, letting go of him.

Nesbitt scrambles to his feet and runs from the cave.

The other men look questioningly at me. They do not understand why I did not kill him and are waiting for me to tell them. I cannot and I wave them away from my skins. After a while the light in the fire pit wanes and I sleep.

XVI

The day is warm. The sun hangs in a cloudless sky. The branches of the trees along the bank of the river are beginning to leaf and shoots of grass like green spears thrust themselves up through the dark earth; the air throbs with the return of life to the forest.

I do not go far from the riverbank. I sit or stand and watch my people. I no longer hunt for them and I no longer live in the cave with them. They chose to follow their path and not mine. I do not know what makes me watch them.

Nesbitt—I see him when he returns from the hunt. He is skilled at snaring rabbits and other small game. But his skill is seldom enough to feed everyone.

As for my own needs, I do not lack for meat, though I do not seem to need it as much as I did in the past. Sometimes I even think I have lost my taste for it and would be content to live on the nuts and fruits of the forest.

Day follows day and the leaves grow bigger. The grass now mats the banks of the river and the open spaces in the forest.

Each evening Nesbitt brings his kill back to the

others in the cave. Then one evening he returns with nothing. The following evening he again brings nothing and from the cave comes the sound of crying children. The next evening when he has nothing to show for his effort the women begin to wail.

I sit by my fire pit and slowly roast a plump bird. I brought it down with a single arrow a short distance upriver.

Twilight comes and deepens.

The crying and wailing from the cave disturbs the silence of the forest.

I cut a leg from the bird and begin to eat it. The meat is tender and sweet-tasting. I look at the rest of the bird in the fire pit. I do not know its name. It lives by the river in the tall grass. It can move about on the top of the water. There is skin between its toes and it has a flat beak.

I shrug and drop the bare bone into the fire pit.

I start to cut the other leg from the bird, but I stop. The forest is silent. I look to the cave. The people are slowly walking along the riverbank toward me.

I stand and pick up my spear. My heart is racing. I do not know their purpose. If they come in anger and are determined in their actions my life spirit will be freed from my body. I glance over my shoulder. I can flee into the forest.

"Ronstrom?" Ogg calls.

I face them!

They stop.

I wait for Ogg or any one of them to speak again.

"Your magic is very strong," Ogg says after a while.

I do not understand the meaning of his words.

"The game has gone!" Dargen shouts.

I shake my head and answer, "The forest is full of animals and birds."

They look at each other and then Ogg says, "But Nesbitt cannot make a kill."

"My arrows are taken by the wind," Nesbitt complains, "or the quarry suddenly runs off."

"And what have I to do with wind or the whim of an animal?" I ask.

"When you hunted," one of the women says, "we never went hungry."

The other women loudly agree with her.

They are quickly silenced by Shute, who then speaks to me. "We know it is your hand that moves the wind and your whispers that make the animals bolt."

My hand tightens on my spear. The first one of them that takes a step toward me will die.

"Such power," Ogg says, "is beyond our understanding. We know now that you can take our life spirit from our bodies should you desire to kill us. We do not wish to die——"

I shake my head. They are foolish to think I possess such power and I say, "I do not have the power of life and death over you. I do not move the wind as the wind moves a branch of a tree, and my whispers are heard only by the one close to me. I am only a man."

"No," cries Dara, "a man would have taken me, but you did not. I tell you," she says to the others, "he is more than a man—much more."

"We have come to beg you to forgive us," Ogg says.

Suddenly all of the people are on their knees, crying for forgiveness. Even the children plead with me to forgive them.

I cannot believe what I see, but I am not asleep.

I do see them. The flames from the fire pit dance across the faces of those who are closest to me and the sound of their voices rises up in the cool night air like a column of white smoke.

And then above the sound of their lamentation is a deeper, dark voice that says, "Hear them, Ronstrom, hear them!"

I nod. The Giver of Life has spoken to me and I must speak to my people!

"I will hunt for you!" I shout. "I will hunt for you!" My voice echoes and re-echoes all around us.

Their wailing ceases. With fear cut into their faces they listen as my voice repeats over and over again, "I will hunt for you."

And when the sound of my voice dies they answer as one, "We will do your bidding, Ronstrom. We will do your bidding."

Their words, too, are echoed from bank to bank across the line of trees on either side of the river and finally to the upper reaches of a night sky filled with flickering lights.

They are pledged to me as I am pledged to them. I walk toward their kneeling forms, knowing that I am not alone, that He who has chosen me is at my side.

With the passing of several suns, the shelters for the families begin to take shape. They are spread out on the bank of the river just below the entrance to the cave. I now live in the cave alone. In the evening after our bellies are full, the people gather in front of the cave and we talk about the other things that must be done, who will do them, and how they will be done.

Of all the men, Nesbitt seems to show the most skill as an arrow and spear maker. He has found good rock for the heads and has managed to make some fine arrowheads.

Ogg and Shute work together on the huts. They bicker with each other like women, but already are talking about a way of using the bullrushes that grow along the bank of the river to keep the wind and the rain out of the huts.

Dargen has tried his hand at making clay pots. He has not yet learned how to fire the molded clay. Perhaps he will before the summer ends.

Thorp has not yet chosen for himself any one thing to do. He goes from one man to another as his whim dictates. He helps for a while and then moves off. But he goes to anyone who calls him and in that way he serves all of us.

As for Clegg, he comes with me to hunt. He is a skillful tracker and knows much that I do not know about the forest's plants. He says that his father's mother taught him to know the plants when he was very small. Some plants, he says, can make a sick man well and a well man sick. And some can make a man sleep, while others can make him feel like a giant. I listen to his chatter but I do not believe him.

Summer comes. The days are hot; the sun's journey across the sky is long. And the light lingers on the world as though it is reluctant to give way to darkness. My people want for nothing.

XVII

The sun is in that part of the sky where it will soon slip below the edge of the earth, but the light is still strong. Its long shafts turn the river water yellow below the ledge on which I sit.

Though the earth and everything on it is in the fullness of summer, I think about when the summer will be gone, the leaves turn, and sharp jaws of the wind and snow take hold of the land. It is not a pleasant thought, and I sigh wearily.

Standing, I catch sight of a movement in the willows, a short distance down river. My blood begins to race. There is a pounding in my ears. I look toward the huts of my people. We are small in number and should we be attacked few of us would escape.

My eyes go back to the willow movement. I see nothing. Perhaps some stray breeze wafted through the slender branches or maybe a bird—I see it again. Such a quivering of the willow branches is not made of a breeze!

An animal?

Perhaps.

Even as I am watching the willows, I am called by Ogg. I glance in his direction. He is coming toward me from the far side of the bank where his hut is. With him is Thorp. Thorp is carrying something black in his hand.

"Ronstrom," he calls, "Thorp has found something."

I start to wave them away. But immediately stop. If there is a man he can see me better than I am able to see him. I do not want him to know I am aware of his presence.

My thoughts race. If there is one man, there could be many. Fewer than the number of fingers I have on one hand could, if they are skilled hunters, kill all of my people. I think of Rigga and grind my teeth in anger. Should he be the one lurking in the clump of willows——

"Ronstrom," Ogg yells, "Thorp has found another cave!"

His shouting has brought all of my people from their huts. They are following closely behind Ogg and Thorp, talking almost as loudly as he is shouting.

I flick my eyes back to the willows. Nothing stirs. My chest is suddenly too small to hold the giant pounding of my heart. I expect the air to be filled with singing arrows.

I look down at my people.

"The cave," Ogg gestures, "is that way, where the sun moves across the sky. Thorp has——" He suddenly stops and looks at me questioningly.

"Do not stop," I tell him, hoping that the sound of my voice will not carry.

"The cave——" he begins and falters again.

"Do not stop!"

"Thorp," Ogg says, looking at his companion, "you tell Ronstrom."

"Tell me in aloud voice," I request. With my

142

eyes I try to indicate that something is taking place downstream.

"I found this cave," Thorp explains, "several suns ago."

"Is it a big cave?" I ask, and in a much lower voice I say, "No one move. In the clump of willows, downstream. Something is there!"

Thorp nods and continues, "The cave is very big and goes deep. I took some meat there, built a fire, but it was too smoky. I left the meat. At sunrise today I returned to the cave and found the meat. It was still there, but it did not stink and there were no white crawling things on it.

I listen to Thorp, but what he tells me does not mean anything to me. I am unable to think of anything except the movement in the willows. I cast my eyes downstream and see it again. I am now certain that a man is hiding there.

"The meat we do not eat," Thorp says, holding up a piece of blackened meat, "we will be able to keep."

The people crowd around him. He quickly cuts off pieces for all to eat. He cuts a piece and throws it up to me. I catch it and quickly bite into it. It is tough but has some flavor. When it is chewed well it becomes stringy.

My eyes seek out and find Clegg. I move my head toward the willows.

He nods and slips away from the rest of the group. "Now," Thorp says, "even if you do not make a kill on the days when the snow flies, we will still have meat."

"It is a good thing you have done," I tell him.

Everyone agrees.

Thorp smiles broadly.

"From now on," I say, "a portion of each kill

143

will be exposed to smoke and placed in Thorp's cave so that we all will have meat when the snow flies."

There is much back-slapping and more laughter than I have ever heard. I look toward the willows again and tell my people, "Walk slowly back to your huts . . . And do not stop making noise. When you reach them, each family must slip——"

"Ronstrom!" My name is shouted from the clump of willows. I wheel around and stand motionless, waiting for the cry of those who are here to destroy us.

"Ronstrom?"

Clegg is calling me. Perhaps it is his death shout?

The willow branches suddenly open. Clegg comes running out and up the far bank toward us. The others quickly ford the river and run to meet him.

I do not move.

Clegg does not stop until he is standing before me. The others are now in back of him. He is winded and breathing hard.

I am impatient to hear what he has to tell. But he must find the words and the breath to say them.

Though his chest is still heaving, he speaks, "People . . . more people have come."

"Who are they?"

"From our tribe," he pants. "More people than are here now. . . ." He is forced to suck in air before he continues. "They are hungry. They——"

"Why were they hiding?" I ask.

"They are afraid——"

I wave him silent. "Nesbitt," I say, "go to the willows and tell those who are there to come into our encampment. Tell them that we will feed them."

"They want to stay!" Clegg exclaims.

I do not think there is any other reason for them to be here. But before I let them join my people I want to know who has come. I already know why!

"Tell them," I instruct Nesbitt, "only what I have said. To come into our encampment and that we will feed them."

Nesbitt nods and begins to run down toward the willows while Clegg looks at me questioningly.

I answer him by saying, "It is not enough for them to want to join us; we, too, must want them to join us and that can not be said until we know who has come."

Clegg does not answer. But from the furrow on his brow I know either he does not understand or does not agree. Perhaps he neither understands or agrees. I wonder why. I am at the very most two summers older than he and it is very clear to me.

Nesbitt is already leading the newcomers out of the willows and up along the bank toward our encampment.

I tell my people to prepare meat for them.

Those who come are starving. The children's bellies are swollen. Their progress toward the encampment is very slow. With the children there are more of them than there are of us . . . many more.

When they ford the river none look up at me. But from where I stand in the fading light I see all their faces. Some I know by name and others I know because I have seen them in the forest grubbing roots or trying to catch a rat.

When they are all across the river, Nesbit halts them. He comes closer to the ledge and says, "Hasel wants to speak."

145

"Is he their leader?" I ask.

"So it would seem."

"Let him speak," I say.

Nesbitt retreats to the head of the column, which is bent back on itself several times so that all of the people who have come are standing in front of me. He speaks to a medium-sized man, with broad shoulders, whose bones jut out from beneath his dark skin and whose face is covered with a beard of brownish hair. He is a hunter of some skill.

The man approaches me. He raises his right arm. "Ronstrom," he says, "we are here to follow you and do your bidding." His voice sounds like the grinding of rocks against each other.

I find it strange that he recalls again the words I spoke to the tribe.

"We only ask that we be given meat," Hasel says.

"You will be fed," I answer.

"Many have died," he tells me, speaking of the rest of the tribe. "Children and old ones are not safe. Many have been forced to eat their own that they might survive the time of snow and darkness."

I remain motionless and force my face not to reveal the sudden churning of my stomach. I have never eaten human flesh, but others I know have. My skill as a hunter has always provided me with some kind of meat, even if it is nothing more than a rat.

"And when the snows vanished and the wind stopped howling, the grass and the leaves did not come in their usual time. And when they did it was already in the long days and short nights. There is no game where we come from, no game other than——"

"We will talk again," I say. "I do not want to hear about one man hunting another for food."

He nods and lowers his hand.

"Nesbitt," I say, "let these people stay where they are. Have our men and women bring meat and water to them."

"Yes, Ronstrom," he answers.

The newcomers immediately drop to the ground. The gathering twilight is filled with the mournful wail of hungry children and deep sighs of exhausted men and women. Even before the fire pits glow red in the darkness of night those who claim they are here to join my people are fed.

Some cannot take the feel of meat in their belly and are forced to vomit. Others who eat less rapidly manage to hold the meat down.

After a while my men walk around and speak to the men, who are more than willing to talk to them. I do not join them, but I sit and I watch all that is happening from my ledge.

Fires spring up in the midst of the newcomers. Some of the men go off into the forest and return with what wood their strength permits them to carry. In the light from the fire nearest to me I see Hasel. Sometimes I catch him looking at me, but when I do his eyes never stay with mine. He always turns away.

The fires slowly die until nothing but red embers are left. The night is warm enough to sleep without a fire.

All of the newcomers are asleep and so are my people. I move back against a large rock near the entrance to the cave and close my eyes.

Hasel's words have given me strange feelings.

There have been those who have boasted about having eaten the meat from a man's body. And

Rigga once told me before I left for the mountains where the sun never travels that he and some others once found a young woman from the Rock People. After they used their manthings on her they killed her. I remember him telling me that her breasts tasted good, but not nearly as good as her rump. He said it tasted sweet, like fowl.

I close my eyes and shake my head, hoping the movement will make me stop thinking about those who eat human flesh.

I slip easily into sleep and just as I expect to hear either Gendy's croaking voice or the thunder-like boom of The Giver of Life I feel someone shaking me.

I open my eyes.

Clegg is bending over me. "Ronstrom," he says, "I have heard that some have eaten——"

"Hasel has told me the same thing," I say.

"Do you think it is so?"

I nod.

"Do you think any of them has done it?"

He has asked the very thing I have not dared ask even myself.

"A man who has eaten the flesh of another man," he comments, "is never again satisfied with the meat of an animal."

"Who told you that?"

"Thorp," Clegg answers.

"I do not know if he is right," I say with a shrug. "Get some rest. We must spend the day hunting. There are more stomachs to fill."

"There is something else," Clegg tells me.

I wait for him to speak. I hear him sigh.

"Rigga has taken Alvina for his woman," he says.

His words are whispered, but they sound like

148

thunder in my ears. "Taken," I question, "or was she given by Gibben?"

"I do not know."

"Who told you?"

"Hasel."

I am on my feet and look to where Hasel sleeps. I wonder if he had wanted to tell me about Alvina but could not bring himself to.

"There are other women——"

"Go," I tell Clegg. "Go. At sunrise we must be on our way."

He leaves me. I watch him cross the space crowded with sleeping forms. The moon is high enough in the sky to make the tops of the trees glitter.

My vision becomes blurred. Water flows from my eyes. I hammer my fist against the stone. I whisper over and over again, "no . . . no . . . no . . . She is my woman. . . . She is my woman . . . she is my woman. . . ."

My hand bleeds and I suck the blood from it. Slowly I sink to the stone ledge and resting against a large boulder, I close my water-filled eyes. I swallow to ease the ache in my throat.

From somewhere in my skull come images of Alvina. I see her inside my head as I have often seen her near Gibben's hut. I see her long black hair and her bare breasts. The ache in my throat forces me to cough.

That I will never know the nearness of her naked body to mine, or have my manthing in her body is enough to make me whimper softly. Then suddenly I whisper into the night, "I will not let it be . . . I will not let it be!"

I crawl into the cave and, finding my skins, I stretch out and wait for sleep to come. But I grow hot with lust and cannot sleep. I have lived without a woman and feel the need for one.

Eventually a hot sticky fluid gushes from my manthing. I breathe easier, close my eyes, and soon feel myself drifting downward.

I know I am sleeping. And then I hear Gendy's croaking and he says to me, "Do not spend your strength and lose what you have gained."

I do not want to listen to him. He is beyond caring about a woman.

XVIII

Before the coming of the sun I wake. When I leave my cave Clegg is already bending over the red glow in the fire pit before his hut. I join him. We eat without speaking. Other people begin to stir.

I had not slept well. Gendy's spirit, for all my efforts to silence it, had not kept silent. I know what I must do to undo what Gibben has done. If I could I would do it without waiting but I must wait.

"Are you angry, Ronstrom?" Clegg asks.

"I did not sleep well," I answer.

"Yes," he comments, "sleep was hard to find last night." And then he gestures toward those who are behind us and says, "Hasel comes."

I make no reply. I look above the trees toward the sun. The sky is filled with the color of blood.

Hasel squats down next to the fire.

Clegg hands him a piece of meat. He tears huge chunks from it and quickly swallows them. His eyes look up at the sky. He nods and says, "Rain."

"It has been dry for many days," Clegg tells him.

Hasel takes more meat, tears at it, and swallows. Then he says, "I will hunt with you."

I am about to tell him to remain in the encampment, but I do not. There are many more bellies to fill. If they do stay with us, then we will need more meat. The longest of the summer days are gone. And in the evening when the sky is clear one of the sky's wonders shows bright in the trail in the dying sun. This is a certain sign that days will soon be cooler and the leaves will turn. We must bring in all the meat we can before the snows begin to fly. . . .

"Are there many with you who are hunters?" I ask.

He holds up one hand and then folds two fingers down.

"And the other men, what can they do?"

"Some weave baskets," he says. "A few can shape wood and still others are not skilled in any way. They spent most of their time digging for roots and insects."

"Are there men with their women and children?" I question.

He nods.

"Any old ones?"

He shakes his head. "Those who started with us gave up their life spirit," he explains.

"Are there any children who belong to no one?"

"Several," Hasel says. "And there are some girls who, even as we searched for you, passed their first blood."

"And of those boys and girls who are not yet men or women," I ask, "are any——"

Hasel waves his hand. "They could not keep pace," he says, "and soon gave up their life spirit."

I nod. My eyes meet Clegg's. In their blueness I read my own thoughts. The question I dared not ask, Hasel has just answered. I look away.

Clegg is told to fill his pouch with enough meat for the three of us. I return to my cave and take my weapons.

In a while we are moving swiftly and silently through the forest. The signs of game are everywhere.

"It is hard to believe that there is so much meat here," Hasel whispers, "and nothing in the other part of the forest."

"It is as I said it would be," I comment. I tell them that it is better to hunt separately. The others agree and I set off alone.

The clouds are the color of slate. They slide across the sky and dim the light in the forest. The rain starts falling softly at first. But soon the rain giants stride over the earth. The drops, though they pound on the leaves, are warm.

I pick up the trail of a boar. As I follow it, I think of Alvina. My throat aches again and my vision is blurred.

"I will have her," I whisper aloud. I wipe my eyes with the back of my hand.

Other thoughts enter my mind.

I do not know what to do about Hasel and those with him. There are too many of them to be driven away. If they stay will they satisfy their hunger with meat from the kill, or will they seek to eat the flesh of a man or woman?

When I was ten or twelve summers I remember being told by the man who was my father that when he had as many summers as I did then, his father had said that in times of trouble, when the game left the forest or death walked amongst the people of the tribe, a man or woman was given to a god. But the body was eaten by all in the tribe.

I stop. In front of me is a heavy thicket of undergrowth. The boar is in there. He has my scent. I hear his low grunt. From the sound of him I know he is big.

I make no movement. I listen.

He is trying to break out of the thicket, but, from the grunting and snapping of branches, cannot get through.

I will let him tire himself. Then I will go in and kill him.

The tread of the rain giants is heavier.

The sound from the thicket lessens. His panting becomes louder.

I take one step. Two steps. I breathe hard.

The boar comes charging out of the thicket. He is huge and black. Two curled tusks are thrust forward and end with points like spears. His head is bent low as he grunts furiously.

I do not think. When he is almost on me I leap to one side. My spear goes into his bristly black hide.

The beast squeals in pain, runs to one side, and breaks the spearshaft against the trunk of a tree. He stops, whirls around, and bobs his head up and down, hoping to see or catch the scent of me.

Blood flows down his side, but the wound is not deep enough to free the life spirit from his body. He is breathing hard. His mouth is open and his red tongue lolls off to one side. His coat is wet with rain.

I watch him carefully.

He paws the ground.

My own chest is rapidly moving in and out. Blood throbs in my head. I am doing what I was meant to do. I am a hunter and will always be a hunter. Between me and the beast there is a simple understanding. I will try to kill him and he will try to kill me. Neither of us would be satisfied to leave the other wounded. Each of us will do our utmost to live.

He has my scent. He rushes at me.

In my haste to move, I lose my footing in the rain-soaked earth.

The beast looms up over me.

I roll over and twist to one side. He charges past me.

I spring to my feet.

He is enraged. Whirling around, he comes at me again!

I am ready for him.

He is almost on me when I leap to one side. As he rushes past me I hurl myself on him!

The shock of my body striking his almost knocks him off his feet. He struggles to keep his footing.

The forest is filled with the noise of his grunting and squealing. To dislodge me he shakes himself furiously.

I hold tight and manage to free my knife.

He drags me at a run through the forest. He tries to break my hold on him my smashing me against the trunk of a tree. His panting is almost as loud as his grunting.

I cannot hold on much longer. I take my knife and slash at him with all the force I can.

He squeals!

I slash again and again. His hide is soon slick with blood.

He rolls over and tries to pin me under him.

I leap free. As soon as he is on his feet again, I am at him. This time I stab and stab until the churned-up mud is the color of his blood.

He begins to wheeze and his front legs splay. He falls.

I reach under him and just as I am about to slit his throat he tosses his head up.

My arm is seared with pain. His tusk has gouged out a long strip of skin and flesh. I leap away. My knife drops into the bloody mud. My blood flows down my arm and drips into the already red-stained ooze.

I try to wrench the head of the spear from his body. But the pain in my arm forces me to stop.

He struggles to get to his feet and almost stands when he drops to one side, rolls over, and dies.

I pick my knife up and cut a strip from his hide. I tie his forelegs together with it so I can pull him back to the village.

I am weak. The forest grows hazy in my eyes. I feel as if I am falling into a deep pit. I stop, lift my face, and let the rain wash over it. Then I take a few more steps.

The forest blurs again. The pit of swirling darkness is very close.

My knees do not hold me, and I stagger and fall.

The great swirling darkness closes over me. I try to fight my way out of it. But it is endless and it continues to suck me into it.

Then suddenly I am free of it. My eyelids open. I am looking up at Clegg's face and beyond him the tops of the trees and the sky.

"I will help you to your feet," he says.

I nod. It takes awhile before I am able to stand. My legs do not seem strong enough to hold me. The rain has stopped, but the earth is still wet. I move my eyes slowly toward where I left the boar. The beast is not there. I look questioningly at Clegg.

"It was taken to our encampment by several of the men," he says.

I nod. Later I will ask him how long I lay in the forest and who found me.

"Here," Clegg says, putting my good arm around his shoulder, "I will help you."

I nod and look up at the sky. It is very blue and from where the sun is I know it is still morning. Slowly we walk back to the encampment. I cannot take more than a few steps at a time.

When I finally reach my cave I drop to my skins and sleep.

XIX

After a few days my strength begins to return. Using mud and spider webs, Clegg has gotten the wound to heal. It itches and I am tempted to scratch, but do not. My arm is badly scarred.

I ask Clegg to tell me what happened. He says that when I did not return to the encampment at twilight he, Hasel, and all of the other hunters went searching for me. "Nesbitt found you and summoned the others," Clegg explains. "Then I stayed with you."

"How long?" I ask.

He waves his hand.

"How long?"

"Many days," he says without looking at me.

I nod. Not too long ago neither he nor anyone else would have remained with me. "I will not forget," I say.

Again he waves his hand. "There is nothing to remember," he answers.

As soon as I am able to walk, I go through the encampment. The people who came with Hasel are now part of it. Their huts spread beyond those of the few who first came here with me. I am no longer faced with the question of what to do with the newcomers. They are joined to my people now, whether I want them or not.

Each morning hunters leave and enter the forest and at twilight return with many kills. Those newcomers with women live in their own huts. The young women have their separate huts and the young men occupy several shelters of their own.

The people with skills are already working and those who possess none dig fire pits or gather fruits, nuts, and berries in the forest.

All of it has been done without me, even to saving a portion of each kill for Thorp to smoke.

I return to my ledge, sit down, and ponder what I have seen. I do not know my own thoughts about it. What has been done gives me an uneasy feeling.

As the light of day fades Clegg returns from the forest with a large deer slung across his shoulder. The women relieve him of his burden.

I call to him.

He comes.

But even before Clegg reaches me I see on his sun-darkened arms one of the curved tusks of the boar I slew. I now know he was the one who told the people what to do. The other would be the man who wears the second tusk.

He sits down opposite from me and says, "The kill was good."

I nod and wait for the other hunters to return.

Each has made a kill. And one by one they join me on the ledge. Hasel is the last to come. I look at his bare arm. Though the curved tusk is not on either of them, I am still certain he has it.

The talk is about the hunt.

I listen and say few words. My thoughts are still on the missing boar's tusk. I do not know why Hasel does not wear it as Clegg does!

The young women bring us meat.

I see that the best pieces are placed before the hunters. I eat very little. My eyes range beyond the group of men with me. The bank of the river is spotted with the red glow from fire pits. The dark shadows of the people move in and out of the flickering light. We are now many.

Hasel sees me looking at the encampment and he says, "Everything goes well, Ronstrom."

"Yes," I answer, "so it seems."

"While you were sick from your wound," he tells me, "Clegg told my people what they must do."

I nod.

"Everything is as though you had ordered it yourself," Hasel says.

"He has done well," I replied, looking at Clegg.

"The others helped," he is quick to explain. "Without them I could not have gotten anyone to do my bidding."

"Who were those who helped?"

Clegg gestures to the other hunters. "All of them," he says.

"And what of Ogg, Thorp, and——"

"It is sometimes better," Hasel says, "if people are told what to do by men who are stronger than those they speak to."

"But Ogg and the others who first came here with you, Ronstrom," Clegg offers, "did not hinder us."

"You did very well," I tell them with a nod.

Hasel comments, "We hoped you would say that. And perhaps you should say as much to the people."

I look at him questioningly.

"There are always those who are discontented with whatever is done," he tells me.

Though Hasel speaks earnestly I do not like the sound of his voice or the meaning of the words. I shrug, but do not answer.

When the hunters leave me I do not go into my hut. Instead I walk through the encampment and seek out Ogg. We walk without speaking. Then he says, "You seem none the worse for your encounter with boar."

I run my hand along the scar on my arm. "I will always have this to remind me of it," I answer. And I ask how it is with him and the others.

"Well," he says. "Very well indeed." He stops and gestures toward the encampment. "You can see for yourself."

"I see," I tell him, "but I feel I do not see."

He starts to walk again, and I pick up his stride.

"I am not sure," he tells me in a quiet voice, "that I see all, either."

His words puzzle me. But I do not push him to give them more meaning. "And of the others," I ask, "Thorp, Nesbitt, and——"

"All are well with the exception of Dargen."

It is I who stop. "Is he sick?" I question.

"No one has told you?"

I shake my head.

"His life spirit, Ogg says, left his body."

"Sickness——"

"He was beaten until the blood flowed from his mouth, nose, and ears," Ogg explains.

"Beaten?"

Ogg nods. "His pots did not please several of the hunters. There was an argument and he was dragged across the river and beaten. But I do not think he was beaten because of his pots. They were getting better ever since Thorp showed him a new way to bake the clay. I think he angered the hunt-

161

ers when he complained about them taking the best cuts of meat for themselves."

"And his body," I ask, "was it placed in the earth?"

Ogg shrugs.

"Was it burnt?"

"No one knows what has happened to it," he tells me.

My heart skips a beat and then begins to race. What little I ate feels as though it will spew out. "We will talk again," I say.

"Perhaps we should," Ogg answers.

I nod, turn, and hurry away.

XX

I do not sleep deeply. I am like a man who is thirsty, but cannot reach water. Many times I am startled into full wakefulness by the hoot of an owl or the bay of a wolf. My head is full of swirling thoughts. To confront the hunters with what I know they have done would probably result in more killing or perhaps my own death.

I leave my skins and stand on the ledge. The sky is dark blue. Some of the lights are already beginning to fade, but one of the brightest of the sky's wanderers hangs just above the tops of the tallest trees on the far bank of the river.

I decide to do nothing. I will wait to see what happens. Perhaps the hunters did not eat Dargen.

Though I am not cold, I tremble. I return to the cave and stretch out on my skins. I close my eyes and purposely fill my skull with images of Alvina. My manthing hardens and I am filled with the need for a woman. I make the hot fluid gush from my body. The tightness in my groin is gone. I get up and go to the river, where I swim. The water is very cold. I climb out on the bank and rest.

Just as I am ready to leave, I see a woman. She is not far from where I stand, but cannot see me in the darkness that lays over the earth before the coming of the sun. She is naked. Her hair is black or brown. It touches the nipples of her breasts. She is one who came with Hasel.

I watch her swim. Her body is very white and there is a leaf-shaped dark patch above her slit. She is pleasant to look at.

She stops swimming and looks straight at me. I know she can see me. She does not swim away and I walk closer to where she is. She looks up at me. Her eyes are wide and even in the gray light of dawn I can see that they are dark like her hair.

"Do you swim here often?" I ask.

"Only to cleanse my body after the blood flows from it," she answers.

I nod and ask, "How are you called?"

"Nan," she answers.

I repeat her name, turn, and start to walk away.

"And you," she calls after me, "are you not Ronstrom?"

"Yes," I answer, looking at her over my shoulder. "I am Ronstrom." She comes out of the river and her wet body is streaked with water. Her nipples are hard and she is smiling.

A flash of heat passes through my body. I pause, knowing that if I want her I can have her there on the riverbank. My manthing throbs with lust. But I force myself to turn away. There are matters more important than satisfying my lust. Perhaps I will take her to my cave when I once again feel the need for a woman.

The sun comes up and hangs like a red lip in the blue face of the sky. I eat with Clegg and take part in the day's hunt. Game is plentiful and all of us return to the encampment with our kills.

I am more tired than I thought I would be. My

body is soft from so many days of rest. But I know it will soon harden.

The hunters join me on the rock ledge in front of my cave. The young women bring food to us. Among them is Nan. I look at her and the wisp of of a smile touches her lips.

The next day when the sun is not very high in the sky and I am walking through the forest with Clegg he asks, "Is The Giver of Life a man?"

I shake my head and say, "If he is, he is not like any other man."

"Then what is he?"

"I am not sure."

"But you have seen him. You spoke with him."

I stop and so does Clegg. "What does his form matter," I ask, "as long as we know he is there?"

Clegg shrugs.

We start to walk again. "He is a shaft of light brighter than thunder and when He laughs the earth trembles."

Clegg says nothing more.

We continue to walk together . . . and I wonder why Clegg has asked about The Giver of Life.

Several days pass. I am no longer tired at the end of the day. Each evening the hunters sit with me and eat. Other than the young women who bring our meat, no one comes near the ledge.

As many evenings pass as I have fingers on my hands before Hasel asks, "Ronstrom, have you decided what to tell the people?"

His question takes me by surprise.

"All of us," he says, gesturing to include the other hunters, "feel that it would be good for the people."

"But what should I tell them?" I ask.

Hasel rubs his beard. "Something . . . something that would give them courage," he answers.

"And," another hunter comments, "that they must do our bidding."

"Our bidding?" I question.

"He means your bidding, Ronstrom," Hasel quickly says, "which is what we all agreed to do."

I nod.

"And you should say something," another of the group says, "about The Giver of Life."

The other hunters immediately agree.

"I will think about it," I say.

Hasel shakes his head. "It must be done," he tells me, "if we are to hold the people together. They must be told——"

"When I am ready, Hasel, I will tell them what they must be told."

"Of course," he stammers, "we all know that."

The hunters are very quiet as, one by one, they leave the ledge. Clegg is the last to depart.

Before he goes, I say to him, "You should have let me die!" He does not answer.

I, too, leave the ledge and walk along the riverbank.

The hunters have set themselves above the rest of the people. I do not know whether this is a good or a bad thing. In any tribe, they are the leaders. The people depend on them for their food and should be willing to give something in return.

But what should be given? The best part of each kill?

That is not beyond my understanding or willingness to give them.

I sit down on a large rock and look at the black water.

I will tell them what is rightfully theirs and

166

what is not. I will tell all of the people that anyone of them who eats the flesh of a man or woman will be driven from the encampment.

The thought of devouring the meat of a man makes me gag.

When the bad feeling is gone I start back to my cave. I feel certain that I know what must be done, and I will do it. My body is filled with a surge of strength. I quicken my step.

When I am near my cave I see Nan.

She is talking to another young woman.

I slow my pace. My groin is suddenly tight with lust.

She sees me.

The presence of other young women prevents me from speaking. I quickly pass. I am scarcely three steps beyond them when I hear the light footsteps of someone behind me. I do not look back. The footfalls pursue me. When I reach the ledge, I turn.

"Do you always walk so fast?" Nan asks.

I circle her waist with my hands and lift her on to the ledge.

She laughs as I take her hand and lead her into the cave.

I pull her coverings over her head and toss it to the ground. Then I remove my skins. When we are both naked, I put my arms around her.

"I have never been with a man," she says.

"Then I will teach you," I tell her.

"Will I be your woman?" she asks as we stretch out on my skins.

I do not answer. My hands are all over her naked body and soon she is eager to have me mount her.

She cries out as I push my manthing into her slit and cause blood to flow.

Soon she is as eager to be ridden as I am to ride her.

167

XXI

Nan leaves before the sun comes. Her going wakes me. I do not make any attempt to stop her. I do not want her for my woman, but I would use her again to satisfy my lust.

When I am alone my thoughts quickly turn to what I will tell my people. As the darkness lessens I become less sure that I know what I should say to them.

I join Clegg at his fire pit. His head is bowed and he says nothing to me. I do not breach the silence. It thickens between us.

When Clegg raises his head, his eyes are wide. He looks at me but I do not think he sees me. His body is within the reach of my arm but his life spirit is somewhere else. At his side is a small clay pot. I take hold of it and sniff at it. I do not know the scent. I put some of the liquid in my mouth. It is bitter and I spit it out.

Hasel comes and I ask him about Clegg.

"The brew he drinks," Hasel explains, "makes him that way."

I pour the rest of the liquid in the clay pot on to the earth. "He will drink no more of it," I say. "Today he does not hunt."

Hasel shrugs and answers. "If that is your word——"

"It is my word," I tell him and go into the forest alone.

I am angry with Clegg for separating his life spirit from his body. To do that leaves the body weak and defenseless. And there is always the danger that the life spirit will not be able to find its way back into the body. Some of the old ones who were priests in their time suffered greatly because their life spirits were separated from their bodies.

I wander through the forest. Though I could easily make a kill I do not. When I return to the encampment the sun is on the far side of the sky. I am the only hunter who has not brought meat that day.

I go to my cave.

After a while the other hunters join me.

The young women bring our food; among them is Nan. Her eyes try to snare mine, but I do not give her the chance. I keep my head down and eat in silence.

"You brought no meat, Ronstrom," Hasel says.

I nod.

"Was there no game?" he asks.

"There was game," I answer.

"Then I do not understand why you did not make a kill."

I do not answer. But I hear the roaring of my blood in my ears.

Hasel rubs his beard, and looking at the others he says, "There are things that must be said."

"Then say them," I answer.

"As leaders we demand that certain things be

169

ours," he says. "We are the ones who supply the meat——"

"What is it that you want, Hasel?" I ask.

"Only that which is rightfully ours."

"Say what."

"The people should know who we are."

"They already know you are hunters."

Hasel shakes his head. "You must tell them that we are better and more important than they. That at all times they must do our bidding. That some of them be given to us to be our slaves and that when one of us takes one of their women it is——"

I slowly stand and ask, "And you will give them a blood sacrifice?"

"That, too," Hasel says. "We will give them what they want. When we are joined by more people we will be able to make war on other tribes. From these wars we will gain more land. And each of us," he explains, gesturing again toward the other hunters, "will be set over a tribe. A portion of the forest will be ours. We will become a leader even as you are now."

I nod and in a low voice I say, "Gather the people together; I will speak to them."

"You will tell them what I have said?" Hasel asks.

"Gather them together!" I roar. The sound of my voice falls on them like a thunderclap. I turn and go into the cave.

I stand with my back toward the entrance. My blood is surging through me. I am hot with anger. I reach down and lift the robe made from the skin of the giant stag. I place the skin of it across my shoulders and set the crown of antlers on my head. In my hand, I hold a spear.

I walk out of the cave and stand on the ledge. The hunters are on one side. The people are below me. A murmur like the sound of a sighing wind rises in the still air. The light is still strong and I can recognize several faces: Shute and his woman, Nesbitt and Ogg, and, slightly off to one side, Nan. She looks at me with wonder on her young face.

A bird calls and is answered.

"All of us," I say, raising my hands toward my people, "know why I have summoned you. Our bellies are full. We are strong. The Giver of Life has kept his word." I stop. I do not have any more words. My tongue gropes like a blind thing in the darkness of my mouth for something more to say. I look down at the upturned faces. What can I tell them?

I close my eyes. I do not sense the presence of The Giver of Life. I am alone.

I look at my people again and I say, "All that you have, all that you are . . . is His. He alone holds sway over life and death. Each one of you have eaten of His meat and need no other. He gives you the meat of the deer and the boar and the meat of the birds, whether they are earth-bound or fly like the hawk."

The hunters stir uneasily. . . .

"There are none among you who are either higher or lower in His eyes. . . .

My throat is dry and my lips are cracking. I do not know where the words are coming from. They do not rest in my brain before they are on my tongue.

"We are His and none among us is less or more His than the man or woman next to us . . . we are to do his bidding——"

"Ronstrom!" Hasel shouts. "Tell them how The Giver of Life has chosen——"

"I was chosen by The Giver of Life," I answer, "and none other."

"You have played us false!" Hasel yells.

The people back away from the ledge.

"Ronstrom!" Hasel roars. "You have played the people false!"

I am too stunned to answer.

"The Giver of Life has cast you from him," Hasel proclaims. He steps away from the other hunters and on his arm I see, for the first time, the other curved tusk of the boar I slew. "This very day," Hasel tells the people, "Ronstrom returned from the hunt without having made a kill."

The people murmur among themselves.

"And was it not true that he could not kill the giant boar? When Clegg found Ronstrom he was too frightened to move. The boar still lived until I joined with Clegg to kill him. The tusks on our arms are proof of what I tell you."

Hasel's words sound in my ears with such a clamor that I cannot find the beginning or the end of my own thoughts.

"How can he speak," Hasel questions mockingly, "for The Giver of Life when he has been cast from Him?"

I shake my head and my answer is locked between my clenched teeth.

"We are your leaders," Hasel tells the people, waving toward the other hunters. "We have given you meat. Even on this day, when Ronstrom has brought nothing back from the forest, we have returned with our kills. In that way The Giver of Life has spoken to us. We will tell you what must be done and how it is to be done. There will be no other way but ours. To set yourselves up against us is to go against The Giver of Life. He is the one

172

whom we serve and by serving us you serve Him."

The light has gone from the sky. Darkness lies over the earth and over my people.

"The flesh of animals is food for us, but a God needs a different meat——"

Suddenly Clegg leaps forward and drops to his knees. "I see Him!" he shouts. "I see The Giver of Life!" He points to the other side of the river. "He is a bright and beautiful light!"

Where Clegg points there is nothing but darkness and in the darkness the still darker shapes of the trees.

"He is brighter than the brightest sunlight!" Clegg cries.

"Yes!" Hasel shouts.

The people turn, look, and see only darkness.

"His voice comes!" Clegg yells.

"He is telling us," Hasel roars, "that he wants——"

I am no longer dazed. I lift my arm and hurl my spear. It hardly makes a sound as it rushes through the air. The head slips into the side of Hasel's chest, crunches through his bones, and knocks him to one side.

Before anyone can move I pull the spear free from Hasel's chest and plunge it into Clegg's throat. His blood leaps free!

Both men lay on the blood-soaked ledge. They die slowly. No one moves.

I look at the hunters and say, "There is nothing on the other side of the river but darkness."

None answers me.

And I say "You will live like the others—none above or below those around you."

I look down at Hasel and Clegg. They are not yet dead. To ease their pain I drive my bloody spear into the heart of each one of them. Then I say to the hunters: "Take them and put them deep in the earth."

I look at my people. It is too dark to see their faces, but I can feel their eyes on me. I can say no more to them.

I am weary almost beyond feeling. Slowly I turn toward my cave. A breeze stirs and as it passes I hear it whisper, "Ronstrom . . . Ronstrom . . . Ronstrom. . . ."

I pause and nod. Then I go into my cave, knowing that I did what had to be done.

XXII

Summer is over. The days are cooler. A fire is needed at night to keep warm. The hair on the skins of the animals taken in the hunt is unusually thick. This is a true sign that the winter will be bitter cold.

No one ever speaks of Clegg or Hasel. Each day the hunters go into the forest and return with meat. I join them and never fail to bring back to the encampment a large kill.

There are days I do not hunt. I spend these days in the encampment, talking with my people. They are concerned about the coming of the snow and I tell them not to fear, that we have enough meat to eat. My words are greeted with nods.

I discover that Ogg is a man full of wisdom and listen carefully to the things he tells me. And in Thorp I find a man who is always searching for a better way to make things. He has helped Nesbitt form better arrows and spearheads. He is everywhere and nowhere. When ever I see him, he tells me about some new thing he would like to do.

There are nights that Nan comes to my cave because she says, "I need to be filled by your manthing." And there are nights when I seek her out because I must satisfy my lust.

But I will not have her as my woman. Often she shouts with anger, telling me that no man will have her because everyone knows she is my thrall.

Her words do not ever say that she craves my manthing as much as I crave her slit. She never says she comes to my cave without my bidding nor when her screaming becomes too much for me to stand I beat her. . . .

Though there is still some warmth left in the day, all of the nights are cold. The leaves change color. Life in the forest is dying. The wind comes. It rips the leaves from the trees.

My people wait for the snow to come.

I go to Ogg's hut, sit before the fire pit, and say, "I am bringing my woman to the encampment."

He shifts his weight from one haunch to the other, holds his hands out to the warmth of the flames, and says, "Nan would be your woman if you would have her."

"She has spoken to you?"

He nods and says, "She has no one else."

I rub my hands on my knees. "There are other men who are in need of a woman," I answer.

"They will not have her," he tells me.

"I do not want her," I say. "I will bring Alvina back. She will be my woman. You tell the men who do not have a woman that the one who chooses Nan——"

"There are several who would be willing to share her."

I think on that.

Even in my time such an arrangement has not been uncommon. The woman lives alone and gives her slit to various men to satisfy their lust. The men leave meat, skins, or whatever else——

"She will then belong to any man," Ogg says.

"Are there many willing to share her?"

Ogg nods.

"Then the matter is settled," I tell him.

"And if she refuses?" he questions.

I shrug. "Why would she refuse?" I ask.

Ogg shakes his head, but says nothing. But when I stand and am about to leave the hut he asks, "When are you going for Alvina?"

"Soon," I tell him.

"And what if Rigga should——?"

"He will not stop me!"

"Alvina was given to him."

"She belongs to me," I tell him, "and I will have her."

Ogg does not answer and I walk out of the hut into the cold night. . . .

The next day before the sun shows yellow above the trees Nan comes running to my cave. I know Ogg has spoken to her.

"You would want me to be used by many men?" she shrieks.

I stand and answer sharply, "That or be the woman of none."

"I would be your woman," she tells me in a softer voice.

"No!" I shout. "I do not want you!"

"But when you want this," she cries, uncovering her slit, "you do not hesitate——"

The truth of her words angers me; I strike her.

"Take it!" she screams. "Take what you so easily give to others!"

Shamed, I start to turn away. She suddenly flings

177

herself at me and tries to claw my eyes. I cannot hold her off. I beat her to the floor of the cave. Blood flows from her nose.

"If you ever do that again," I tell her, breathing hard, "I will kill you!"

She crawls to me. Wrapping her arms around my legs, she whimpers, "I want no other man——"

I push her away.

"Ronstrom," she pleads, "do not do this to me!"

I take my weapons and a heavy skin cover.

"Where are you going?" she cries.

I do not answer. I leave the cave and go out into the forest.

Nan is no better than a she-wolf. I run until I lose all thoughts of her.

I move swiftly and silently. I am careful to leave no trail.

After many days I pass from one part of the forest into the other. Where I come from, the trees are not stunted and the signs of game many; where I now tread, the trees are stunted and the signs of game few. I reach the place where my hut once stood. I do not pause to let old memories make me stop and remember.

I am careful to let no man see me, though I see many. Before the sun is gone from the sky I am close to Rigga's encampment.

I hide in the forest. The moon comes. It is full and very white; its light is very bright.

I keep to the shadows of the trees. I move closer to Rigga's encampment.

The wailing of hungry children fills the night. Now and then women shriek. There are few fires burning. I do not see any men.

It is bitter cold. To bring some warmth to them, I rub my hands together. But it does not help.

I leave my spear, bow and arrows, and skin covering in the shadow of a tree. I crawl closer to the clearing.

There are many huts in the encampment. Rigga's is in the center. Covering its entrance is the skin of the bear I slew the day I met Gendy. . . .

The children stop wailing. The women are quiet. The fires die.

I take a deep breath, leap up, and run toward Rigga's hut. I am bright in the moonlight. My knife is ready. I reach the hut and pull aside the bearskin. I am inside the hut. Smoke rushes from my mouth.

I see Alvina. She lies with her back toward me. In front of her is a fire pit filled with glowing embers.

Silently I go to her. I kneel down and place one hand on her mouth. With the other I shake her gently.

"Alvina," I whisper, "it is Ronstrom."

She turns her head toward me.

Even in the dimness of the hut her face shows nothing. I touch her hair. It is stringy and unkempt.

I do not understand what is wrong. "Come," I say, "I have come for you." I try to lift her. She is bound hand and foot with strips of skin.

I cut her free. As soon as she is on her feet, I take her hand. Pulling her after me, I race back into the forest, pausing only to pick up my skin covering and my weapons.

We crash through the forest!

I want to be far away from Rigga's encampment when the sun comes. Alvina stumbles, falls, and does not get to her feet. I pull her up and race forward. I would speak with her but do not have the breath.

She falls again. She cannot keep my pace. If we are caught by Rigga, our life spirits would leave our bodies slowly.

I life Alvina in my arms and carry her through the darkness.

The new day comes gray and cold. The wind is up and makes the dark clouds fly swiftly across the sky.

I stop and set Alvina down. My chest is heaving and smoke rushes from my nose and mouth. Though it is very cold, my body is wet with sweat. My arms and legs ache.

I take my skin robe and cover Alvina. She does not even look at me. Her face betrays nothing. No light is in her eyes.

When I am able to speak, I call her name.

She does not hear it.

I do not understand what has happened to her, but something has covered the light in her eyes. I shake my head, take her hand, and start off again.

She will not walk, and I am forced to carry her.

I leave many false trails to hide my own. Through many days and many nights I move, pausing only to rest my body and ease my breathing. I no longer carry Alvina in my arms. Wrapped in the skin cover, she is slung over my shoulder.

I am too weary to think about her sickness, for that is what I am sure it is. I do not ever remember seeing anyone suffering from the same malady. The more I look at her the more uneasy I become. I chide myself for thinking like a frightened old woman.

Alvina has always been my woman. I knew this whenever she looked at me with her bright black eyes. She will be my woman when her sickness passes.

The smell of snow fills the air. I force myself to move even faster. But I can not move faster than the snow. It comes whipping down on a howling wind from the place where the sun never travels. The earth, the sky, and the forest are soon all one whirling whiteness.

I do not stop. I ache for sleep. If we sleep we would both die. My hands and legs are numb. My brain is numb.

To keep myself from falling into the huge drifts, I speak to Alvina, but she remains silent.

The storm makes the day and night run together. I do not know the difference between one and the other. I continue to move back toward my people. I do not need to see where I am going to find the encampment. I am guided by something inside me. If I survive the storm, I know I will reach the riverbank where my people live.

The wind suddenly dies and the snow ceases. The sun comes through the clouds and as its light fades, I see the encampment. Before I reach it Ogg, Nesbitt, and Thorp are running toward me.

Nesbitt and Thorp take Alvina from me, and all of us walk swiftly to my cave. A huge fire is built in the fire pit. Food is brought. Next to the fire, Alvina lies covered by the skin in which I wrapped her. . . .

The three men sit silently by and wait until I have eaten.

I ask about my people and I am assured that they are well fed and warm.

"And what of Rigga?" Ogg asks.

"He and his followers were not in the encampment," I say.

"Did they follow?" Nesbitt asks.

I glance toward Alvina. "I do not think so," I answer in a low voice.

Ogg looks at me questioningly.

"I will speak with you tomorrow," I say. "I must sleep now."

Nesbitt and Thorp leave immediately. But Ogg hangs back. "You should take that skin off her," he says, gesturing toward Alvina, "and put her on your skins."

"She will not know the difference," I answer.

"Is she dead?"

I shake my head. Then I stand, go to Alvina, beckon to Ogg . . . when he is close by I take the skin off her.

He looks at her face. She is awake. Her eyes are wide and staring.

"She is sick," I say and then looking at him I ask, "Do you know the nature of her sickness?"

Ogg shakes his head.

I drop the skin over her again and say, "She will get better."

Without answer, he turns and leaves the cave.

I look at Alvina and suddenly water flows from her eyes. I kneel down, take her in my arms, and as I press her to me she begins to whimper and then scream. When I release her she stops screaming. But her whimpering keeps sleep from me through most of the night.

XXIII

Many days pass and many more follow. The sun seldom shows itself. It snows often and the wind howls without letup.

Alvina's sickness does not pass. She is more like a child than a woman. She sits close to the fire and eats only when food is set before her. She says nothing.

I sit and watch her. I no longer think of her slit or the pleasure it might have given my manthing. I no longer think of her as a woman. She is there when I leave the cave and there when I return.

"The people," Ogg tells me, "say that Alvina is possessed by demons."

We trudge together in the snow. I cannot answer him. I do not know. Finally I say, "I should not have gone for her."

He shrugs. "It is always easy," he says, "to say what we should have done after we have done something else."

His words give me little comfort. I leave him and walk back to my cave. I do not know the nature of my own feelings. I ache inside. I want to scream, but dare not. At night I wake up as my manthing throbs with lust, and I cannot move toward her.

I have been hungry and cold and I have known physical pain almost beyond endurance, but never did I feel the way I do now. I am filled with a grayness inside so dismal that I wonder if I will ever know anything else.

The days hold little of the sun. The darkness becomes greater and greater. The people are more afraid than ever that the sun will not find its way back. Once gone over the edge of the world, it might be gone forever.

Their fear is my own. And at night I close my eyes with the hope that Gendy or The Giver of Life will give me some sign that I am not abandoned, that the sun will come back to me and my people, and that it will burn away the heavy grayness inside of me.

Another storm comes howling through the forest. There is no way to know whether the sun has left us forever or will return as it has in the past. The days are separated from the nights only by lesser and greater darkness.

Ogg visits my cave and sits by the fire to warm himself. His eyes move from me to the flames in the fire and then back to me. He pulls on his beard and says, "Nan still has not let herself be shared by the men."

I nod.

Ogg says nothing more to me about Nan. We speak of other things, and he tells me that some of the other animals of the forest are coming into the encampment in search of food. "Even the wolves are prowling about," he says.

"Do we have enough meat?" I ask.

"Yes."

"Then let the deer and the other animals live,"

I tell him. "But the wolves must either be driven away or killed."

"Thorp would like to capture a few," he tells me.

"For what purpose?"

"He says," Ogg explains, "the cubs that come after the snows could be trained to help us in our hunting."

"That is because he has never hunted a wolf," I answer.

"Do you forbid him to try?" Ogg asks.

I shake my head. "Only tell him," I warn, "and those who help him, to be very careful."

Ogg nods and leaves the cave.

I sit and look into the flames for a long time. I look at Alvina. She is stretched out on a skin not more than five steps from me. I sigh deeply, stand, and walk out of the cave.

A light snow is falling. I make my way to Nan's hut. I push the skin covering the entrance aside and enter. She is at the fire pit. She looks up and sees me. Light comes into her eyes.

"You have not lain with any other man?" I ask, without moving closer to the fire pit.

She stands up. "And you have not lain with your woman," she says.

My words to her were a question but hers to me were something she and everyone else knew. I do not answer. The tightness in my throat grows.

"It is said," Nan says, "that she is sick."

She questions now and I answer, "Some go so far as to say she is possessed by a demon."

Neither of us speaks. I see the rapid rise and fall of her breasts under her covering. She seems more womanly to me. There is a tightness in my groin.

"For a woman who can give you nothing," she

185

says, looking straight at me, "you beat me to the floor. For her you were willing to——"

Her words cut deep. They slice through the knot of tightness in my groin. I move back, pull the skin covering aside, turn and step into the night. I cannot beg!

I hurry back to my cave. But when I reach the ledge I hear Nan call my name. I do not look over my shoulder. When she reaches me I turn and, putting my hands around her waist, I lift her up on the ledge. Together we enter the cave.

Nan goes to Alvina, look at her, returns to me, and says "She is asleep."

We move to the back of the hut where my skins are spread out. She does not hesitate to remove her covering and as soon as I am naked we drop to the skins and press our bodies together. Her breasts are warm and firm in my hand and her slit becomes wet with lust.

I mount her. My manthing slides into her slit and she groans. Her arms close around my neck. I move my manthing in and out of her slit.

Her body keeps pace with my movements.

Soon soft throaty sounds come from her lips. Then she says to me, "My feelings for you are——" She closes her eyes. Her lips part and under me I can feel her body tense.

"Ronstrom," she whispers in a voice sounding as I have never heard hers sound, "Ronstrom, my slit belongs to you. It belongs to you. To you. . . ." Her body leaps against mine and I know her lust is pushing her against me.

My fluid pours out of me and when it is completely gone I do not move. I think about her words. I do not understand them.

The slit of any woman belongs to the man

186

who can take it. A woman's slit belongs to the man who gives her meat and skins, whose hut she lives in. But if a man stronger than the one who uses her slit claims it for his own and can keep her then he uses her slit.

I am so filled with need that before the day comes I fill her slit with my manthing until sleep takes me.

Nan stays in the cave with me. She is my woman and everyone in the encampment treats her as such. She tends Alvina and makes sure that she lacks for nothing.

One night as I sit by the fire pit, Nan says to me, "Alvina's belly is swollen with the life spirit."

"Are you sure?" I ask.

"Yes," Nan answers.

"Then she will bear a child?"

"In time."

"But why would the life spirit choose to enter a sick woman?" I ask.

"Perhaps it entered her," Nan says, "before she became sick and was trapped inside of her."

I shrug. I know very little about why or even how the life spirit enters a woman's body. But whenever it happens sometime later a new child comes from her body. It is something that puzzles men as well as women.

"You will be the child's father," Nan says.

"She is not my woman! You are!" This is the first time I say that to her.

She does not answer, but her eyes glisten with water. And when we are naked on my skins she says to me, "That night when I saw you dressed in your great stag robe and crown of antlers I could not believe that you ever had lain with me. I could not believe that you were anything but some kind of a giant. And even before you said I was your woman, I knew that I would be your woman no matter who or what you were. I knew it when I saw you watching me in the river."

I do not know what she is talking about. Her words make no sense. But I do not stop her. She talks until my hands are on her breasts. Then she stops and taking hold of my manthing she gently strokes it.

Her hands feel like the swirl of water or perhaps the movement of a breeze. I spread her naked thighs and enter her slit.

My movements are slow.

She wraps her arms around my neck and pushes my head down toward her breasts. Her bare nipples are full. Each looks like a dark cherry. I put my lips to one.

Nan moans.

The more I suck on her nipple the more she moans and writhes under me. I am lost in the taste of her nipple and the pleasure I find in her slit.

Then suddenly she cries, "Ronstrom, look out!"

I look up! Alvina stands over us. She holds a firebrand. The flaming tip rushes toward my face.

I thrust out my hand, grab hold of hers, and stay the torch's movement.

I push her back, leave Nan's body, and wrest the torch from her.

Nan is on her feet.

I toss the burning faggot into the fire pit and lead Alvina back to her place against the wall. Alvina is coaxed to lie down.

I take some strips of skins and bind her as I found her in Rigga's hut.

Nan kneels down and, pressing Alvina to her

naked breast, she says, "I will stay with her until she sleeps."

I return to my skins and wait.

When she comes, Nan says, "She sleeps."

Neither of us speaks. The lust we felt for each other is gone. "Why do you think she did something like that?" I ask.

"She thought you were Rigga," Nan answers. "She called his name when she tried to burn you."

"I did not hear her."

XXIV

Each night I bind Alvina's hands and feet. The task is not done without some strange feeling inside me. When I let myself think about her, I wonder if she is the way she is because of me.

The days pass. The snow does not leave. Our supply of meat is low, and I tell the men to kill several of the deer that come into our encampment. Their blood stains the white snow along the frozen riverbank.

Alvina's belly continues to swell. She seldom moves from her place along the wall of the cave. More and more she looks like an old woman.

One day the sun rises in a cloudless sky.

The wind is still and a new warmth comes to the earth. The snow turns to water and the ice in the river breaks with loud, snapping noises.

My people come out of their huts and shout their welcome to the sun. I stand at the entrance to my cave and shout with them. Nan is at my side and she is shouting, too. Only Alvina remains away from the bright, yellow warmth of the sun.

The snow is gone. Buds begin to show. Everyone in the encampment is busy. The hunters seek fresh meat; the children and women forage through the forest for firewood. Huts are mended. Several of the women bear children.

The trees come to leaf. The grass is thick and soft in the glens of the forest. Game is plentiful for everyone.

With all The Giver of Life has provided, I am still filled with a grayness that rises inside of me like mist over the lake. Though I can see the sun and feel its warmth on my body, there is a part of me that neither its warmth or light ever reaches.

Gendy's spirit does not come to me, nor do I hear The Giver of Life speak. At night I close my eyes and think about them, hoping my thoughts will bring them to me, but they remain away. I can not summon either of them, even if I go deep into the forest and on my knees to call to them.

With each day that passes I feel more and more uneasy.

I look at Alvina. She is near her time. I do not want to be the father of the child she will bear. A child, though, must have a father; that is the way it is with my people.

I sit on the ledge outside my cave and try not to let the heavy grayness inside of me spoil the things I see.

The sun is low in the sky. The light in the encampment is soft. The air is warm and filled with the scent of the forest. Nan is coming up from the river. She is carrying a large clay pot filled with water.

The cry of a hawk pierces the stillness of the twilight. Another answers. And still another.

Suddenly my blood begins to race. I shout at Nan to hurry. But even as my words die the wild shrieks of men sound from every side of the encampment.

I leap from the ledge and rush toward Nan. I come too late.

An arrow strikes her in the back and frees her life spirit!

I run back toward the cave.

Men are swarming over the top of it and stand on the ledge.

My people run in every direction. The hunters try to fight back, but the attack is too swift. They cannot drive back those who have fallen on us.

Women are screaming. Children cry.

The attackers sweep down on them with the fury of a summer storm. They sweep over everything. Their spears sparkle with blood. Huts are set ablaze and black smoke rises into the sky. . . .

I fight with my bare hands, and hurl rocks. I close with one man. He drives his spear toward me. I grab it, stay its motion, and push the end of the wood shaft back against his chest with such strength it breaks through the skin. He falls. I wrench the spear from his hands and kill him. I run to find another man to kill.

I kill and kill. . . .

I do not think of my people, of who is fighting, and who is not. I see only the red of blood.

The earth is slippery with the blood of the dead and wounded.

Arrows fly toward me. I am hit in the shoulder. I tear the head out and hurl my spear at the man who wounded me; it strikes him in the stomach and he dies.

I run for the river, ford it, gain the other side and pause to look back.

No hut has been spared the fire. The cries of the wounded fill the deepening twilight.

Suddenly I hear my name called. It is Rigga!

"Ronstrom," he says, "I have Alvina!"

"Ronstrom," Rigga shouts, "watch and see what I do!" He lifts Alvina high above his head and throws her down to the earth below the ledge. "Ronstrom," he calls, "blood flows from her body. Ronstrom, her blood and the blood of the others is on your hands. Ronstrom, your followers are scattered like the leaves before a raging wind, your encampment is no more. I have destroyed you, Ronstrom . . . I have destroyed you. . . ."

Silently I stand and watch my encampment burn. Darkness comes. The light from many fires glow red on the surface of the river. Through the night I listen to the screams of the women as Rigga's men satisfy their lust.

Gendy's spirit warned me not to spend my strength and lose what I have gained. I have lost all of it; my people and their purpose; Nan and also Alvina.

I wait for the night to pass.

When dawn comes smoke hangs heavily over the encampment. Even from where I am, I can see the earth is littered with dead. Rigga and his followers are still there. And from the limb of a tree not far from the ledge near my cave, Alvina has been hung by her feet.

I seethe with rage and would run in their midst to kill as many as I could before I myself would be slain. But I do not move. My legs do not obey my will. Perhaps I am afraid to die after all.

I hear a noise behind me. I whirl around and see Ogg. His face is gray and the whites of his eyes are red.

"Are there many left?" I ask.

"Some men and a few women," he replies. "Thorp

still lives . . . Shute's woman is still there!" He points across the river.

"And your woman?"

"There, too," Ogg replies.

We do not speak. The sun climbs high above the trees.

Rigga stands on the ledge and shouts, "Ronstrom, hear me. I and those with me claim this part of the forest. We claim all of the forest. There is no place for you. Those of your followers who join me will be welcomed. Those of them who choose not to join me will be hunted down and slain. I give you warning Ronstrom, I will——"

"Rigga," I shout, "I will hunt you down and when I find you I will kill you!" My words boom out like summer thunder.

Rigga laughs.

"You have done your worst," I tell him. "You have set your men against my people when it was me you wanted. I will not do the same, Rigga. But I will go after you. It is you I want and it is you I will kill!"

He laughs again but the sound of his laughter is weak.

It is many days before Rigga and those with him leave the encampment. The stink of death hangs over the riverbank.

The dead are burned and their ashes covered. I do not speak to the living and they do not speak with me. In their eyes I am responsible for their misfortune. I do not even speak with Ogg or Shute. Their women were taken captive by Rigga and his men.

At night I sit alone in my cave and stare into

the flames in the fire pit. My head fills with swirling thoughts.

I do not understand why The Giver of Life has allowed Rigga to destroy the encampment and scatter the people.

I do not understand why Nan was the first to die.

I do not understand why He let Rigga kill Alvina.

I do not understand how I am to complete the task He set before me, if I do not have the men to do the building.

When my wound is healed I take my weapons and my great stag robe and begin my hunt for Rigga. Many days pass, and I do not find him. Now and then I see his followers, but it is not them I pursue.

The summer ends. The leaves turn and when the snow begins to fly I am still hunting for him. The wind and the snow claw at me, but I do not stop my hunt. I feel neither the claws of the wind nor the cold of the snow.

The sun vanishes from the sky and I move through a long twilight.

The sky becomes blue again and the sun gives warmth to all the living things. Leaves fan out on the limbs of trees. Grass covers the paths and open spaces of the meadows.

I seldom eat or rest.

Those men I pass in the forest pause and look at me, but none raises his weapon against me.

Then one day I leave the forest and walk out on to the open plain where Gendy's bones lie buried. Dark clouds slip over the yellow face of the sun.

I do not have to search any further. I know Rigga is somewhere close by.

"Rigga!" I shout. "Rigga, it is Ronstrom!"

He comes up over a slight rise in the earth.

"I have been waiting," he answers.

The sky grows darker. I hear the roaring of my blood in my ears. Rigga comes within hurling distance of our spears.

He stops and calls out, "And when you are dead, Ronstrom, the crows will eat your body."

I do not answer.

I raise my spear.

He does the same.

The two weapons like birds in flight pass each other. His falls behind me. Mine drops in front of him.

Neither of us bothers to retrieve the other's weapon. Instead we rush together, each willing to use his strength to kill the other. I hurl myself against him. Our bodies come together with a sound like the crashing of a great tree.

Rigga's body is pressed against mine.

We grunt and strain as each tries to hold the other.

His body is wet with sweat.

I feel his hands locked on my arms.

We move backward and forward from one side to the other. The sound of our breathing is loud. Neither can bring the other down. Our movements grow larger. We grapple with each other over the entire plain. The earth trembles where we tread.

I am no longer a man even as Rigga is no longer a man. We are giants whose heads touch the upper reaches of the black sky. And all around us there are those who watch our contest.

In front of me, or somewhere in my skull, are

two huge forms. They are black. They are white. They swirl around each other, much the same way that Rigga and I circle one another.

One cries, "I have won!"

But the other shouts, "Not yet!"

"Ronstrom will die!" the first proclaims.

"He will live and do my bidding!" the other answers.

"He has already failed!" the first howls.

I lose my footing. Rigga is on me. The images leave me and I fight for my life.

Rigga's hands are around my throat.

I gasp for air. But suddenly I break his hold. I roll free and suck air into my lungs.

Both of us leap to our feet.

We are still giants and the earth quivers beneath us. We close again and I am able to toss him over my head.

I fling myself on him, but he rolls out from under me. He is on my back, and, grabbing hold of my head, he pins my face into the earth.

Blood flows from my nose. My eyes become dim. I reach back, take hold of his foot, and twist it with all my strength. The sudden wrench pulls him off me. I scramble to my feet.

He comes at me and drives his fist into my stomach.

The blow robs me of wind. I sink to my knees. He runs at me and, lifting the bottom of his foot, he sends it crashing against my head!

My sight blurs and I am close to falling into a whirling blackness.

Rigga comes close again.

I fling myself forward against him to stop myself from falling into the black water. I lean on him. He tries to free himself but cannot.

Soon the black water is gone. My sight is no longer blurred, but there is the taste of blood in my mouth.

I push myself free of him. His face, too, is bloody. I wonder if he knows we have become giants.

"I will kill you," he hisses.

I do not answer. I do not know which one of us will die, nor do I think he knows.

Once more we are locked together. Our bodies strain to fell the other.

The visions come again and one says, "Neither one will win."

The other says, "It is in our wager that one will triumph over the other."

"But I have already won," the first one claims. "After the famine, after the fire, after the hunger, your people became less than animals in the forest. They abandoned you. They will not return. None has come from their issue to bring them back."

"Ronstrom," the other answers, "I have chosen him."

"Only if he lives!"

The visions slip away.

"Ronstrom!" Rigga shouts. "I will cease to fight if you will do the same!"

I do not answer, but try to throw him.

"We are equally matched," he croaks.

I still do not answer.

Suddenly Rigga breaks my hold and runs.

I go after him. When I am close enough I fling myself at his feet.

He tumbles down.

I am on top of him. Now it is I who have my hands around his throat. I press.

His eyes push out of their sockets.

I press harder. I feel his body thrash under me. And then something inside his neck snaps. His head slips limply to one side. I let go of his neck. Still breathing hard, I take my knife and sever his head from his body.

I take his head, impale it on my spear, and, leaving his body for the crows to feed on, I stumble my way back into the forest.

I am no longer a giant. I am only a man who has slain his enemy and I hold the bloody trophy to prove what I did. Perhaps I was never a giant.

I walk slowly. My body is battered and I am covered with blood. From time to time I look at Rigga's head.

I do not shout my victory to the people of my tribe. I let them see Rigga's head.

They do not ask what has happened. They know.

I return to my cave and, planting my spear on the ledge of front of my cave, I wait for the people to gather in front of me. They will come. . . .

First Ogg, Shute, Thorp, and Nesbitt come. They look at Rigga's head and then at me. None of them speaks. Soon the others who survived Rigga's attack come. As the days pass more join in.

Huts are built. Fire pits are dug. The work of providing meat and shelter occupies everyone. The long days of summer are over. The snows will come and the cold wind will blow. My people must be ready for the winter.

I join the hunters. Game is plentiful and widespread, even to the edge of the forest where the plain begins.

Though there are many who follow me, there are many more who will not join me. These I do not think about. Among them is Gibben, Alvina's father. He and those with him remain in their encampment.

To prevent another attack on my people, large fires are kept burning throughout the night around the encampment and men keep vigil while the others sleep. Thorp will soon have several wolves trained to help guard the area around us.

Often I think about the vision that came to me while I fought Rigga. I do not understand all I saw or heard. And the best I can make of it seems foolish. Who could believe that The Giver of Life and The Keeper of Darkness continually exchange identities, so that it would seem one could not be without the other? Or who would believe that such gods would design to play with me even as children play with other creatures? These are foolish but persistent thoughts.

From my victory over Rigga I know that The Giver of Life has not cast me aside. It is His power that has filled the forest with meat. I wait for Him to speak to me again so that I might fulfill the task for which He chose me. I become once more the hunter I had been.

The days of summer pass. The sun's journey across the sky lessens. The nights are cold and the leaves turn red, yellow, and brown.

Then one day when the sky is filled with gray scud and our breaths smoke in the cold air Gibben comes to the encampment. With him are several hunters.

From my ledge I watch him. He fords the river and comes straight toward me. His beard and hair are grayer than I remember.

"Ronstrom!" he shouts when he is almost at the ledge. "Ronstrom, call your people together so they will hear me!"

His voice is loud enough to be heard all over the encampment, but I nod and order my people to come before me.

I do not have good feelings toward Gibben. He knew I wanted Alvina and yet he gave her to Rigga. He has always been a spiteful man.

When all my people are in front of me I tell Gibben "They are here. Say what you have come to say."

He leaps up to the ledge. Then, facing my people, he cries out, "Do not follow him! Ronstrom will bring death to all of you! His magic will desert him! The Giver of Life will fail him!"

The people shift uneasily.

Gibben looks at Rigga's head. The skin around the face is now dry and rotted. He gestures toward it and says, "I gave my daughter to him. But her spirit was not her own. Ronstrom took it from her."

He looks at me and I see fire in his eyes.

"With his magic," Gibbon shouts, "Ronstrom took her spirit and then he came for her body. He came at night. With Rigga watching him, he made off with Alvina."

"Rigga was not there," I say. "None of the men were there."

Gibben points to one of the hunters. "Answer him," he orders.

The man looks up at me and says, "I was there. I saw you. We all saw you. But we could not move. Something held us."

I shake my head. "I saw no one!" I tell him.

"Ronstrom did not fight Rigga!" Gibben cries. "He did not slay him!"

The people murmur among themselves and the smoke of their breaths rises like mist over their heads.

"I was there!" Gibben shouts. "I was there. I saw them. I saw Ronstrom and I saw Rigga. Ronstrom became a giant. It was the giant who slew Rigga!"

"Yes!" I roar. "We were both giants. We fought and the earth trembled where we trod. But I was a man when I took Rigga's head. Tell them more, Gibben, tell them of the gods," I challenge, "who also fought there. Tell them how Rigga waited for me. Tell them that the sky turned black. Tell them, Gibben, that though we fought as giants, I killed as a man and Rigga died as a man. But more than all of those things, Gibben, tell them that you do not understand what you saw. I who fought there do not understand."

Gibben is silent.

My people are silent.

Gibben leaps from the ledge. He and those who came with him leave the encampment.

That night when I am sitting close to the fire pit and staring into the flames Ogg comes into the cave.

He sits down opposite me, and says, "Gibben's words have frightened the people."

I nod.

"But your words have frightened them even more," he tells me.

I throw another faggot into the fire. The flames devour it. As they grow from what they feed on, their light casts our huge shadows on opposite sides of the hut.

"What do they say?" I ask.

"Many things," Ogg answers with a shrug. "Some claim that you can move without being seen. Others say that you can become a giant at will. And a few——"

"And what do you think?" I question.

Ogg rubs his beard. He looks at me across the fire. Then he says, "I think you hold powerful magic."

"Is that all?"

"That your magic comes from The Giver of Life."

I nod.

"You serve Him as we serve you."

"We all serve Him," I say.

For a while Ogg is quiet, but then he asks, "Can you move without people seeing you?"

"No."

"Then the man with Gibben lied?"

"Yes."

"But why?"

I shrug. "Who knows why a man will lie?"

"And when you fought Rigga," Ogg asks, "were you a giant?"

"That is the way I felt," I reply. "I felt that we were both giants."

"And of the gods who fought there?" Ogg questions.

I tell him of the vision that came to me while I fought Rigga. He listens. When I finish he says, "If the gods play with us, what is their purpose?"

"I do not know."

Ogg falls silent again. He sits and stares into the fire. Then with a long-drawn-out sigh, he says, "They must have a purpose. All this must have some meaning."

"Perhaps," I answer, "we give it meaning. Perhaps we can do what the gods cannot."

He nods and asks, "Then it is you who bears the burden for what must be done?"

"Yes."

"And what is it that must be done?"

"We must build——"

"I remember," Ogg says. "You told us that we must build something for The Giver of Life——"

I nod.

"But what is it?"

"I cannot tell you, but when the time comes I will show you."

Ogg stands up.

I follow suit.

"The trouble with magic," he says, "is that the people who see evidence of it once must see proof of it over and over again."

"I understand," I answer. I walk with him to the skin that hangs over the entrance to the cave.

When Ogg is gone, I return to the fire. I am tired. I stretch out on my skins, close my eyes, and sleep.

The snows begin to fly. The days are dark and dismal, but my people are warm and well fed. Whatever fear Gibben stirred by his words or I by mine seems to have died with the coming of the snow.

I am alone most of the day and all of the night. I have no need to take another woman. The lust I once felt for a woman's slit I no longer feel. My thoughts move in a different direction.

My thoughts move like a flock of birds toward a place of their own. But to where or what I know not. I cannot stand. I find no rest when I sit, and sleep flows past me, unwilling to take me within its movement.

My thoughts return to the cave in the mountain, to that place where The Giver of Life first spoke to me, where I saw—I know not what I saw. All my effort now is bent toward remembering its form.

It is difficult for me to find the right images in my mind. I see many things, but they are the wrong things. I know they are wrong because as soon as I see them they are gone.

When it is not snowing and the wind has stopped blowing, I leave the cave. In the snow on the ledge I try to make an image of what I saw. My efforts are wasted. Nothing that I cut into the snow is anything like the things I saw in the cave.

Then one day when I am staring into the fire, as several pieces of burning wood fall together, I remember!

I close my eyes and I can see the altar and everything that was on it. I waste no time: I begin to carve what I see in my head. But I am not skilled with my hands. Nothing comes right. I call Thorp and tell him what I want.

"What are they for?" he asks.

"We must begin to think of the days to come," I answer.

He gives me a questioning look.

I do not offer to tell him any more.

XXV

Impatiently I wait for Thorp to finish carving. Days pass. I walk back and forth in my cave. Food means little to me—sleep less. When I can no longer stay within the walls of the cave, I prowl through the encampment. My people call to me. I answer their calls, but I do not stop to speak.

Ogg comes to my cave and asks, "Are you sick?"

I shake my head.

"Your cheeks are hollow and your eyes look without seeing," he tells me.

I do not know what to tell him, and I say, "It will pass. It will pass."

He does not answer, and when he is gone I stretch out on my skins. I close my eyes. I hear the thumping of my heart, the roaring of my blood. Those sounds soon fade, and I slip into the warm flow of sleep.

The river is soft. The sky above me is blue and cloudless. I go where the waters take me. The sky darkens. Night comes. The lights in the deep darkness flicker and the bright wanderers move through the blackness.

The sky brightens with the coming of the sun. I

watch the sun move. Night follows and then day. One follows the other many times.

"Ronstrom," Gendy's spirit calls, "Ronstrom, mark the path of the sun. See where it rises."

The river is gone. I stand on the plain where Gendy's bones lie buried.

"There is a summer light and a winter light," Gendy says. "Mark where each begins and ends."

I would answer Gendy, but am caught by the strange movement of the sun. It rolls across the edge of the plain, moving toward a place where it never goes, stops and then rolls far to the other side where it always travels, stops again, and then rolls back to where it started from.

"Mark the light from the sun, Ronstrom," Gendy croaks. "And around where it falls on each side of its journey, you will build. Mark the light, Ronstrom. Mark the light. . . ."

"How?" I cry. "How can I mark the light of the sun?"

"It must be done," Gendy answers. "It must be done."

The sun begins to fade. "Gendy," I call. "Gendy?" But he is gone.

I wake wet with sweat. I go to the entrance of the cave and step out on the ledge. The sky is filled with gray clouds. Snow drifts down from them. I rub my eyes. I do not understand the dream. I do not know how to mark the light of the sun.

All day it snows. When night comes Thorp enters my cave.

"I cannot do it, Ronstrom, I cannot do what you asked."

I look at him. Thorp, who can do anything, cannot carve for me.

"The wood will not take the knife," he explains. "I could not find the shape you wanted in the wood. I do not think it is there."

I nod. I should have known I could not give my task to another man. I ask Thorp to stay and share meat with me.

He does and we speak of many things. He tells me, "When the ice on the river melts, I will be able to catch fish. I made something from the rushes that grow upstream. It will trap the fish."

After a while Thorp leaves and I once again begin to carve.

I work slowly. I am not skilled. Often the wood splits. I start over again.

Each piece takes many days for me to complete.

I need three pieces with which to build. When they are finished I set the uprights in place. I try to cap them with a third member. The three of them fall.

I bring snow into the cave and pack it around the bottom of the uprights. They stand firm when I cap them. But now the third member rolls off.

I do not know how to keep it in place.

I am filled with anger. My hands are cold. I go to the fire and hold my hands out toward it. I look at the spaces between my fingers. Immediately I know how to keep the top pieces from rolling off the other two.

In each of the uprights I cut a notch, shaped like the spaces between my fingers. Into this notch I set the third piece. It is held. It does not roll off.

I continue to carve many more pieces, as many as I need to make all the things I saw on the altar in the cave.

Many days pass. The light of day grows less and less. The sun, despite the wind and cold, shows itself more than usual. As it climbs into the sky I see it sit in the fork of a tree. Later it has moved up and rests on a high limb.

I go back into my cave and continue to work on my carvings. I remember how the sun rolled across the earth in my dream. And suddenly I realize that when I saw the sun in the fork of the tree and then on the limb, I marked its light.

I set my carving down and walk out on to the ledge. The sun is shining in a brilliant, cloudless sky. I breathe deeply and whisper, "I will make the light, Gendy. Tell The Giver of Life I found the way." My breath smokes in the cold air.

I seek out Ogg and say, "I am leaving the encampment."

"Where are you going?" he asks.

"To the plain beyond the forest," I answer.

"Will anyone go with you?"

"What I must do must be done by me alone," I say.

"And what do I tell the people?"

"Tell them," I reply, "that I have gone to mark the light of the sun."

His jaw loosens and his mouth falls open. His red tongue slips along his lips. He closes his mouth, nods, and asks, "When will you return?" '

I shrug.

Ogg pulls on his beard and says, "Do not stay away too long. The people must see you to know that you are their leader."

I leave the encampment before the last rays of the sun give way to twilight. I move through the forest. I do not feel I am moving. I feel as though I am being carried by the wind. I do not feel the cold. I am filled with the heat of the sun. It is inside of me. I am one with it.

Never have I known such an overpowering excitement. Never in the heat of mortal combat did I experience a small portion of what I now feel. And never when my manthing was deep in the slit of a woman did I ever gain the satisfaction that now is mine.

Of all the men in my tribe, perhaps of all the men who live in the mountains like the Rock People, or in other forests even as my people do, I alone know the secret of the sun. I alone know that at the very time it dies it is born again and when it lives at its fullest is already beginning to die. Its death and birth are one. Its life and death are one.

The plain stands white in the moonlight. I walk to where Gendy's bones lie. And though the snow lies over his grave I kneel down and softly call to him, to his spirit.

"Gendy," I say, "I will do all that must be done. I will mark the sun and I will build for The Giver of Life."

The earth trembles and Gendy's answer comes with the sighing of the wind. "It will not be enough, Ronstrom. It will not be enough."

"What more must I do?" I cry.

"All that you must do, you will do," Gendy answers.

"Am I never to be free?"

He does not answer. The wind begins to howl. The snow flies wildly around me. I wrap myself in my robe made from the skin of the great stag and wait for the dawn.

All night the storm rages and then just before

the first light it stops. The clouds fly apart. I see the very last of the night sky.

The sun comes up over the edge of the earth and where its rays first touch the snow I plant my spear. Later in the day I replace my spear with the limb of a tree.

Each dawn I mark the place where the light of the sun first falls. Days pass. There are many markers in the snow. I add more. From where Gendy's bones lie buried, the markers extend in a long straight line.

Then one day when the day is born with a golden dawn the light that first touches the earth remains on my last marker. I have marked the light of the sun! It will not go any farther toward the mountains. It is at its end and at its beginning. And I am the one who has marked it.

"I have marked the sun!" I shout. "I, Ronstrom, have marked the light of the sun!"

My voice swells up in the cold air and rolls across the plain. The smoke of my breath climbs in a white column above my head. And as the sound of my shout lingers over the plain, another deeper dark voice calls out, "Ronstrom, you are the instrument of my will!"

I fall to my knees and bow my head.

"Your idle boasts anger me!" The Giver of Life roars. "Do not anger me, Ronstrom. What I give I can take away. I have chosen you to build——"

I lift my head and cry, "I did not want to be chosen! I did not want this task. You have chosen me to do your bidding, but I am a hunter and not a builder."

"You will do what must be done!"

"Then I say," I shout, standing erect, "that I

have marked the light of the sun! I, Ronstrom, have done it!"

The Giver of Life does not answer. Only the sound of the wind moves across the plain. I pick up my spear and slowly make my way back to the forest. There are many things that must be done before I return to my people.

When I come to where Gendy's bones lie, I stop and tell his spirit, "I will lead my people forth, Gendy; we will build around you."

Suddenly The Giver of Life's voice comes on the wind. "You have marked the light of the sun, Ronstrom," he calls. "You have marked the light of the sun."

I look up. The sky is very blue. The sun is already high above the earth. I breathe deeply and go toward the forest.

XXVI

At the place where I marked the light of the sun, I burn away the snow. Then I build a mound of stones. Before the sun finishes the journey across the sky the clouds come. The wind becomes stronger and, as the light of day dims, snow is flying.

I hurry to the forest. The trees offer some protection from the blast of the wind. I spend the night in the hut where Garth and I hunted together. I sit wrapped in my great stag robe and look into the flames of the fire pit. Outside the wind howls and the snow falls thick and fast.

So many nights in the past I have been alone that by now it should not matter to me. Yet it does. I have a longing to speak with another man. Perhaps I have a longing to be with a woman. It is not that my lust is strong within me, but I wish to tell her about the things I did today. If Nan were here, I would tell her. She might not understand all I would say, but would listen.

I stretch out close to the fire. Its flames are lower now. There is a strange quality to my thoughts about Nan. They are warm and soft like her body was when I pressed it against mine.

I roll over and look at my shadow on the wall of the hut. It is much larger than I am. I wonder if The Giver of Life has a shadow? A foolish thing to bother myself about!

Suddenly I bolt up. Something has changed between myself and The Giver of Life. Though I am only a man and He a god—there is a new bond between us. I look at my shadow. I wonder if I am His shadow? Another foolish thought. I smile, close my eyes, and sleep.

When day comes it is still snowing. But I am anxious to return to my people and continue my journey. After several days I reach the river, cross its ice-covered surface, and enter the encampment.

As soon as I am among the huts I know something is wrong. An uneasy stillness hangs like a heavy robe over the encampment. I go immediately to Ogg's hut.

A fire is burning. Thorp is there. He is at the fire pit and looks up at me. Behind him, stretched out on several skins, lies Ogg.

I squat close to the fire pit.

"He is wounded," Thorp tells me. "His life spirit is trying to leave his body."

Anger boils inside of me. "Who," I ask, "who raised his hand against him?"

"I do not know," Thorp answers.

"He cannot speak?" I question.

"He has not," Thorp replies.

I move to where Ogg lies. His breathing comes hard. It sounds like a low growl. Those parts of his face not covered by his beard are very white. His brow is wet with sweat. I kneel down and say, "Ogg, tell me who——"

His eyelids flutter.

I speak again. "Tell me, Ogg, and I will take his life from him."

His eyes open. His lips tremble. "Did you mark the sun?" he asks haltingly.

"Yes," I answer, "it is done."

He nods and closes his eyes.

From the sounds he makes I know his life spirit is still with him.

"Ogg," I say, "tell me who——"

His lids flutter again and open. He says, "Beware, Ronstrom, beware. There are those who challenge your power. Those who seek to pull you down."

"Who Ogg? Who?"

His eyelids flutter and close. He says, "I did not think it would be so hard to die, so very hard!" He wheezes, coughs, and blood flows from between his lips. His hand grasps mine. "Ronstrom," he whispers, "oh, Ronstrom——" He is silent!

The hand is limp in mine. I let go of it and it drops like a stone. "His Life Spirit is gone," I say. My voice is tight in my throat.

Thorp turns from the fire. His eyes go to Ogg and with a tightness in his voice, he whispers, "I would rather it would be me than him."

Ogg, never a big man in life, now looks even smaller in death. I shake my head, leave the hut, and go to my cave.

The flames in the fire pit bring me no warmth. I am cold within. I sit and watch the fire die and think perhaps The Giver of Life took the life spirit from Ogg in return for the words He gave me? If that is what he did, then Ogg's blood is on my hands and not on those of the man who opened his body with the spear.

I do not understand the way of The Giver of

215

Life. He is a god and what is stronger than a god?

Does he envy me for having marked the light of the sun? Would he set some of my own people against me because of it? Would he let one of them kill Ogg? Was I not told by Gendy to mark the light of the sun?

The fire burns low and the glowing embers are many. What man can answer for what a god does? I roll my eyes upward and ask aloud, "Why? Why? Why Ogg?"

The Giver of Life does not answer.

Sleep does not come. I leave the cave and stand on the ledge. The encampment is still. My breath smokes in the cold air. Dawn has yet to come. The night sky is filled with bright flickering lights. Here and there, in their midst, I see a sudden movement, a streak of light, and then it is gone.

Against the bigness of the sky I am very small.

I lower my eyes to the dark trees across the river. I am even smaller than they are. But a tree cannot move. A tree cannot make a spear nor a bow and arrow, much less use them. A tree can do none of the things I can. I am even smaller and less powerful than some of the animals I slay. Yet, I can slay them.

I look up again. Never before have I had such thoughts. I am different from the trees and animals in the forest. All men are different. The things we can do can be done by no other creature.

I take a deep breath and the smoke rushes from my mouth. I look toward Ogg's hut. Had he lived, I would be table to tell him my thoughts. I am sure he would have understood. But now I must keep them to myself.

Once more I look out over the encampment.

Sheltered in some of the huts are those who would pull me down, who would challenge my power.

I will not give them the chance. And I must protect those who have done so much to help me. Thorp, Shute, and Nesbitt will not die at the end of someone's spear. I will place them beyond the reach of all the others.

I return to the cave. I stretch out on my skins; just before I close my eyes, I say aloud, "I am stronger now than I was before. If a man can mark the light of the sun. . . ."

The low sound of laughter moves through the cave. It soon swells and moves from wall to wall, shaking the earth beneath it.

I do not tremble.

When the laughter dies I sleep!

XXVII

It is twilight. I and my people stand at the base of a nearby hill. On the top of the hill a huge fire pit has been dug. It is filled with wood and Ogg's body rests on top of the wood.

Each man who lives in the encampment has a torch. In the cold gray twilight the flames from the torches bend with the wind and give the snow a reddish color.

I am covered with my great stag robe and on my head I wear the crown of antlers. In one hand, I, too, hold a torch and in the other my spear.

Thorp, Nesbitt, and Shute are close by. I have told them to stay with me.

I have led my people from the encampment to this place and now I walk slowly up the side of the hill. Thorp, Nesbitt, and Shute come with me.

I stop, turn, and look down on my people. Their flaming torches now seem like a lake of fire that is stirred by the wind.

I raise my torch and my spear and in a loud voice I say, "Ogg was slain by those who would pull me down, who would challenge my power. To those who thrust their spears into him I say you will be found out and when you are discovered you will give your lives to satisfy Ogg's spirit."

There is no movement or sound from my people.

"From this day on," I tell them, "a man who slays another in any manner but an open contest will suffer death. We cannot do what must be done when we kill our own."

This does bring a loud murmur from the people.

"He who takes anothers life and frees his life spirit from his body will die and have his own life spirit freed."

Many voices are raised against what I say, but I cannot see the faces of those who cry.

"There is no other way!" I shout. "We will no longer kill our own!"

"How then," challenges a voice, "will we settle our differences?"

"By an open contest," I answer. "The man who wins such a contest gains the advantage of the other."

"That has not been the way of our people!" the same man shouts.

"It will be their way now!" I thunder.

"You take our manhood from us!" the man cries.

"Then you think those who slew Ogg were men?" I ask.

The man does not answer.

"Let the one who hurled his spear at Ogg," I challenge, "hurl that same spear at me. I cannot see your faces and will not know who hurls it. I will stand here without my great stag robe. Let that man hurl his spear!"

I drop the robe from my shoulders and walk several paces down toward my people. They are silent. None raises his spear.

After a while I return to where I stood and replace the great stag robe around my shoulders.

"There will be no more killing of our own!" I thunder.

"We will obey!" my people cry. "We will obey your word, Ronstrom!"

I wait until their shouting ceases and then I say, "From this day on the men who stand here with me—Thorp, Nesbitt, and Shute—are to be held in your eyes even as I am. Should those who slew Ogg do the same to any of them I will have The Giver of Life take from you what he has given. The game will leave the forest. Your children's bellies will swell from hunger and you will know the pain of hunger."

The people shuffle in the snow. They whisper to one another.

"I will let you eat rats again," I tell them, "if a hand is raised against any one of them." The wind picks up and the flames on the torches bend toward me.

"A sign!" a man shouts.

"It's a sign!" a second calls.

The cry is taken up by all of them.

I have done all I could to protect Thorp, Nesbitt, and Shute. I nod and beckon them to follow me. Slowly we make our way to the top.

I hold my torch over Ogg's body.

I am filled with those gray mists again. My throat aches and water flows from my eyes.

I bury my torch in the dry kindling under Ogg's body. The tongues of the flames leap up through the dry wood; a larger fire erupts! I step back.

Thorp places his torch on the kindling. Nesbitt and Shute thrust their torches forward. The three of them stand with me as the rest of the men move past the fire pit and add their torches to the flames.

Soon I stand alone and watch Ogg's body burn. The flames work quickly. The air is filled with the stench of burning flesh. When the fire begins to die I walk slowly down the hill.

I do not know where the words I spoke came from. But this time I do not doubt their wisdom. I look back toward the hill. I cannot see the fire. But the smoke still rises from the pit.

XXVIII

I go back to my carving.

On the day that the ice on the river erupts with loud cracking sounds I finish making as many pieces as I remember. I put together those made from the uprights and the crosspiece. Then I place everything on the floor of my cave. Where I marked the light of the sun I place one piece of wood stripped of its bark. I know not what to do with the other pieces of wood I cut and scraped clean.

Those pieces that are joined together to form one are set around the place where Gendy's bones lie buried. There is enough land inside the ring for my people to live. But I still do not know what to do with all the other pieces.

For many days and nights I look at what I have done. I take a burning faggot, one with enough fire on its end to cast some light. In the darkness of my cave I slowly move the torch over the pieces I carved. I do not see its light touch the marker I have placed on the floor of the cave.

Over and over again, I try to make the light of the torch fall on the marker. I cannot do it. Yet I know it must be done if I am to show my people.

Each dawn I stand on my ledge to watch the

coming of the sun. There is a soft warmth in the air. The sky is filled with birds.

After I see a single shaft of sunlight slip from behind a tree I know how to make the light from the torch fall on my marker. I take a large flat rock and carry it into my cave. On top of the rock I put all the things I carved. I take a burning faggot and hold it below the rock. From where I am I can see its glow. Slowly I move it up the other side as I have seen the sun move. Light brightens, and as soon as enough of it is above the top of the rock it touches my marker!

That day I summon Thorp.

When he comes into the cave and sees what is on the flat rock he looks at me with wonder in his eyes. "So this is what you wanted me to carve?" he asks.

I nod.

"You have done it better than I could," he tells me. "The things you made were in the wood for you; I could not find them.

"But what is it, Ronstrom?" he asks.

I do not know its name, and I say, "It is what we will build for The Giver of Life."

"But what purpose does it serve, Ronstrom?"

Again I cannot answer and I say, "Watch." I take a piece of wood from the flames; I move it as the sun moves.

Wide-eyed, he looks at me and then at the burning wood.

I do the same thing many times.

"What is it?" he questions.

"The firebrand is the sun," I say.

"And that piece of wood?"

"Its marker."

"Then all this is to mark the coming of dawn?" he asks, shaking his head.

"More, Thorp," I answer, knowing he does not understand what he is looking at. "Much more than that. But we must build it."

He nods and asks, "Where will we build it?"

"In a special place," I tell him. Then I ask, "Will you set all these pieces on a flat piece of wood so they can be moved from place to place?"

"Yes, Ronstrom," he says, "I can do that."

There is an unfamiliar sound in his voice and I ask him, "Is anything wrong?"

He shakes his head.

He does not know what we are to build or its purpose, and I cannot help him to know. Other than marking the light of the sun when it is at its end and its beginning I do not understand any more about the purpose of the pieces I carved than Thorp does.

"Do you think our people can build this?" I ask, waving toward the pieces on the rock.

"Yes. But it will not be easy."

"I do not think it was meant to be easy," I answer.

"Will I have time to try my fish traps before we move?" he asks.

I nod.

Thorp smiles and says, "If I catch a big one I will give him to you."

He leaves the cave. I am alone with the pieces of wood I carved. I look at them and then I close my eyes. Deep in my skull I can see what it will look like when it is finished!

I open my eyes and look at the pieces on the top of the rock. Even though my people will have them to look at, they will not see what I have seen.

Those pieces of wood will remind them of their debt to The Giver of Life. But what we build around the place where Gendy's bones lie buried is in my skull.

I turn away from the rock and think about what I must tell my people.

The leaves on the trees are pale green. The days are warmer. The hunters go into the forest, and each returns with fresh meat. Thorp is busy with his fish trap at the river. Several new children have come to the women of our encampment. But, as always, more give up their life spirit within a few days after coming out of the woman's body.

Thorp has set my carvings into a broad piece of wood which he himself cut from an oak that was felled by the winter storms. Now all that is lacking to put my people on the march are my words. I hesitate to speak to them. But I know I must.

One day when the hunt has been very good and each man comes back to the encampment with nothing less than a good-size deer, I dress in my great stag robe, place the crown of antlers on my head, and summon the people to stand before my lodge.

Thorp, Nesbitt, and Shute are behind me. In the space between us I have placed the carvings that Thorp has mounted for me. In my hand I hold a spear.

I take a deep breath and say, "The time has come for us to do that which The Giver of Life asks. He has kept His word to us and we must keep ours to Him, lest He withhold the game from the forest."

There is a murmur of agreement and one man asks, "What is it we must do, Ronstrom?"

"We must do his bidding," I answer.

"And we will!" several men shout.

I step to one side and with the head of my spear pointing to it, I tell them, "He bids us build this."

A sudden silence sweeps over my people.

"He bids us build this," I repeat.

"We are hunters, Ronstrom," a man shouts angrily. "We will hunt for Him, but we can not build——"

"He bids you build this!" I thunder. "It is not what you will do for Him, but what He bids you do. This is what we must build if we are to keep our word to Him and His——"

"But how, Ronstrom," someone calls, "how are we to build?"

"We will build," I assure them.

"Where will we build?" another man questions.

"I will take you there," I answer.

"We will follow. We will follow. We will follow."

I turn and look at the three who are behind me. I nod, and then facing my people again, I say, "We will leave this encampment at dawn after as many days pass as I have fingers on one hand."

XXIX

We move in a long line through the forest. The day is bright with sun and the sky above the light green of the new leaves is very blue.

I walk in front of my people. Thorp and Shute follow directly behind me. Slung between them is the board on which my carvings are mounted. I do not want my people to lose sight of their purpose.

The faces and eyes of many are clouded with doubt. They all are leaving a place where there is food and shelter; they are going to a strange place where they must not only provide for themselves, but must also keep their word to The Giver of Life. That they must turn their effort from hunting to building is something that troubles them greatly. It also troubles me.

I do not know whether I will be able to hold my people together when they actually begin to build. I do not know whether our skill can make out of felled trees what I carved out of small limbs.

The days and nights are warm.

I do not lead my people directly through the forest to the plain where Gendy's bones lie buried. I take a winding course. Some days we do not move at all; we rest. The hunters go out and bring back fresh meat. When we are well fed and no longer footsore, we move on.

When we started I did not think of moving my people from our encampment on the bank of the river to the plain in anything but a straight line of march. Even now I cannot say why I do not go to the plain. But each day we spend in the forest seems to give my people something they did not have before we left our encampment.

Nightly as I move from fire to fire, I hear talk about what we will build.

Some claim it is for one purpose; others say it is for something else. People often come to look at my carvings. The task that lies before us is beginning to bind my people to one another.

If I can think of any reason to remain in the forest, it is to overcome my people's fear of leaving the forest, of moving out on to the plain to live in a place where the spirits of the dead also live.

My people are of the forest. And I am taking them out in the open where they will do what they have never done before.

Our march through the forest brings other people of our tribe to us.

Some follow at a distance. These I have our hunters watch. I do not want to give these silent watchers the chance to raid our column.

There are also others who come and speak with me.

They ask our purpose and I tell them, "We are going to build for The Giver of Life." Most do not understand. They shake their heads even when I show them my carvings and go their way. Several ask if I will give them meat when the snow flies. I tell them that The Giver of Life will keep His word if we keep ours. A few join our line for no other reason than to receive meat when the snow comes.

The days pass. The sun gives the day more light than there is darkness at night.

My people are weary of moving through the forest. I have taken them from one end of it to the other and back again.

Some of the men ask me if The Giver of Life has given me a sign where we are to build.

I shake my head and the next morning we are on the march again.

When the same question is asked over and over again, and when the people speak about it over their fires at night, I know they are ready to leave the forest.

The next day as the sun is almost at the end of its journey across the sky and the clouds are pink I lead my people out of the forest.

They do not follow!

I stop and turn. Even Thorp and Shute hang back.

"Come," I call. "Come!"

They do not move.

"The place where we will build is there," I tell them, gesturing toward the plain.

"Ronstrom," one of the men shouts, "no man lives here! Spirits of the dead claim this for their own!"

"We will build there!" I answer, pointing to the distant slight rise in the earth.

"This is not for the living," another man calls.

"We come for The Giver of Life!" I shout back. "He will protect us. He has given us food. He will protect us from harm."

Still none move. The people talk among themselves. Then one calls out, "Let Him give us a sign that He is with us!"

Anger rises up within me. "I am your sign!" I thunder at them. "I am your sign." I turn and without looking back I continue to walk to the place where Gendy's bones lie buried. A wind comes up. It tugs at my hair and my beard. And in its sighing, I hear, "You have spoken well, Ronstrom. The people come."

I turn. Moving slowly toward me are my people. "Ronstrom," Thorp calls out, "Ronstrom. . . ."

I stand on the small hill and wait for my people. I look up at the clouds. Shafts of light come through them and touch the earth where we will build. What must be built suddenly comes before my eyes and I say aloud, "It will be built!"

My words ride on the wind and rise up over the plain until the sky is filled with their sound.

My people fall to their knees and cry, "He has given us a sign. He has given us a sign."

XXX

My people begin to build a new encampment. Everything they need must be brought from the forest. Everyone works.

Because I am their leader my hut is the first to be built. It is larger than I need.

When I say this, those who built it answer, "You will need a large place when you take a woman." Then they laugh.

I laugh, too, but I have not thought about taking another woman. I have not felt the lust for a woman's slit, though there are several in the encampment who would be more than willing to let me use theirs.

As soon as the huts are up for shelter, others are built to store our meat for the winter.

Living on the plain is more difficult than it was in the forest. Even the flint for arrow- and spear-heads must be brought from where it comes to the surface in the forest to where we are. Those who make clay pots must carry their clay from the bank of a lake to the encampment. Wood for the fire pits must also be brought out of the forest.

When the rain giants come we have no shelter, but our huts. The wind blows without hardly ever stopping. When it does stop, the silence over the plain makes my people uneasy.

Everyone seems to know that when the snows fly what is difficult now will become even more difficult. But game is plentiful and the people are well fed.

Nesbitt has rejoined the hunters. There are men more skillful than he at making arrows and spearheads. Shute has taken over Ogg's place, but it will be a long while before he gains Ogg's wisdom. Thorp helps everyone, even though some days he does nothing except looks at the carvings, outside my hut. He is trying to understand them.

The days of summer are long, warm, and bright with sunshine. When I do not hunt I walk out upon the plain where I marked the light of the sun and look back toward the encampment, to the place where Gendy's bones lie buried. There is something darting around inside my skull as a bee darts over a brightly colored flower.

Whatever is in my head does not come out. But one day I look down at the carvings in front of my hut. I pick up one of the extra pieces and hold it in my hand. I still do not know where it belongs!

I shake my head and put the piece down. I turn and look to the place Gendy's bones lie buried. My eyes move across the plain to where the sun rises each day.

Suddenly I realize that to know the sun's complete movement I must mark its light when it is at its fullest and begins to die. I look down at the extra pieces on the board. I have found a use for one of them.

For several days I am up before the first light spills across the plain. Where that light touches the earth, I place a marker. After setting as many markers as I have fingers on my hands, the sun touches the last marker with a burst of yellow light. In the days that follow it goes no further.

When Thorp sees that a new piece has been added to those on the board, he asks, "Why is it placed there and not in another place?"

I explain the movement of the sun.

"I do not understand," Thorp tells me, shaking his head. Then after a long pause, he says, "Everyone knows that when the snow comes the sun always tries to run away."

"But why does it come back?" I ask.

Thorp shrugs and answers, "It just does."

"Then why is everyone so frightened when——?"

"Because," he tells me, "no one is ever sure that it will come back."

I nod. I do not ask him any more questions. No matter what the people believe, I will be able to tell them how the sun will move. They will doubt me until they see it for themselves; then they will say Ronstrom has magic so strong that it controls the movement of the sun.

The days pass quickly, and I look over the ground where we will build. The earth is soft enough to be dug out and the uprights set in the holes.

With Thorp and several others following me, I plant stakes where we will dig. We are all so occupied with the task of putting two stakes on a straight line some distance from each other that none of us sees or hears the men who come on us. Suddenly one of them shouts, "Ronstrom, this plain is for the spirits of the dead!"

I look up. Gibben is there with several of his hunters.

He comes toward me. There is a strange look in his eyes. "Go back to your riverbank," he says.

"I have come here to build," I answer.

Gibben shakes his spear at me. "Hunters do not build!" he shouts.

"I will build," I tell him. "And those with me will build."

"Leave this plain, Ronstrom!"

"We have come here to stay," I answer. My old dislike for Gibben fills my head. I cannot forget he gave Alvina to Rigga. I take a deep breath and say, "Leave us to our work, Gibben; we take nothing of yours."

He mutters something, leaps forward, and rips out one of the stakes. "You will not build here!" he shouts. He goes for the other stake.

I leap at him.

He falls, but springs to his feet.

We are too close for him to use his spear.

"Oh, Ronstrom," he bawls, "I have been waiting to kill you for so long——!"

"You are a fool, Gibben," I tell him in a low voice.

He draws his knife.

I draw mine.

Gibben is skilled with a knife. He feints to one side.

I try to block his thrust. But he is off to the other side and the point of his knife opens my shoulder. My arm is wet with blood.

"I will stick you," Gibben says, "so that you will bleed from many places before your life spirit leaves your body."

I rush him. We close and grapple with each other.

Gibben tries to find my stomach with the point of his knife.

I push him back and free myself from the hold of his strong arms.

We are both wet with sweat, and we suck in great gulps of air.

He slashes at me!

The sudden pain across my chest feels like fire as blood mingles with my hair.

"Ronstrom!" he shouts, "I should have killed you long ago. I should have——"

I rush at him. He cannot leap clear of my sudden movement. I push my knife against him. His blood gushes against my hand. It is warm. I push harder. His mouth opens. He drops his knife, and then he screams.

With a sudden upward movement I gut him as I would gut an animal.

Gibben screams again!

I pull my bloody hand and knife out of his belly.

Gibben holds his bleeding guts in his hands. He staggers a few steps and falls face-down on the earth, staining the green grass with his red blood.

I bend down and roll him over. His eyes are wide and staring. I look up at those who came with him and say, "Take him and tell all those who live in his encampment that Ronstrom and his people will live on the plain." My vision begins to blur. "Tell them what we have come to build——" The earth whirls around me and I sink to my knees.

When I open my eyes again, Thorp is bending over me. I try to move.

"No," Thorp orders, "rest now!"

I do not have the strength to argue.

I close my eyes and feel myself slip into sleep.

XXXI

Many days pass before I am able to leave my hut. The summer is gone. In the distance the trees of the forest look like red and yellow flames. I do not have the strength to continue the work I started before I slew Gibben.

During my sickness other people have come into the encampment. Those who followed Gibben are now here. Among them are Ansgar and Mayne, the man of his bloodline who makes clay pots. When I see them, they fall to their knees and beg to be allowed to stay.

"All those who are willing to work," I answer, "have a place here. I do not think much of a man who kneels to another man."

"Ronstrom," Ansgar says, "I have another son. He is called——"

I wave him silent. I do not wish to hear about his other son. If it had not been for his actions, Garth would still be alive.

"Do not tell me about your new son," I say sharply.

His face twitches and the skin above his beard turns white.

I say nothing to drive the whiteness from his

face. I leave him and Mayne on their knees and continue to walk through the encampment.

I go to the place where I first marked the sun. From where I stand I see the second marker. Each marker is like the tip of a bird's outstretched wing whose body covers the grave where Gendy's bones lie buried.

Soon the wind has a bite to it.

My people stay close to their fire pits away from the whirling snow. They are not hungry because there is enough food for everyone.

Several of the women become filled with the spirit of life. A few of the children born in the summer die. Their small bodies were not yet strong enough to hold their life's spirit.

The sun does not linger in the sky. And the darkness grows more and more. Even when it is not snowing, the sun is hidden by thick gray clouds. Then the day is but a long twilight for the long deep night that follows.

Before the light comes into the sky, I go to the place where I first marked the sun's light. Some days the clouds hide the coming of the sun. The deep darkness that is night lessens, but does not become day. Then for several days the sun comes full and yellow. I see its light and I know it will soon touch my marker.

I gather my people together. With the wind howling in our ears we stand in the snow and wait for the sun. I have my great stag robe across my shoulders. On my head I wear the crown of antlers.

Our breaths smoke in the cold air. The wind takes our smoke and quickly blows it away. My people stamp their feet and beat their arms to keep the knifing cold from them.

I look to where the sun will come up over the

edge of the earth. Then I turn to my people and with a voice louder than the howl of the wind I say, "I, Ronstrom, have marked the light of the sun for all to see it."

My people are too cold to care about what I did.

I tell them, "You do not have to be afraid that the sun will run away and never come back."

I point to the marker behind me and say, "When its light touches that, it will go no further. The sun is at its end and its beginning. When it rises above the edge of the earth again its light will have started to move back that way." And I point toward the other marker.

My people stop moving.

"The sun," I tell them, "will move no farther this way when the snow flies." Again I point to the marker behind me again. "And no farther that way when the days are long and the leaves on the trees." And once more I point to the second marker.

A murmur rises from my people. The murmur soon grows into wild shouting. "Ronstrom," they scream, "Ronstrom has power over the sun! Ronstrom holds the sun in his magic! Ronstrom is The Giver of Life!"

"No!" I shout. "No, I am a man. I hold no power over the sun. I am not The Giver of Life. I am Ronstrom the hunter. The sun moves as it wills; I have only marked its light when it is at its end and its beginning and when it is at its fullest and is already beginning its end."

"Ronstrom . . . Ronstrom . . . Ronstrom. . . ." The people shout.

Then suddenly they fall silent. The only sound is the howling of the wind.

I turn. The sun is up. Its light has tipped my

marker with a brilliant yellow! I glance over my shoulder. . . .

My people are in the snow on their knees.

"The sun," they cry. "The sun . . . Ronstrom has trapped the light of the sun!"

I would deny it, but it would not change what they think. Though they have eyes and see, they are blind. I am not The Giver of Life. I am Ronstrom the hunter!

I shake my head and look at my marker again. The yellow light is gone. Clouds hide the sun.

XXXII

As the days grow in length I begin to set the stakes in the earth where we will build. Thorp is at my side. When each carving on my board has its place marked around the place where Gendy's bones lie buried, I go into the forest to choose the trees that we will use to build. The tall trees are thick of trunk. The usable trees are cut on the trunk with my knife.

When I am finished, I return to the encampment. The trees I have chosen will last beyond the day when my life spirit leaves my body. They will last even beyond the life of the children who have recently been born.

To build something that will last so long gives me a strange feeling. I do not know whether it is a good feeling or a bad one. I only know it is there.

Those who came to the forest with me and Thorp go to their huts as soon as we reach the encampment. Thorp lingers with me.

I know his ways and ask, "Do you think I have chosen the best of the trees?"

He nods.

Getting Thorp to speak is hard work. I say to him, "It will take many summers to build everything."

"I do not think our stone axes will cut them down," he says softly.

"Is there another way?" I ask.

He shakes his head.

"We will try," I answer, not knowing what else to say. "If we cannot fell the trees then we cannot build. And we must build!"

Thorp leaves me and I go into my hut.

The next day and for many days we try to fell one of the trees that has my mark. The thud of our stone axes against the trunk of the tree startles the birds. They fly up and wheel against the blaze of the sun. The stone does not bite deeply enough into the trunk and it quickly loses its edge.

All of us try our strength against the strength of the tree. The tree is stronger than the swing of our arms and the stone edge we smash against it.

We leave the forest when the sun sits low in the sky. All of us are wet with sweat and weary. Our strength is nothing compared to that of the tree.

I eat little meat now that the forest is filled with wild nuts and berries. At night, when I have eaten enough to satisfy me, I stretch out on my skins.

I try to think of another way to fell the tree. Our tools are too weak. They are made from stone, wood, or bone. We have nothing else. I know of nothing else.

I close my eyes.

Suddenly my body is filled with a warmth. My manthing stirs. I have not felt this way for many, many days. I have not lain with a woman since Nan's life spirit was freed from her body. I grow hot with lust. I close my hand over my manthing and, when the pleasure comes, I grunt loudly. The hot lust is gone and I sleep.

At sunrise Thorp comes to my hut and says, "I think I have a way to bring down the trees."

I nod and listen.

"We will burn them down," he says.

"I do not understand," I tell him.

"Around the trunk of each tree," Thorp explains, "we will dig a fire pit. Over the fire pit we will build a hollow mound of clay. This will stop the fire from creeping up the trees. Once the fire eats the base of the tree we can put the fire out and pull the tree down. We can even use the fire to eat away the part of the tree we do not want to use."

That day and many days afterward the men who come with us to the forest dig fire pits around the bases of all the tree I marked. Hollow clay coverings are built. And then the fires are started.

All day and all night, for many days and nights, tall columns of gray smoke grow over the green of the forest. At night the fires are kept burning. The air in the forest smells of fire and smoke.

One tree does not wait for us to pull it down but comes crashing to earth without warning. One man is crushed to death. His life spirit leaves his body in the gush of blood that comes from his mouth. Two others are hurt.

Thorp tells me the dead man has recently taken a woman to his hut. The next day we do not go back into the forest. Instead we stay in the encampment and watch the body of the dead man being burnt.

When his flesh is no more and only his bones remain, the pit is covered with earth.

I sit outside my hut, letting the warmth of the sun flow over my face. I think about the man whose body has just been burnt.

Nothing of him is left. His bones lie in the pit. His life spirit is gone. Even his woman will soon be claimed by another man. Neither his life nor death seems to have had a meaning.

I shake my head. There is a darkness in me that I do not like!

The next day we are back in the forest. One by one we burn the trees through until they are weak enough for us to pull down.

At dawn on the day when the light of the sun will touch the second marker, I gather the people. We stand in the grass and wait for the sun to rise above the edge of the earth. The air is warm and filled with the fragrant scent of grass. Overhead in the night sky one of its wanderers still glows brightly.

The sun comes. Its light hangs like fire on the top of my marker. It is enough to make my people utter exclamations of awe. Then they shout, "Ronstrom holds the movements of the sun with his magic!"

I wait until they are finished screaming and I say to them, "The sun goes no further than this marker. Tomorrow, when it rises, it will have moved toward the other marker. Its movements are held between the two markers."

"And you have put it there, Ronstrom," Ansgar cries, pushing his way toward me. "You alone Ronstrom have captured the sun!"

The man is a fool!

"Listen!" Ansgar shouts. "All of you know me! All of you knew my son. All of you know how I wronged Ronstrom. And all of you know how he did not keep me from you. I tell you that Ronstrom is a god. He is more than all of us. He is——"

243

"Stop!" I shout. "Stop bleating like a goat. I am a man. I am not a god. I do the bidding of The Giver of Life. He is a god. He has chosen me to bring you together. He has given you meat and He has shown me how to mark the light of the sun. He is your god. I am a man!"

"If He is a god," one of the men asks, "then why must you do His bidding? He should be able to mark the light of the sun. He should be able to build what He asks us to build."

The others quickly voice their agreement.

"I have been chosen by Him," I answer, not knowing anything else to say, "to gather you together to do His bidding. He has put meat in your bellies. Now you must do——"

"We will build, Ronstrom," the same man says, "not for The Giver of Life but for you. It is you who has given us all we have. . . ."

"No!" I shout. "What you have comes from Him. He is——"

"We build for Ronstrom!" the man yells. "We build for Ronstrom!"

Others soon shout the same thing. The plain is filled with their yelling. I cannot quiet them. As I stand and silently watch them, my throat aches and water flows from my eyes.

They are foolish beyond the use of words to think that I am anything more than I am. They have seen me bleed. They have seen me take a woman into my hut. They have seen me filled with anger. They have seen me in all the ways of a man and still they think I am more than a man.

I look up toward the sky. It is already filled with light. The brighter wanderer is gone. I do not want my people to think that I am a god. Silently I tell this to The Giver of Life. "I want them to think of me only as Ronstrom the hunter——" I say. I do not know if The Giver of Life has heard. If he has, he does not answer!

When the summer is gone, most of the felled trees are stripped of all their other limbs. But we must wait until after the snows come before we start to move them.

It is Thorp's plan for men to pull the trunks in the snow from the forest to our encampment. He has made a harness out of strips of skin. Part of the harness goes around the waists of several men and the other part is tied to the trunk. When the men pull against their part of the harness, the other part pulls at the trunk of the tree. It will move by fits and starts.

Thorp claims it is easier to move things on snow than on the earth. I do not know if he is right. Until now I never thought about moving anything as big as a tree trunk.

The wind comes howling down out of the place where the Rock People live. The gray clouds pile up in the sky and block the light of the sun. We anxiously wait for snow to come. We need snow. We need a lot of snow. Still it does not snow.

The wind continues to howl and the clouds are heavy with snow though hardly any falls.

At dawn on the day when the light from the sun will touch my marker, the people stand and wait. The sun comes!

The first light turns the tip of my marker yellow. And the people cry out, "Give us snow. Oh, God, Giver of Life, send us snow!"

That winter the snow does not come. And when the cold is gone, the wind remains. It blows the rain giants across the plain until the earth runs between our feet.

XXXIII

Even as the days grow long the rain giants possess us. Seldom do we see the sun. The skins that Thorp braided into a harness rot. Many of my people are sick and the chidren die slowly. But the hunters never return from the forest without meat.

On the morning when the first light of the sun would touch my marker the clouds cover the sky. My people stand under the slate-gray covering and wait. The darkness of night gives way. The light of day slowly seeps through the clouds, but the sun does not show itself.

The disappointed people make their way back to the encampment. A thin wind-driven rain begins to fall. Soon the rain giants will follow.

I do not know what has happened to the summer.

I do not know why the sky is always filled with clouds.

I do not know why the rain giants batter us.

I am as wet and miserable as my people.

Shute comes to my hut. He is wet with rain. He sits down at the fire pit and says, "The people say it was a bad omen when the sun did not touch your marker."

I nod. I did not expect them to say anything else.

"Some claim," Shute tells me, "that you have lost your magic. That the sun became angry at you——"

I wave him silent. "Enough," I say. "Enough!"

"You must do something, Ronstrom," Shute tells me. "You must do something or the people will begin to leave the encampment. Already there is talk that the forest would offer more protection from the wind and from the rain giants."

"I cannot stop the rain," I answer sharply. "I cannot move the clouds away. I cannot make the sun shine on us. I can do none of those things."

He shrugs and says, "If the men could work they would not spend each day talking. It is their talking that makes them grumble more than the wind or the rain giants. The words they speak make them restless."

I nod and pull on my beard. Shute has become much wiser since we left the forest. He has learned the ways of the men.

"If you think that work will help them, we will work," I tell him. "We will begin to drag the trunks of the trees out of the forest."

"I will tell Thorp to make several more harnesses," Shute says as he leaves the hut.

Though the rain giants are all around us and the sky is blasted by lightning and thunder we begin moving the trunks of the trees. To move one just a short distance taxes the strength of many men. Our feet find no solid hold in the soft and oozing earth. Over and over again we lose our footing and fall.

We attempt to move felled trunk after felled trunk. We exhaust ourselves trying to do what

247

cannot be done. The suck of the mud is stronger than the strength we pit against it.

Days pass, but I will not stop. I keep urging the men to pull harder. I am in the harness with them. When we slip and slide in the mud I scramble to my feet before any one of them regains his footing. And pushing myself into the harness again, I call the others to join me.

At night when I am in my hut I am often too tired to eat. I do not sleep deeply or long. I lie awake in the darkness. I listen to the beat of the rain on the roof of the hut and the sighing of the wind as it rushes over the plain. I do not know how much more my people will endure.

I go to where Gendy's bones lie buried and silently tell him what is in my head.

He does not answer.

I go to the place where I first marked the light of the sun and, raising my eyes to the cloud-filled night sky, I call to The Giver of Life to stop the rain. I tell Him to let the sun's light and its warmth fall on my people.

But He, like Gendy's spirit, remains silent.

The summer is over. The wind is now cold and raw. It will soon become colder. It will soon blow harder. The rain stops; the cold comes. The mud turns hard. The trunks of the felled trees are frozen into the earth. To dig each one out and roll it free of its hold takes many days. The earth does not yield easily to our stone axes.

The clouds cover the sky again. The smell of snow is in the air. Then one night the wind blows howling out of that place where the sun never goes and brings with it snow. It comes down on the plain in a whirling whiteness that quickly covers everything.

When day dawns, the snow is still falling. The people leave their huts and run wildly about. They have waited for the snow and now it is here.

I lead the men into the forest. We attach one end of the harness to a tree trunk and we pull against the other. Slowly the trunk moves behind us. We sweat. We groan. We gasp for air. And still we do not stop pulling. When the gray light of day lessens and the deep shadows of twilight gather over the earth we stop. We have moved the felled trunk from where it lay in the forest to the beginning of the plain.

The snow has gone. The clouds fly away and the night sky is brilliant with flickering lights.

Thorp is at my side and as we walk back through the snow, he says, "If we pour water on the snow and it freezes, it will be easy to move the trunk."

"We will do it," I answer. "We will do anything that will help us build!"

The day comes when the sun is at its end and its beginning. My people wait for its light to touch my marker. The sun rises up over the earth; my marker is tipped with yellow light!

My people shout and I know they are happy.

It takes several winters to move all of the felled trees from the forest to our encampment. And several summers pass before each trunk is stripped of its bark and cut to size. Those trunks that will be the uprights are cut to hold the crosspiece. Holes are dug and the first uprights are planted. But we cannot get the crosspiece up to where it can be rolled into the notch.

Thorp spends several days looking at my carvings and then he says, "We will put the crosspiece in the notches while the uprights are still lying on

249

the ground. Then when we plant them, everything will be in place."

The uprights already standing are dug out. They are set down on the ground. The crosspiece is fitted into its grooves and bound in place with strips of skin. The newly made piece is placed near the holes where the uprights will be planted. Strips of skin are tied around the crosspiece so that some will fall on one side and some on the other when the entire piece is upended.

Thorp oversees the men. They begin to pull the piece upward. The men on one side pull while the men on the other play out the strips of skin until the piece is upright. To keep the piece from falling backward or forward each man holds his line taut.

Together the two uprights with the crosspiece stand very tall and wide. It is very heavy and the men who hold it upright use all their strength to keep it from falling.

Thorp and several other men slowly move the bottom of one of the uprights toward the hole where it will stand. Thorp calls for the men at the lines to give him slack or to tighten their hold.

The bottom of the upright moves out over the edge of the hole a bit at a time. Then suddenly it falls into the hole. The lines are torn away from the men holding them. The piece creaks and groans and then falls forward. The sides of the notches on the uprights splinter. The crosspiece tears itself away from the uprights, and then it rolls free.

I rush forward to see if Thorp is hurt. His arm is badly scratched. None of the other men is injured.

Thorp looks at the three pieces of wood and, shaking his head, he says, "I did not think that would happen."

I do not know what to answer and so I keep silent.

Over and over again Thorp tries to set the uprights and the crosspiece in place.

He can think of many different ways, but he cannot do it. Something always goes wrong!

Most of summer passes. Thorp makes another attempt to set the uprights and the crosspiece into place. At his command, men move the bottoms of each upright. None goes beyond the other. When most of the bottoms are over the holes, other men cut the remaining earth out from under them. They slide easily into the holes.

The men see what has happened. They begin to shout.

The holes are quickly filled with earth. To make it more secure rocks are set around the base of each upright. Then at Thorp's order the men holding the lines let go of them.

It stands alone! It stands!

Through it I can see the place where I first marked the light of the sun. Now when the sun reaches its end and its beginning, when its light touches the tip of my marker, it will flash yellow midway between the two uprights and midway between the crosspiece that sits above them and the earth into which they are set.

"It is the beginning," I say to Thorp. "The beginning."

He shakes his head and answers, "No, Ronstrom —the beginning was many summers and many winters ago when you stood in your great stag robe with your crown of antlers on your head and told us you would give us meat." Thorp waves his hand in front of him. Its movement takes in what he has just set into the earth. "The meat was the promise, the bait. But that," he says, "and the others we will build was always its purpose."

I nod.

"And yet," he says softly, "we cannot name what we build and do not know its purpose, or even why The Giver of Life would have us build it."

Again I nod. I have often had the same thoughts though I never spoke of them to anyone. I have led a people—my people—from the forest to the plain. All that I have done has been done in order to build what no man before has built. And now that I see the first part of it standing I know no more about it than I did when I first saw it on the altar of the cave so very long ago.

Word of Thorp's work spreads through the encampment. The people flock to see it. Though none of them knows its purpose they all marvel at it.

At night when the sky is alive with bits of flickering light, I leave my hut and walk to where the two uprights and the crosspiece are. Though it stands because of Thorp's work, I run my hand over the rough wood and realize I, too, helped make it stand.

The moon comes up full and white. The light from the moon is very bright. The shadow of the uprights and the crosspiece is huge. My shadow, too, is big, almost as big as a giant's.

XXXIV

Before the cold comes and makes the earth too hard for us to dig, we set another structure into place. It is similar to the one already standing.

Neither I nor Thorp can discover its purpose. There is one like it among those I carved. It is on the board that stands outside my hut.

The leaves turn red, brown, and yellow. The wind howls. The snows come. But my people are warm and well fed. No man or woman or child gives up their life spirit and dies.

When the sun is at its end and its beginning I gather my people behind the first structure to see the sun's light touch the marker. The sky is very clear. Our breaths smoke in the cold air. My great stag robe is across my shoulders. I wear the crown of antlers on my head.

The sun creeps up over the edge of the earth. The tip of my marker turns yellow. The people shout for joy and stamp their feet in the snow. The sun will move no farther. Its yellow circle is framed by what we have built!

After many many days pass, the snow gives way to grass. The green leaves come back on the limbs of the trees in the forest. My people begin to build again.

More structures are set into place.

Winter comes and is followed by summer.

I do not know how many winters or summers pass, but the many structures we build rise above our encampment as trees rise above a grove. Most of what I carved and had Thorp set on the board now stands around the place where Gendy's bones lie buried.

Other tribes see what we have done and come to marvel at it. Some join us, while others go their way.

Some who come to us tell of a place where the land ends and there is water as far as a man can see. They also say that men come in long wooden things that move on the water. These men I am told bring women and children with them. They even claim that the water that stretches as far as a man can see is filled with the taste of salt.

I do not believe these stories. But when I ask Thorp about the wooden things that carry men on water he says, "If a log stays on top of the water, many logs bound together will do the same."

I accept what Thorp tells me.

The days pass and the building continues. Soon there will be nothing left for us to build.

I am restless. I prowl through the encampment and realize that my people are also restless. I feel the need for a woman's slit and yet I cannot go to any woman in the encampment.

I look at the structures we have raised, and I think about the place where the land ends and the water begins. I have never seen such a sight and would like to look at it.

I spend more and more of my days in the forest

hunting. Thorp and Shute take care of what must be done in the encampment.

Often at night when all the others in the encampment are sleeping, I walk from my hut to where Gendy's bones lie buried. Around me are the dark shapes of the structures built for The Giver of Life.

What he bade me do so long ago is almost done. But I do not now feel that strange feeling that came to me when I first marked the light of the sun. What I see I do not understand. Inside I feel as empty as a dried gourd.

I do not know if I will be able to hold my people together.

I do not know if I want to hold them together.

I wonder what will happen to them if they return to the forest.

And I wonder what will happen to what we have built if we should leave it. That others would come and destroy what we labored so long to build sends a flash of anger through me. I shake my head and say aloud, "I will not let that happen. Too much of me, of all of us, is here to let that happen!"

I run my hands over the rough-hewed timbers. I do not know why, but there is an ache in my throat and a heavy feeling in my chest.

I turn and, as I go slowly back to where my hut is, I meet Thorp. He is walking toward the structures he has built. We stop and I ask, "How many days before it is finished?"

"Perhaps when the next summer comes to an end," he says.

"You have built them well," I tell him.

"Would that there was more to build, Ronstrom," he says.

I look back toward the dark shapes. "Perhaps," I suggest, "we can learn their purpose."

Thorp shrugs and asks, "What will happen, Ronstrom, when it is finished?"

"I do not know," I reply. "I do not know."

Thorp utters a deep sigh and says, "I did not think a man could become so much a part of what he does. Each of those structures, Ronstrom——" His voice cracks.

I put my hand on his shoulder and tell him, "It is the same with me, Thorp. It is the same with me."

He nods and goes to walk among the things he has built.

I return to my hut, stretch out on my skins, and discover that water is flowing from my eyes. I wipe it away, but more comes. I drift into sleep with it still leaking out of my eyes. . . .

XXXV

Not many days after speaking with Thorp, Shute comes to my hut and says, "A man was killed trying to prevent another man from taking his woman."

"Was it an open fight?"

Shute nods.

"Then I will not seek the blood of the man who slew the other," I say, and I ask if I know either of the men or the woman.

"I do not think so," Shute answers. And then he says, "There will be more killings for the same reason. There are not enough women for the men in the encampment. We must bring more women here or——"

"And how am I to do that?" I ask.

"The way our people have always gotten their women," Shute replies.

"By raiding another tribe?"

He nods.

I shake my head. I do not want to raid another people. I do not want to give another tribe a reason to attack us. I still remember what Rigga and the men who followed him did to my people.

"Then the killing here," Shute tells me, "will———"

"No," I say, "I will not let it happen."

"You will not be able to stop it, Ronstrom," he tells me. "The need for a woman's slit runs strong in every man. Stronger perhaps when he has fewer summers or winters than men like us, but even I still enjoy my woman's slit."

I know he speaks the truth. "I will think about it," I tell him. And then I say, "I am not so old that I no longer feel the lust for a woman's slit." But as soon as I speak, I feel foolish. I do not look at him when he leaves the hut. I am sure there was a smile on his face. My lips crease into a smile; I begin to laugh. I look around the hut.

It would be good to have a woman with me. I would not hestitate to bring a captured woman to my hut.

That night when I stretch out on my skins to sleep, my manthing stirs with lust. I close my eyes and let my skull fill with images of a woman's body. Her breasts. Her stomach. Her bare thighs. Her uncovered slit. The fluid pours out of my manthing. I sigh deeply and sleep takes me.

I lead a raiding party. Nesbitt is with me. He is still not a very good hunter, though he thinks he is.

We travel for many days toward the edge of the earth where the sun comes each dawn. I do not want to take women from a tribe near our encampment. I am anxious to look at the water that stretches as far as a man can see. I want to taste it for myself to see if it is salty.

We move swiftly and silently.

The sun stays bright and there is still some

warmth in it. At night it is cold enough to light fires, but we do not want to risk being seen.

Finally we crest a hill. But even before we get to the top we hear an unfamiliar roaring sound. Below us is a bank of soft tan earth, and there is water as far as a man can see.

The water stretches until it touches the sky. It moves and heaves itself upon the land over and over again.

In the sunlight it looks green and blue. Far from the bank the green and blue is flecked with white.

It is unlike any river I have ever seen. It is vast and angry-looking, so angry that it bares its white teeth all along the narrow bank. Birds cry and wheel over it. Sometimes these birds drop straight down into the water and from it seize a fish.

I climb down the hill and walk on the soft bank. The earth beneath my feet is bits and pieces of crushed rock. I look at the water rushing up on the bank. Could that water pound a rock to pieces?

I go closer to the water. It rushes up and wets my feet. It is very cold. As the water draws back into itself my feet sink into the earth. I reach down and, cupping some water in my hand, I taste it. I spit it out. It is salty.

"What do you think?" I ask, looking back at Nesbitt, who stands higher up on the bank.

"I did not think those stories I heard were true," he says.

"Nor I," I tell him. "But there it is. Water that stretches as far as I can see and it tastes salty." I make my way up the bank. "It has a strange sound. I almost like it."

Nesbitt waves his hand and says, "It makes me uneasy. It roars like some giant beast. Even to look at it makes me uneasy. In the forest and on the plain, I know where one ends and the other begins. That," he tells me, "has no end and no beginning. It is too big."

I shrug. I do not know if he is right. I look to where the water and the sky are joined and wonder how men move on it in wooden things. What signs do they follow to guide them across its emptiness? Do they use the sun and the lights in the night sky to guide them even as we do?

Nesbitt says, "We would be safer on the other side of the hill than down here."

I agree with him and lead the men back up the hill. We make camp on the other side of it. I listen to the roar of the water. Clouds fly across the sky at night. The wind comes off the water, bringing with it the rain giants. By daylight we are cold and wet, and some of us are angry that as yet we have not taken any women.

The rain giants move off. The clouds twist into long strands. Then vanish. The sky is very blue. And the sun, though it is halfway across the sky, is bright and warm.

We leave our camp. Climbing the hill again, we follow its crest. The sound made by the water, as it rushes on to the bank below, is now less of a roar and more like the whispering of the leaves. The water is not as restless as it was. I look to the very end of it, where the water and sky meet. I wonder if that is where the sun begins its journey each day. I would speak of this to Nesbitt, but suddenly I pick up the scent of smoke.

I halt the column and pointing up ahead I say to Nesbitt, "A cooking fire." From the blank expression on his face, I know he has not yet smelled anything.

I sniff again. The scent is sharp. Whoever is at

the fire is using wet wood. Even as this passes through my mind, a tall thin stalk of bluish-white smoke pushes itself above the tops of the stunted trees that follow the long sweep of the hillcrest.

I look back at the men. They have seen the smoke and are eager to move toward it.

"How far?" Nesbitt asks in a whisper.

"Just beyond where the crest of the hill slopes downward," I answer. I move forward and motion the others to follow.

My chest heaves with excitement. I can hear my blood roaring in my ears. I sniff at the air. The scent has become sharper. Meat is on the fire.

I begin to trot.

The hill slopes downward. There are wind-blasted trees on the slope. Their trunks slant away from the water and toward the land. Their leaves are dark red.

I halt the men. From where I stand I can see the camp. It is on a bank where a river flows into the water that stretches as far as a man can see.

On the bank next to the camp is something I have never seen. It is made of wood. It is as long as a very tall tree. It looks like a seedpod. The head of some sort of a monster rises above each tapered end.

"The wooden thing that moves on the water," I whisper to Nesbitt.

He nods.

"But where do the men come from," I ask, "that they need to move on water to get here?"

"I do not know," Nesbitt answers. Then he asks, "Will we attack the camp?"

"Yes, if there are women there," I tell him. "But we will wait until the night comes before we do anything. Now we will move——"

Suddenly a woman's laughter flutters up from the camp. Her laughter is joined by the laughter of others.

"There are women there," Nesbitt says tightly.

I nod and signal the men to withdraw back up the slope to the crest of the hill. When we are a distance from the camp where the women are, I gather the men around me.

"We will go against them when they sleep," I say. "Nesbitt will take some of you from one side. I will take those who are left against the other side. We will leave through the center and move up the slope to this crest. From here we will move back to our own encampment without stopping."

To be sure that every man understands, I repeat what I have said. This time I make marks with the point of my spear in the earth to show how Nesbitt and I will move against the camp and how we will leave it.

Then I say, "All the men and boys must be killed. If there are children with the women you take, you will also take them. No one must be left who can tell their people what happened."

The men murmur among themselves and one asks, "Are there many men in the camp?"

"I do not know," I answer.

"If there are more men there than——"

"We will have the advantage by attacking at night," I answer.

"Do we fire the camp?" Another man asks.

"No. Fire and smoke might warn others of their tribe. I do not want to have them track us back to our encampment."

"And if some of us should be wounded?" another man asks.

I look at Nesbitt, but he looks away. I turn my

eyes back to the men. They are young. Though they have hunted in the forest, this is the first time they will go against another man. To hunt an animal is something few men do well. Few animals ever strike back at a hunter.

Man against man must always leave one dead. Often both combatants die, locked in each other's death grip; or if one lives awhile longer his wounds are so many and so deep that he can not keep his life spirit in his body.

"It is one thing," I say to them, "to talk about taking women from a strange camp; but when it comes to doing it, it must be done with the spilling of blood. You must be prepared to shed your own blood for the women you want. You must be prepared to give up your life spirit for——"

"Our men will fight bravely," Nesbitt says. "It is the other men who will die. Our men will live."

The men agree with Nesbitt.

"They will fight bravely," I answer, "and some will give up their life spirits. Those who are wounded and cannot keep the pace of our retreat will be killed. Those who are wounded and fall in the fight——"

The men shake their heads. They do not like to hear what I am telling them.

"Are you asking those of use who are wounded," one of the men questions, "to free the life spirit from our bodies?"

I nod and say, "If you do not do it and are captured it will be done for you."

"Come, come Ronstrom," Nesbitt says, "you are talking like the croak of a bird."

"We come," I answer, "as raiders—and as such we will be treated. I do not want the men to think that what will be done will be done easily. If none of us fall, then——"

"I, for one," Nesbitt says, "would rather talk of the woman that we will take. It is far better to talk of that than what will happen to us if we are wounded."

"You are right," I answer with a nod, realizing that my words of truth are wasted. The men would rather hear Nesbitt boast of their untried skill, of a victory they have yet to win. His words are a comforting breeze while mine are harsh and cold, like the wind that brings the snow. "All will go well," I tell the men. "Rest now. Night has yet to come."

I move away from the men. I sit looking out over the water. I am uneasy in myself. I listen to the sound made by the water. It is strangely soothing.

Nesbitt sits down next to me. He says, "You make the men doubt themselves, Ronstrom."

"That was not my intent," I answer without looking at him.

"They are untried," he says. "Had I spoken to them I would have told them how well they would fight. How the women they take will please them. I would not have spoken as you did."

I face him.

He is looking at me.

His gray eyes do not waver from mine, and in a low voice I say, "We are not boys, Nesbitt. We must know what we are about. Neither you nor I know whether they will fight well. But even if they do fight well, some are bound to fall——"

"I am sure they know that."

"Those who die are no danger to us," I answer. "But those who are wounded are."

"Do you think any of our men would reveal our encampment?" he asks.

Nesbitt suddenly understands why I spoke as I did!

"I do not know what another man will do," I tell him, "if he is tortured. I do not know what I would do if I were tortured. But I do know that I would take my own life rather than risk the lives of the others."

Nesbitt does not answer. After a while he leaves me. Alone, I sit and look at the place where the sky and the water come together. I am still uneasy in myself.

The sun is low in the sky. The water turns dark. The wind picks up and the water begins to roar.

Night comes. Only a small thin moon is in the sky. It is very cold and our breath smokes.

I assemble the men. We move toward the camp. When we reach the slope, we stop.

"I will hoot like an owl," I tell Nesbitt. "Answer me the same way. Then we will both attack."

"I will wait for your signal," he says.

We remain hidden among the trees. There are sounds of men and children in the camp. We watch the fires. They burn a long time. When they begin to dim I send Nesbitt to one side of the camp and I take the men with me to the other side.

We ford the river upstream and come close to the camp. There is no sound coming from the camp. To be sure that everyone there is asleep I wait.

I am stretched out on the earth. I can hear the thud of my heart. My blood is racing and it roars in my ears. The insides of my hands are wet with sweat and, though it is very cold, there is sweat on my body. The fires are nearly out.

Suddenly the night's stillness is slashed by the

blood cries of Nesbitt's men. They sweep into the camp without waiting for the signal. I can do nothing but follow.

I leap to my feet and shout to my men, "Now . . . now . . . now!" I race toward the camp. Those with me are close behind.

Nesbitt's men are already fighting. There are enough defenders to drive his men back.

The night is filled with the cries of the wounded and the dying.

We fall upon the defenders from their rear. It is not difficult to cut them down. There are fewer of them than there are of us. They do not stop fighting. My spear is red with the blood of several men.

One of the defenders runs for the fire. He seizes a flaming brand and dashes toward the wooden thing that rides the water.

I go after him. I hurl my spear; it drives into his chest. With all the strength left in his body he hurls the flaming brand up into the wooden thing. Then he cries out, "Odin! Odin! Odin!" He falls. The fire blazes up, drenching the camp with red and yellow light.

I pull my spear from the man's chest. I join my men in running from shelter to shelter looking for the women. Some of them have already found a few and are dragging them to the center of the encampment.

The camp is littered with dead. Many are wounded. Those I see, be they theirs or ours, I slay.

I am at the edge of the camp, near the beginning of the woods. I see Nesbitt. He is trying to force a woman to ground. She is fighting to keep him off her. I am about to turn away and let Nesbitt claim what is his by right of victory. But the woman breaks free from his hold. She bounds past him and comes straight toward me.

In the light of the fire I see she is very young. Her long yellow hair streams out from behind her. Her covering is torn. I see her breasts.

As she rushes past me I put out my foot; she stumbles and with a cry she falls.

Nesbitt is in front of me. He is panting. His breath smokes. He grabs hold of the girl and, twisting her arm, forces her to stand.

She looks at me. The hate in her eyes burns through me.

"Once I get my manthing into her," Nesbitt says, "she will not fight as hard." He brings her to him and rips away the rest of her covering. Her body is very white and her hair above her slit is the color of dark honey. He puts his hand on her breast. "Not much there," he says, laughing, "but she is still young enough to grow."

The girl's body begins to tremble. Water comes from her eyes.

Nesbitt puts his hand on her breast and eases his hold on her arm.

She whirls around, pushes her knee into his manthing, and runs again.

I go after her. She does not get very far before I grab hold of her.

Nesbitt comes running up to us. His hand smashes against the girl's face. I let go of her.

Nesbitt knocks her down.

She struggles to her feet.

Again he strikes her and sends her sprawling to the ground.

Again she stands. Blood flows from her nose and from her mouth.

Nesbitt's hand smashes against her face.

She falls.

"I will take her," he says, pulling her up.

"This one," I tell him quietly, "is mine."

"What?"

"This one," I say again, "is mine."

He glares at me, turns, and walks off. Had he challenged me, I would have killed him.

The girl looks at me and then at Nesbitt. She nods. I know she will not try to run away. As we walk I look at her. Even in the glow of the fire her eyes are blue.

The bodies of the dead are put into the fire. The men push the wooden thing into the river. Burning, it slowly moves out on to the water that stretches as far as a man can see.

Our losses are fewer than I thought they would be. Each man has found a woman. Even Nesbitt has one.

We begin the trek back to our own encampment. The girl walks at my side throughout the long cold night.

XXXVI

Just before the first light of day comes over the edge of the earth we pause to rest. The sharp scent of the water is no longer with us. We are hungry. But we dare not light fires. We eat pieces of smoked meat. I give one to the girl. She bites into it with the vigor of a young she-wolf.

I eat, but I cannot take my eyes off her. I know that by taking her from Nesbitt I have caused bad feelings between us. During the night's march he has not been at my side. But I also know that he will not speak of it to any of the other men. He would not want them to think less of him. Should those who look up to him discover I took his woman and he did not challenge me they would not hold him in such high esteem. Nesbitt will keep silent. He will bury his feelings.

As for the girl—she is surely more girl than woman—I do not know why I claimed her for my own. I am sure I will ask myself that question many, many times. But as I watch her tear at the piece of smoked meat, I know no other woman would have moved me to act as I did.

We resume our march. I do not go directly back to the encampment. I swing toward the mountains where the Rock People live. The men leave signs that we went into the mountains. Then covering our real trail as much as possible, we move along the hills that stand before the mountains.

I lead the column toward the place where the sun ends its journey each day.

Many days after taking the women we reach the forest and plunge into it. Already the limbs of the trees are bare. The earth is covered with red, yellow, and brown leaves that crackle when we tred on them.

The girl is always with me. At night when we stop to sleep, she sleeps close to me, under the skin covering. I do not put my manthing into her slit. From the sounds around me, I know the other men are already using the women.

Again I choose not to go straight through the forest to the encampment.

Nesbitt comes to me and says, "The men are anxious to return to their shelters and have fresh meat in their bellies."

"And so am I," I answer. "But I would rather stay in the forest a few more days and leave as many false trails as possible than leave one trail that would lead directly back to the encampment."

"But we are not being followed," he said. "Each day we have sent men back to where we were the previous day and they tell us when they return that no one is behind us."

I nod and answer, "Another few days and we will all be back in our warm shelters and have meat in our bellies."

Though he does not say so, he cannot hide the look of resentment that comes into his eyes.

"Tell the men," I say to him, "I am doing what I think is best."

He nods and, without casting a look at the girl, leaves us.

That night the girl sleeps so close to me that with each breath she takes I feel the push of her breasts. My manthing swells and I put my hand on her body.

She wakes!

I can see her eyes, and I do not know whether they are lit by fear.

She does not move.

I open the top of her covering and touch her breasts. Each fits into my hand. Each is smaller than the span of my hand. Her nipples swell. Her breathing is fast. I open the bottom of her covering and put my hand on the tuft of hair above her slit.

When I roll over her and push my manthing into her she utters a small cry!

I do not want to hurt her and start to pull away.

But she wraps her young arms around my neck and holds me to her.

She is soon moving to my movements, soon sighing and thrashing under me.

I hear her moan when the lust of her body gives way. I, too, gasp and growl when the fluid leaves my body, taking with it my lust.

Clinging together, we sleep until sleep is torn from us by shouting. I am up and on my feet as soon as I open my eyes. I have my spear at the ready. One of the men at the far side of the glen where we are camped is shouting at Nesbitt.

I motion the girl not to move. I cross the open space and coming up to Nesbitt, I ask, "Why is the man shouting?"

"His woman ran away," Nesbitt answers.

The man is still shouting. He is like a child in a temper. I tell him to stop.

"You have your woman," he answers. "I have lost——"

I slap him across the face.

He stops shouting. His lower lip is cut and blood flows from it.

I motion to Nesbitt to follow me. When we are some distance away from the stunned man, I say to Nesbitt, "You and two other men see if you can bring her back. We will wait here until you return. If you find her and she fights you, kill her."

He nods.

I look up at the sky. It is filled with clouds. "It will snow before the day becomes night," I say. Then I add, "if you cannot find her, there will be no reason to remain in the forest. We will go straight to our encampment. I did not think that this would happen. All we did to cover our trails will be undone if the woman returns to her people."

We wait for Nesbitt and the other men to come back.

The other women know one of them is missing. They sit quietly. Fear is in their faces and eyes. They do not know what will happen to them.

The girl with me shows no fear. She does not sit as the others do. Her blue eyes are bright. Sometimes I find her looking at me. I do not know what she sees in my face or my eyes to interest her.

Snow comes. It drifts down from a gray sky.

When the light of day is hardly more than a deep grayness Nesbitt and those with him return. I go to meet him.

"We did not find her," he says. "The snow covered her trail."

I do not speak. If the snow covered one trail,

it also caught her footmarks and held them. Had I followed the woman, I would have continued.

"I do not think she will find her way in the forest," Nesbitt says. "I think she will die in the snow."

I nod and return to the girl. Her face is upturned and in her eyes there is a question. I shake my head. I do not know if she understands my meaning. She reaches for my hand and squeezes it very tightly.

Later, when I have my manthing in her slit, she moans softly and, easing my face down to hers, puts her lips to mine. I do not know why she does it, but her lips are warm and soft.

In the morning we turn toward the plain. The snow has stopped during the night. Little of it covers the earth. But the limbs of the trees are laid over with it.

I keep the column moving.

The clouds gather across the sky again. The smell of snow is heavy in the air. The light of day is like twilight. The wind begins to blow. The snow that has fallen is whipped about us. New snow soon begins to tumble out of the clouds.

We quicken our pace, anxious now to reach the encampment and be out of the storm.

The girl reaches for my arm and, grasping hold of it, keeps pace at my side. I do not know whether to let her hold on to me or to push her hand from my arm. I glance at her. Her yellow hair is crowned with a headpiece of snow and there is snow over her eyebrows.

We leave the forest and set out across the plain. The wind and snow are even more cutting than they were. But after a while I can see the dark shapes of the structures we built. We are back in the encampment!

Each man hurries to his own hut and I take the girl to mine. Without being shown, she quickly sets a fire going in the fire pit. Meat has been left for me by the others in the encampment and the girl begins to cook it.

I watch her at work. I do not know how she is called and I do not know how to ask her. But I must call her something.

She hands me a piece of meat, takes one for herself, and settles down across from me to eat. When she is finished, she stands up and takes the covering off her.

I stop eating. My blood is racing. I can feel my manthing swell.

Her body is as white as the falling snow. Her nipples are pink like berries in the early summer. To see her standing naked is enough to make me gasp. I do not think she could be more than fifteen or sixteen summers.

Her white skin takes the reddish glow of the fire. Even as I stare at her she is chattering in the strange language of her people.

She points to me and then to her slit.

I start to move.

She motions me back.

She looks around, sees my spear, goes to it, and pushes her finger against its point until blood flows from it. Then she points to me and then to her slit.

I nod. I understand. She has told me I am the first man who used her as a woman. I get to my feet.

She runs to me and, throwing herself into my arms, she speaks once more in her own language. Though I do not understand, the sound of her voice tells me that she is saying something about the way she feels when my manthing is in her slit.

I lift her in my arms and then set her down on the skins. When our lust is gone I reach around and put my hand on her buttocks. They are larger than her breasts and pleasant to hold. Suddenly I smile and tell her, "I will call you Pratt. I will call you Pratt which means this." And I give her buttocks a gentle squeeze.

She laughs.

I tell her how I am called. But she cannot say my name.

The days pass. Storm follows storm. The snow is piled high around the structures we built, but the wind and snow cannot tear them down.

The day comes when the sun is at its end and its beginning. With my great stag robe over my shoulders and my crown of antlers on my head, I wait for the sun's first light to touch my marker.

The people rejoice when it happens!

I look at Pratt. There is wonderment on her face, as I remember there once was on Nan's. I am filled with a warmth that comes not from the light of the sun but from her. She is all and all to me.

She alone will make me laugh when she struts and growls pretending she is me. She brings laughter to me when she places the great stag robe over her naked body and the crown of antlers on her head and, speaking in her own language, she makes the sound of my voice come from her mouth. She does not even have to speak to make me laugh. It is enough for me to see her bare breasts bob up and down to make it happen.

Never have I felt such feelings toward a woman

as I have toward Pratt. I am filled in a strange new way.

With Nan I felt the pleasure of her slit and her willingness to give to me whenever I had need for it. With Nan I sensed the feeling she had for my manthing, but with Pratt it is all those things and more.

It is the way she presses her lips to mine.

It is the sound of her laughter. It is the way she touches my manthing.

It is the way she opens her naked thighs to receive my manthing.

It is the way I am on fire when I look at her.

There are nights when the flames in the fire pit are low and she lies asleep. Then I uncover her to look at her naked body. I do nothing more than fill my eyes with it. I did not think a man could feel such pleasure from just looking at a woman's nakedness.

I cannot understand these feelings I have toward Pratt. I do not know if any other man feels toward his woman as I feel toward Pratt. I often think of speaking to Shute about it, but I always stop myself just as I am about to begin.

The winter leaves and each day that passes brings more signs of the coming summer. The sun stays in the sky longer and the snow melts. Buds begin to show themselves.

Thorp begins to build again.

Some days I watch Thorp and his men work. Pratt stands with me. Her hand is on my arm. I would like to tell her about the things I did. I would like her to know that what she sees standing, though built by Thorp, came from inside my skull where it was put by The Giver of Life. From the way that she looks at me, from the way the light comes into her blue eyes, I think she knows that in some way I am responsible for all that is standing.

On the days I go into the forest and hunt, I am impatient to return to Pratt. Then one day I take her into the forest with me. I teach her how to use a spear and how to string and loose an arrow. She learns quickly and is soon as skilled a hunter as many of the young men who follow so eagerly at Nesbitt's heels.

When the sun reaches its fullness and begins to die, I gather my people together and with them rejoice when the first light touches the marker. I tell them, "The word we keep with The Giver of Life is our bond to Him. This place is His and we have built it for Him. He will always provide for us."

The people shout their approval of what I just told them.

Later, when the sun is past its highest point in the sky, Shute comes to my hut. Because it is warm I am outside. Pratt sits next to me. Her hair is bright yellow in the sunlight.

Shute sits down in front of me. He looks at Pratt and nods.

She nods at him.

He says, "Have you thought about the days to come?"

Shute is asking what will happen when Thorp finishes building. I shrug. I have been living too much in each day and each night to think about future days. I glance at Pratt. There is a question in her blue eyes.

"Some of the people," Shute tells me, "say that you have left Thorp to do your work."

"And Thorp," I ask, "what does he say?"

"Nothing," Shute answers. "Thorp knows he is only your tool as you yourself are the tool of The Giver of Life."

"What else do the people say?" I question.

"That she has bewitched you," he replies. "That she has taken hold of your manthing and keeps it in her slit all the time."

My blood begins to race. I feel the anger rise in me.

"And what do you say Shute?" I ask tightly.

He looks at Pratt and then at me. "I say," Shute answers, "that Ronstrom is no less a man now than he was before. I say that Ronstrom's woman has touched a part of him that makes him more like other men than they want him to be."

My anger fades. I smile and say to Shute, "I will not let all that we have done pass. I will think of something."

"Soon, Ronstrom," Shute tells me. "Soon."

"Yes."

He stands, nods again to Pratt, and says to me, "I will silence those who claim she has bewitched you."

"I am sure of it," I answer.

When Shute is gone, I look at Pratt. I want so much to speak with her. I take her hand and before I realize what I am doing I press it to my lips. She reaches up and touches my cheek.

XXXVII

Summer wanes. The season of grass, leaves, and flowers goes away. The sun shortens its stay in the sky and the moon hangs closer to the earth. Some nights it drenches the plain with its white light. Other nights it is the color of a leaf touched by the cold wind.

For many days Thorp has been trying to raise another structure. When it is in place, though, something always goes wrong and it comes crashing down. It has killed two men. Those who work with Thorp claim that the earth does not want to have the structure there. Perhaps they are right.

I walk with Thorp. The day is bright with sunshine. A chill is in the air. I look at the holes he has dug to hold the uprights. They are no different to my eyes from the other holes. He shows me the uprights and the crosspiece. They do not differ from the others he has made.

"I do not understand," Thorp says, "why I cannot raise this one as I raised the others."

"Are you sure it is in the right place?" I ask.

He nods.

I look at the other structures. They stand securely placed in the earth. Why should the earth vomit this one out?

"Perhaps," Thorp says, "The Giver of Life does not want us to finish what we have started."

I shrug. That thought has entered my head. If He does not want us to continue building, why would He not come and tell me?

I look about me. To leave the work unfinished does not sit easy with me. There is too much of me, of Thorp, of all of the people to leave it undone.

"I will not try again," Thorp tells me, "to set it in place until after the snows melt."

"Yes," I tell him, "that will be the best thing to do."

I go back to my hut and sit outside of it, letting the sun warm my face. Pratt comes close and touches my forehead. Not only does it bear the mark that The Giver of Life put there, but now it is furrowed from thinking.

Her efforts make me smile.

She smiles and points to her stomach. It is beginning to swell with the spirit of life that has entered her. She points to it and to me as if I had something to do with it.

I know she thinks that I am responsible for it. Her people must be full of strange ideas. That night when I sleep I am suddenly flung in to a whirling. A whirling the color of Pratt's hair. It comes over the plain and carries me along with it. Nothing I can do gains my freedom from it.

I wake, trembling, and wet with sweat.

Pratt sleeps peacefully next to me. The embers in the fire pit are red and the ash is white. The dream robs me of sleep and I wait impatiently for the dawn to come.

For several nights, the same dream comes.

I know it is more than a dream.

I know it is a presentiment.

And I know that in someway it is responsible for Thorp's failure to raise the structure.

At night I go to where Gendy's bones lie buried. I try to speak to him, but he remains silent.

I lift my eyes to the moon-bright sky and ask The Giver of Life the meaning of my dream. I hear nothing except the sighing of the wind.

When I sleep again, the dream sweeps me up and I cry out.

Pratt shakes me.

I wake. Now I would speak with her and tell her what fills my head when I am asleep. But words cannot pass between us. She cannot even call me as I am called by others.

I motion her to lie down again. I, too, lie back. She takes hold of my hand and sets it on her breasts. Since the spirit of life has entered her, her breasts have become larger. She is pleased with their new size and has me touch them whenever I can.

Sleep takes me again, but the dream does not. I wake after the sun's light is above the edge of the earth.

A cold wind foretelling the coming of the rain giants blows. Clouds rush across the sky. In the distance near the mountains of the Rock People, shafts of sunlight touch the earth.

I am uneasy. I feel the presence of something, but know not what it is, or even how to speak of it to Shute, who walks with me as I go through the encampment.

Together we have watched most of our hunters leave for the forest. Each day's kill will fill our bellies when the snows fly. Only a few of the hunters did not go into the forest.

We reach the place where Gendy's bones lie buried. Shute says, "You have frowned much and said little, Ronstrom."

"I have little to say," I answer.

"And much to frown about," he adds.

Shute points to the structure that Thorp could not raise and asks, "Is that troubling you?"

I do not answer. I cannot speak. I strain to see more of what I have seen—what has taken my speech from me. I do not want to trust my eyes. I touch Shute's arm and point toward the forest, from where the men are coming. They run across the plain. The clouds suddenly open. The sun streams through. Spears flash in the brilliant, shifting light.

"Who are they?" Shute screams. "What are they, Ronstrom?"

"They are my dream," I answer.

He does not understand.

I grab hold of his arm and together we run through the encampment, shouting for the men to take up their arms.

The men I lead are few. Those who run toward us are many. We are the defenders of our encampment. They are the attackers.

I watch them come at us.

They are tall, broad-shouldered men, with yellow hair that streams out behind them from under their horns.

My blood is racing. I cannot fill myself with enough air. I suck into my throat.

My men are ready with their arrows. If we kill

enough of them with arrows, we might be able to hold them off when we fight them with spears.

I wait until they come closer. My men wait. We are one line of men against many. I look at my men. Fear is in their faces and in their eyes. I, too, am afraid. Never have I met an enemy like the one that now runs toward me.

They come closer. I brace my feet solidly against the earth. I take a quick backward glance at the encampment. Those men who cannot fight are with the women and the women are at the place where Gendy's bones lie buried.

I turn away and face the running men.

Their line suddenly stops.

I suck in my breath once more and wait.

They notch their arrows. And then with the wild cry "Odin!" on their lips, they loose them. Those long slender birds of death wing their way through the air.

"Run!" I shout to my men. "Run!"

The arrows move swifter than many of the men. The slender birds drop from their flight and find their mark. Several of my men fall screaming in agony.

Another flight of arrows comes at us. But we are scattered now and none strike any of my men.

The attackers drop their bows and arrows and come running at us.

Now we are the ones who loose arrows at them. Few find the flesh of those who come against us.

"Each man," I shout to my men, "must fight on his own!"

Over and over again the attackers yell, "Odin! Odin! Odin!"

Pratt has called that name. These are her people who come running toward us.

The line of running men reaches us and we fight.

The shouts of both sides are deafening. Our weapons crash together. But theirs are stronger. Many of my men fall. And those who fall give up their life spirit.

But we, too, kill. The yellow-haired men who drop beside our own dead die shouting, "Odin!"

My spear is bloody. My hands are bloody and I am hot with the lust to kill.

The second line comes charging into the encampment. They come with firebrands. Our huts are soon torches and the smoke rises over the encampment.

We fight. And we fight. We kill. And we kill.

I am wounded on my leg and on my shoulder.

I grapple with one of the attackers. He throws me to the ground, leaps on me, and tries to push his knife into my chest. I push my finger into his eye. He roars with pain. I push my finger deeper. He drops his knife. I take it and plunge it into his throat. His blood spills over my arm.

I am on my feet.

Those who fight with me are also soaked in blood. We fall back and fight to protect the women. Their women shout to them and they answer.

Other men come running into the encampment. With huge hooks and other things I have never seen they pull down the structures we have built. One by one, they come crashing down and are set afire.

To see what we have built destroyed is more than I can stand. I bellow with anger and hurl my spear at one of the wreckers. It goes through his body. He dies screaming.

I kill many that way.

Amid the shouts and screams of these destroyers comes the blood cry of our hunters. They have seen the smoke and have come to fight beside us. They come running toward the encampment. Our attackers turn to meet them. But now they are few and we are many.

They fight to break away from us.

We will not let them. The plain in front of the encampment is soaked with blood. The air is filled with cries of agony.

Several of the attackers wheel to one side. Their movement takes us by surprise. They have broken away.

We do not follow. We are too tired to give chase. We have lost too many men to risk losing more, and our encampment lies smoldering. Not a hut is standing. Not a structure remains.

Wet with sweat and stained with blood, I walk to where I first marked the light of the sun. I look around me. The work of my people, the effort of so many summers and winters, is burning.

I sink to my knees and with water flowing from my eyes I cry out to The Giver of Life! "If this was to be the end, why did You have me begin? If this was Your purpose, You have achieved it. If this is Your will, then why did You make me Your tool?" I cannot remain on my knees. I stand and shaking my fist at the dappled sky, I shout, "You have deceived me! You have deceived me! You have put meat in my belly and destroyed the very thing we——"

"Ronstrom!"

I turn and see Nesbitt. He, too, is smeared with blood. Several men are with him.

"Look," he says, "what you have done!"

I shake my head.

"Your work," he shouts, pointing his spear at me.

My weapon lies on the bloody earth. I would reach for it, but I would die before my hand touched it.

"Take him," he tells several of the hunters with him.

They do not move.

"He cannot harm you," Nesbitt assures them. "He will not go for his spear."

"Say I did many things, Nesbitt," I tell him, "but this is not my doing."

"Yours because you let that woman bewitch you," Nesbitt answers.

Suddenly, I understand. He has waited to strike at me for taking Pratt from him. I say to him, "None will believe you."

"They will believe it about her," he says.

"Not about her, either."

"They already have her, Ronstrom," he tells me. "They already have her." Again he orders the men to seize me.

"I will go," I tell him. I make a sudden move toward my spear.

"No, Ronstrom," Nesbitt shouts. "You will go weaponless."

"How long have you waited to do this, Nesbitt?"

"From the day when you took Clegg to hunt with you," he answers.

"You have been a patient man," I tell him. "That happened so very long ago."

"Yes," he answers. "It was a long time to wait." And he prods me with his spear.

XXXVIII

The ground is littered with many dead. The smell of fire is heavy on the air.

I walk slowly. Nesbitt is in back of me. The men with him are on each side of me.

The people are gathered at the place where Gendy's bones are buried. They open a path for me.

My heart is thundering in my chest. I can hardly breathe. And when I see what has been done to Pratt, I stop and shout, "No—no—cut her down!"

Nesbitt prods me with his spear.

I walk to where Pratt is.

She is bound hand and foot to a crosspiece. She is naked. A small swell in her belly shows where the life spirit lives. Water is flowing from her eyes. Her body trembles. She looks at me and struggles to free herself.

I start toward her. But my way is blocked by the heads of many with spears.

"She is to be given to The Giver of Life," Nesbitt tells me. His voice is loud enough for all of the people to hear.

"A blood sacrifice?" I cry.

"Yes," he answers. "All that has happened here

today is her fault. She has bewitched you. She has robbed you of your sight. The people have seen it. Since you took her into your hut, since she became your woman, you were no longer interested in anything but her slit."

The people agree with him.

"Then take me!" I shout, my voice rising above the sound of theirs. "I am to blame. Take me but let her go!"

Even as I plead, my head is filled with the vision of something that happened a long time ago. I remember how, when I was in the mountains where the Rock People live, and I came to the camp of a man and his woman. I remember how I fought him. I remember how he put his body in front of my spear to save his woman from it. I remember and I understand now what I could not understand then.

"Take me!" I shout again. "Take me!"

"You have lost your power, Ronstrom," Nesbitt yells. "She has taken it from you. She holds your manthing in her slit."

Several of the young hunters run to where Pratt is bound and move their bloody hands over her slit.

She cries out.

I shake my head. I can do nothing to help her. I cannot speak to my people. Stained red with the blood of so many, they want still more. It is the way they are. It is the way I am. Once the killing begins, the hunger for it grows. Nesbitt knows this hunger as well as I do, as well as any man who has ever killed. He is using it to strike at me.

"I will beg you," I say to him, "to cut her down and put me there in her stead."

"No, Ronstrom," he answers, "she and she alone

must suffer for bringing her people down on us."

"But there are other women of her people here," I answer, hoping the men who have taken these women into their huts will sense the danger.

"But only she" he replies, "is your woman, Ronstrom."

I take a deep breath and I say, "Tell the people, Nesbitt, how I found Pratt. Tell them, Nesbitt, so that they might know why you do what you are doing!"

"You took her from me," he says.

The truth of his answer silences me. I do not know what next to say.

"From the very first she bewitched you," he explains. "The people know that Ronstrom would never take another man's woman unless he was bewitched. Long ago when Shute's woman offered her slit to you, you would not have it because it belonged to another man."

I did not think that Nesbitt was a cunning man. But he is. He possesses more cunning than he does skill as a hunter.

A cold wind-driven rain begins to fall.

"It is time," Nesbitt says.

"No!" I scream, trying to leap to where Pratt is. Again I am stopped by spears.

"She will be given to the wolves," Nesbitt says.

My skin crawls. I drop to my knees.

Nesbitt goes to Pratt and with one swift stroke of his knife he opens her belly.

"Odin!" Pratt screams.

Nesbitt reaches into the bloody wound and pulls out her guts.

She is screaming.

He holds her bloody entrails in his hand and shouts, "For The Giver of Life!"

The people echo his cry.

I bow my head.

Some of the young hunters lift the crosspiece and begin to carry it to where Thorp keeps his wolves penned.

I hear nothing, but Pratt's screams.

Nesbitt prods me with his spear.

I cannot find my legs. I do not have the strength to stand.

I am pulled to my feet and forced to stagger behind those men who carry Pratt.

The rain giants fall on us. I do not feel either the sting of the rain or the lash of the wind. The blood from Pratt's body stains the mud beneath my feet.

My body is filled with pain. The inside of my head is dark. I cannot stop the water from flowing out of my eyes.

These are my people who are doing this to Pratt. These are my people I have led out of the forest to this plain, so that we would do what The Giver of Life——

I raise my head. We are passing through the encampment. The rain has quenched the fires. The smoke has gone. Ashes are left, nothing more.

Though they surround me, my people are gone. Nesbitt has taken them. Soon they will leave this place and return to the forest.

I shake my head.

I have given so much and for what purpose?

To what end did I strive all these many summers and winters?

For ashes.

To have my woman taken from me.

To see what I had in my skull built and then destroyed.

For what purpose has all of this happened?

Pratt's screaming grows louder when she sees where she is being taken.

I bow my head.

Suddenly I stop! I cannot go any farther. I will not go any farther.

Nesbitt prods me with his spear.

"No!" I shout above the sound of the rain giants. "I will not walk!"

The people stop.

Nesbitt pushes his spear against my back.

"Kill me, Nesbitt," I challenge, "kill me!"

He walks in front of me. His eyes glow with hate.

"I will go no farther!" I tell him.

"Ronstrom!" Shute suddenly yells. He rushes forward and hurls a long flat knife to me.

I grasp it even as it is in the air.

Nesbitt hurls his spear. Its head drives into Shute's throat. His feet give out from under him. He drops into the mud.

The people move back.

Now it is I who has the weapon. A weapon taken from the body of one of the attackers.

Nesbitt looks wildly about him.

I pause only long enough to get a secure hold on the long knife. Then with a blood cry on my lips, I run at him. "Die!" I scream. "Die!"

Fear holds him where he stands.

I lift the long knife and send it slashing down on him. The blade crunches through his shoulder. He is cut apart.

Nesbitt screams and falls into the mud. His blood now mingles with Pratt's.

I wrench the blade from his body and run to

the crosspiece. Those who hold it let it fall and flee.

Pratt screams in agony.

The wolves have the scent of blood and are howling wildly.

I cut Pratt's bonds. I hold her bloody body close to me, sheltering it from the rain and the cold as much as possible.

She whimpers softly. Her blue eyes are filled with water.

I lift her in my arms. I look out over my people. I shout, "Look what you have done to me! Look what you have done to me! You have taken my woman from me!"

They turn away.

"Hear me!" I thunder. "Hear me and know you have killed part of Ronstrom. This woman whose life spirit runs from her did nothing to you. She was my light and now you have plunged me into darkness. There is nothing left inside Ronstrom. Nothing but blackness."

I cannot speak. There is too much hurt in me to let the words pass from my lips.

The people do not move.

Pratt trembles in my arms.

I press her closer to me.

Sounds come from her lips.

I bend my head to hear.

She speaks in her own tongue. Suddenly her hand lifts. She fights to push it higher and higher. She touches my beard. Her fingers spread across my lips and she cries out, "Ronstrom! Ronstrom! Ronstrom!" The sound of her voice, the sound of my name, rises above the howl of the wind. Her hand falls away from my lips.

Pratt is dead. Her life spirit is gone.

I hold her close and walk through my people to

the place where I first marked the light of the sun. All through the night I sit with her body clasped tightly in my arms.

The rain giants pound the earth with their mighty fists and the howling of the wind is louder than the howling of the wolves.

Someone throws a skin over my shoulder.

The new day dawns. Its light is gray.

I set down Pratt's body. Alone I dig a fire pit and gather the wood for it. When I have enough, I place Pratt's body on it and let the flames have what was mine.

The people gather to watch.

I say nothing to them.

After Pratt's body has become one with the fire and smoke, I take her bones and bury them under the place where I first marked the light of the sun.

I go to Shute's body and do for it what I did for Pratt's.

When nothing more is left of him I gather his bones and bury them at the place where we raised our first structure.

I go to Nesbitt's body and as he would have done to Pratt, I now do to him. I throw him to the wolves. I do not wait to see them tear his body apart. I have looked at enough blood to last me the rest of my days.

I still say nothing to the people. I have nothing to say to them. I will not keep them, if they should want to return to the forest.

I will live on the plain. I will live and hunt until the day comes that my life spirit will leave my body. I want that day to come soon.

I walk where we fought Pratt's people. There are many weapons on the ground. They are not made of stone. They are made of something much harder than stone. I take arrows, spears, several long flat knives and several short ones.

After a few days I build a shelter for myself. It will protect me when the snow flies.

The people have not yet left the plain. They have burned the bodies of all those who were slain. The people are building shelters close to mine.

I have not yet spoken a word to them. There is nothing I can say to them. I want only to be left alone. I think it would be good to die. I live so that I might soon die. I have given much thought to freeing the life spirit from my body with my own hand. Though I am eager to die, I cannot bring myself to kill myself.

Then, one day, Thorp comes to me. He sits down on the other side of the fire pit and says, "I have taken Shute's woman into my hut. The life spirit has entered her. . . ."

I nod. What have I to say to him?

For a long while he is silent. Then with a sigh he says, "We no longer have to think of what we will do when everything is built."

I look at him questioningly.

He waves his hand toward the place where the structures stood. "It all must be built again," he says, looking straight at me.

"For what purpose?" I ask. "For what end?"

Thorp shrugs and answers, "Only you know that, Ronstrom, only you know it!"

I am about to tell him that I know no more than he does, but I stop. I look to where those things we built stood. My anger is fired when I see they are no longer standing.

"Then we will build again?" Thorp asks softly.

I nod and answer, "We will build again."

Thorp almost smiles, but he does not. He stands and says, "I will tell the people."

I stand and say, "Tell them, Thorp, that I promise nothing. Tell them that I do not know whether The Giver of Life will continue to give us meat. Tell them that we will build again because that is what we must do. Tell them that if we did not build we would not have a purpose. Tell them all those things, Thorp. If they still want to stay, we build again."

"I will tell them," he answers.

I nod and watch him go to speak to the people.

XXXIX

Winter is not far off. The snow will come whirling down from the dark clouds. The wind will come howling across the plain. We must do what is necessary to survive until the snow melts and the leaves come back to the trees.

Shelters are built. Wood is gathered for the fires that will keep us warm. Before we can store enough meat to keep us from starving the snow comes with its bitter cold.

Days pass and still the snow falls and the wind blows.

The people eat less meat; even the children are given less.

I take several of the hunters with me and go into the forest. The snow falls so fast and so heavily that I can only see short distance in front of me, but it is enough when I catch sight of any animal. The game is there, and we kill as much as we can carry back to the encampment.

The snow stops. The wind has lessened. The sky is blue and the sun is bright. I lead the hunters back into the forest. To keep meat in our bellies we must hunt almost every day.

Though I am often with the hunters, I do not

speak to them. They know what they must do without my having to tell them. What word I speak, I speak only to Thorp. He tells the people what I tell him. I do not know if I will ever speak to them again. Through the long winter nights, I ache with loneliness.

When the pain becomes too much, when the blackness inside me becomes blacker than the darkness, I go to where I first marked the light of the sun, where Pratt's bones now lie buried.

I neither feel the bite of the wind nor the cold sting of the snow. I stand above her grave and whisper her name into the teeth of the wind.

I raise my eyes and look toward the cluster of shelters mounded on the flat plain.

Many people follow me, but there is not one among them who could ever make me laugh as she did; there is not one who would raise their hand and touch my cheeks as she did; there is not one who would cry my name as she did.

I look down at the snow-covered grave.

I do not know how to speak of what I feel. Perhaps in her language there are words that give voice to such feelings? I shrug and some snow falls from my shoulders. If I knew such words, I would have said them to her while she lived and I would speak them now for her spirit to hear. But I remain silent.

On the day the sun is at its beginning and its end, I gather my people together and we watch the first light tip the marker that stands over Pratt's grave with a brilliant yellow light. I no longer wear the great stag robe or the crown of antlers. Both were burned during our fight with Pratt's people. As soon as the light leaves the marker, I turn and start back to my shelter.

Thorp suddenly calls my name.

I stop and face him. He has stepped in front of all the people. The light of the sun is on his back.

"Ronstrom," he says, "the people wait for you to speak."

I push his words away with a gesture from my hand. I turn again and continue to walk.

"Ronstrom!" Thorp calls once more.

I stop; I face him.

"Speak to them!" he cries out. "Speak to them."

I do not want to speak. I have nothing to say.

"Ronstrom, I ask you to speak to them!"

I cannot deny Thorp anything and I nod. I raise my hands and motion the people to come closer. And I say to them, "The sun will begin its backward course. Each day the sun will linger in the sky longer."

I stop and breathe deeply, sending smoke from my mouth in a wild rush. I look at the people. Their faces are all turned toward me. They are my people. Though I lead them, I am of them.

"The past is gone," I say. "We have come out of the forest together. Together we did what no other people could do. We fought and drove off those who came to destroy us. We have shelter and we have meat. None of us will give up his life spirit for want of meat. We have done all this because we have stayed together. We will build again what was destroyed. We will build so that no man will be able to pull down what we raise. This place is our home. We will build again——".

The people cry out, "Ronstrom! Ronstrom! Ronstrom!"

I look at Thorp.

He nods and smiles.

I turn and walk back toward my shelter with the sound of my name being shouted over and over again by my people.

I shake my head. I do not understand them. They are so changeable. They shift even as the wind shifts. But they are my people and with them I will build again.

I, Ronstrom, the hunter, will build again. I will do it because it must be done. Because it binds my people together.

I stop and face them.

They are still shouting my name.

I smile and move my hands at them.

XL

We begin the work of building a new encampment when the snows melt. The battle with Pratt's people has left many scars on the land. The holes in which the uprights stood are now nothing more than wounds. The uprights and crosspieces are nearly burnt through.

It takes many days to clear away the rubble from the place where Gendy's bones lie buried. The earth must heal before we build again.

The crude shelters that withstood the winter storms are replaced with well-built huts. A portion of each day's kill is smoked and put aside for the days when the snow will fly.

Thorp has found that fire softens the spear- and arrowheads of weapons we took from the men we slew. It does the same to the blades of the long knives that some of the dead carried.

He says, "If the fire is made very hot the arrowhead will turn soft as clay. When it is that soft, I can change its shape by placing it on a rock and pounding it with another rock. When it cools, it stays in its new shape and is harder than any stone.

"If we had more of it," Thorp tells me as I watch him change a spearhead into the blade of a knife,

"I could make ax heads that could cut through the trunks of the trees that we will use for our structures."

I shrug. For the few spears, arrowheads, and long knives that we now have, many men died. I would not want to get more the same way.

Thorp holds the new blade up to me and says, "Strike a stone blade against it and the stone will break. Yes, Ronstrom, I could make many things if I had more of it." His eyes are filled with the glow of his thoughts.

The air turns warm. The green tips of the grass begin to push their way out of the earth. New leaves show on the trees.

Many people come out of the forest to our encampment. From men who lead them I discover that they, too, have suffered from Pratt's people. I am told that the men who wear horns, whose blood cry is *Odin!* have killed many and taken many more captive.

The few who escaped death and capture ask to be allowed to join my people.

I nod and say, "Become one with us. We will give you shelter. We will put meat into your bellies. We will protect you. But for all those things you must do our bidding."

They look questioningly at me.

"My people are here to build," I say, "and that is what you will do."

Some say without hesitation they will build with us.

Others shake their heads and ask if they may rest with us for a few days before going back into the forest.

To these I also answer, "Yes." And I tell them,

301

"We will also share our meat with you for as many days as you rest with us."

From all that I hear about Pratt's people I know they will come back. They are our enemies and we are their enemies. In the days to come we will fight them many times.

I do not know what we have that her people could want, though I am told by others that their purpose is to fight, to kill, and die for Odin.

Because I am sure they will come again, I do not let all the hunters leave the encampment. Enough of them remain with the people to defend the encampment from attack. At night large fires are kept burning. Various hunters keep watch while the people sleep.

The day comes when the sun is at its fullest and already begins to die. I bring my people together to watch the first light touch my marker. With the yellow light of the sun still glowing brightly on its tip, I tell my people, "Tomorrow I will go into the forest and mark the trees that we will use to build——"

They shout their approval.

Then I say, "We will build so that what we build will be left standing long after our days."

"Yes, Ronstrom," the people answer. "Yes, Ronstrom. We will build so that it stands long after our days."

They fall silent again and wait to hear me say more.

I cannot speak!

My head is suddenly filled with the vision of what happened to the structures we first built.

I see again how they were torn down.

I see how the uprights were uprooted from their holes.

I see how the crosspieces were torn from their notches.

I see the flames that chewed through the thick trunks of the trees that we used.

I gesture to my people, turn, and leave. The vision of burning wood is still in my head.

If it happened that way once, it could happen again. No matter how thick the trunk, fire can always chew it to ashes.

I stand at my hut and look.

If we build our structures of wood, they will not last after our days. They will become ashes before our eyes.

I shake my head and turn away from the forest.

The light of the sun is high above the edge of the earth. It touches the mountains where the Rock People live.

I glance back to where Gendy's bones are buried. Then I look at the mountains where the Rock People live.

"Stone," I whisper aloud. "Stone. . . ." The whisper becomes a shout. "We will build in stone! We will build in stone!"

My people hear me and come running.

"We will build in stone," I tell them.

They do not understand.

I point to the mountains. "There!" I shout. "It will come from there!"

Thorp is at my side. Behind us are several more men. We have traveled many days. Now we stand at the base of the mountains.

I look up at the living rock. At the top, where

the face is straight up, the grayish-brown stone touches the blue of the sky.

If I could, I would take my stone from those heights, from the place where the rock thrusts itself out of the body of the mountain. I would, if I could build with such rock, as giants might.

Such rock is not for men to use and my eyes crawl unwillingly down the side of the mountain. . . .

Thorp asks, "How Ronstrom—how will we do it?"

He has asked the same question over and over again. I answer, as always, "We will find the way to do it."

He leaves my side and goes to where the stone begins. "This is not wood!" he cries. "We cannot burn it down. Our axes will not chop it down!"

I nod.

"Then say how we will do it?" he challenges.

If I am to use stone to build I must answer him. I can no longer just say to him, *It will be done.* I somehow must tell him how it will be done.

My eyes rise to the heights, where the living rock is touched by the dying sun. Slowly I lower them until I see Thorp.

He is, even as I am, and those behind me are, in the shadow of the mountain. One arm is outstretched and pointing to me. The other arm is extended in back of him. Its hand is balled into a fist. Below the fist and scattered around him are several huge blocks of stone cast off by the living rock that towers high above us and touches the blue sky.

"Then say how we will do it, Ronstrom?" Thorp shouts again.

I bound forward. I move so swiftly that Thorp leaps out of my path.

"There," I say, pointing to the pieces of stone scattered around the two of us. "There is what we will use. The mountain has given us what we need. We will take those pieces and build with them."

Thorp says nothing. His red tongue moves over his lips. He walks among the pieces of stone. Silently he looks at each one.

I watch him.

Once in a while, he glances up at me.

The shadows deepen. Twilight comes.

Thorp leaves the stones.

The other men make camp. In the darkness of the night our fires burn brightly. We eat.

Thorp looks up at the dark mass of the mountain. His face is the color of the flames. Their light glows in his eyes.

"Our days," he said with a soft sigh, "are not enough to finish what we will start."

"We will build," I tell him.

"We will build," he answers.

I nod, stand, and go to where the stones lie at the base of the mountain. "I will raise you up," I whisper. "I will make more of you than you are. . . ."

The wind suddenly comes. Laughter ripples through the night.

I look toward the fires.

They burn low. Except for the two who keep vigil, the others are already asleep.

XLI

We leave the base of the mountain and return to our encampment.

To move the stones will be more difficult than it was to move the trees from the forest to where Gendy's bones lie buried.

Thorp and I speak about nothing else. . . .

He tells me, "When the snow flies we will be able to move a stone the way we moved the trunk of a tree. But we will need many men."

"And in the summer," I ask, "what will we do?"

"I do not know," he answers.

The days pass.

My people are anxious to begin the work of moving the stones. Few if any of them realize how hard they will work.

When the leaves begin to turn and the sun shortens its journey in the sky, several of my hunters fight a small band of Pratt's people. None of the hunters are killed, but some are wounded. One gives up his life spirit in the encampment.

To protect ourselves it is necessary for all of our young men to learn how to use the bow and arrow and spear.

Before the first snow flies, we are joined by

several more groups of people. From those who join us we gain men with various skills. Thorp knows how to make the best use of these men.

I wait until the day that the sun reaches its end and its beginning to stand before my people and say, "Tomorrow some of the men will start for the base of the mountain. They will begin the work of moving the great stones to our encampment."

A murmur of approval comes from the people. They have waited many, many days to hear what I have told them.

Then I say, "We are many. We are no longer a few. There are people from all parts of the forest in the encampment. We are a people, a people who holds sway over the forest and over the plain. And those who come to do us injury will themselves be injured, even to giving up their life spirit. Those who come from where the water stretches as far as a man can see will know the bite of our arrows and the death thrust of our spears."

The people shout loudly.

I point to the first light of the sun as it tips my marker with yellow and say, "That is where I will set the first stone. And where I stand, we will raise the first structure."

"We are a people!" someone shouts. "We are a great people!" The others pick up the cry and soon all of them are yelling, "We are a people—we are a great people!"

Between the base of the mountain and our encampment huts are built. To protect the men, hunters travel with them.

Soon everything is ready. We wait for the snow to come!

Each day the sky fills with clouds. We look up

at it. We sniff the air for the smell of snow, but it is not there.

Then one night the wind comes howling out of the place where the sun never travels. And with it flies the snow. It turns the plain white.

The people run from their huts. They shout and laugh as though they are children.

As soon as the snow stops Thorp, several hunters, and I make our way to the base of the mountain.

Thorp marks the way the first stone will be brought from the encampment.

When we reach the base of the mountain the white snow is red with blood. From the men who are alive, we are told that Pratt's people fell on the camp during the storm.

Those of our people who were killed are burned. The others are left to the wolves.

I send for more men from the encampment and at night I say to Thorp, "They will come again and again to kill. Even as we build, we will have to fight them." I shake my head. "It is strange that we bend our efforts to build and they use theirs to destroy. Why should we be one way and they another?"

"They do not have a Ronstrom," Thorp answers, looking straight at me.

What can I say to that?

It begins to snow again.

The men who come from our encampment take many days to reach the base of the mountain. When they are rested, Thorp ties one end of the harness to the stone. The men take their place at the other end.

Thorp looks at me.

I nod.

"Pull men!" he shouts. "Pull!"

The men strain against the harness. Others push at the stone. Suddenly it is wrenched free. It begins to move. Smoke rushes from the mouths of the men. Though it is cold, they are wet with sweat. They move a short distance and must stop to rest.

I go to Thorp and say, "A better way must be found to move the stone. It gathers snow before it, making its own hill. The men will have to cut through it."

His brow wrinkles and he answers, "The stone sinks low in the snow."

I cannot be angry at him, and I tell him in a softer voice, "I will send you more men."

Thorp nods.

I leave the base of the mountain and return to the encampment.

More men are sent to Thorp. At the end of each day, a runner comes to tell me how far the stone has been moved. It is never very far. On the days that the wind is too strong or the snow falls too heavily, the men are forced to take shelter. On such days the stone is not moved at all.

Once more I begin carving what I saw on the altar in the cave so very long ago. Even as I carve and set the pieces on a new board, I see there are differences between what I am doing and what I did. I do now know which way is right. At night when I stretch out on my skins, I wonder if I now remember more than I did before I have forgotten something that I once knew.

The snows melt.

The stone must remain where it is! Before we can move it again, we must have snow.

Strange people come to our encampment. Their leader tells me that their home is near the water that stretches as far as a man can see. They were driven from the place where they lived by the marauders.

I tell the leader that his people may stay in our encampment to rest or they may become one with us.

They agree to become one with us.

Many of them have weapons taken from the marauders, and Thorp soon discovers that few of the men are skilled in working the arrow- and spearheads which they call metal.

Season follows season.

The stone is dragged closer to the encampment. There are bloody fights between our hunters and bands of the marauders.

One day, when the snow is on the ground, Thorp comes to my hut and sits down on the other side of the fire pit. He holds his hands above the flames and says, "I have found a way to move the stone faster."

I nod.

Using his hands, he shows me and explains, "The stone rests on a flat bed of logs and the front of the logs are cut to move on top of the snow. One of the men who lived near the water that stretches as far as a man can see told me the marauders move heavy things over the snow in the same way."

Before the snow melts Thorp brings the first stone into the encampment.

When my people see it they shout to one another, "The stone is here! The stone is here! The stone has come that will mark the light of the sun when it is at it send and its beginning!"

They drag the stone through the encampment to where I first marked the light of the sun.

When the snow melts and the earth is still soft, a deep hole is dug though not so deep as to crush

Pratt's bones. To set the stone we push logs under one end. As one end is slowly raised, the other begins to slip into the hole. When the bottom of the stone rests against the earth, lines are secured around its middle. These lines are pulled taut. The stone slowly becomes upright. As soon as it stands upright, rocks are put into the hole; then it is filled with earth. More rocks are set around the stone's base to hold it in place.

When the work is done, the people look at the stone and then at me. Over and over again they shout my name.

"It is you have done this," I tell them. My words only make them shout all the more.

I look at Thorp.

He smiles.

Through the summer several of the arrow makers chip at the stone to make it smoother than it is.

I myself shape the top to resemble a woman's slit. This is not something I do without having thought about it. And even as I use a stone tool to cut the shape into the rock I look up at the sky.

The sun is hanging low over the trees. Soon its journey for the day will be done. Darkness will come. But now there are high clouds yellow in the dying sun.

I look at them and remember Pratt's long yellow hair. I touch the stone cut and remember the soft warmth of her slit. A sudden rush of heat fills my body. My throat aches again and I silently call her name.

The snows come even before the leaves are off the trees. Thorp takes his men to the base of the mountain where they begin to move one of the stones for the structure. But they return to the encampment before the sun reaches its end and its beginning.

On the day when the first light of the sun will touch the new marker all my people are gathered before me. They wait.

As the sky loses its blackness and the flickering lights in it fade, I move to where the stone stands.

When the first light of the sun pours yellow over the top of the stone, I say, "This is a woman . . . her slit is carved into the top of the rock. The sun is a man. Its light is a manthing. It enters the woman here——" And I touch the stone. "It will enter the woman again when it is at its fullest and begins to die."

From the looks on their faces, I know the people do not understand what I am telling them. I am not sure that I understand, either. I have been thinking about speaking these words ever since I buried Pratt's bones. . . .

"The sun," I tell them, "is The Giver of Life." I do not know if this is so, but I know they will understand it. "The earth is his woman." That, too, they will understand.

The light has passed off the stone.

I have nothing more to tell my people. I leave the base of the stone and walk back to my hut.

That night Thorp comes and asks, "Why did you tell the people that the sun is a man and the earth a woman?"

"I have been thinking about it for many, many days," I answer.

"The people talk about nothing else.

I shrug.

"They do not understand——"

"Nor do I," I tell Thorp, "but the words I spoke

were in my head. I did not mean to upset the people."

Thorp shakes his head and with a sigh says, "Ronstrom . . . Ronstrom . . . Ronstrom."

I look at him questioningly.

He says nothing more and leaves my hut.

When we begin to move the other pieces of stone from the base of the mountain, more winters have passed than I have fingers on one hand.

By the following summer one of the men tells Thorp that we can roll the stone over a bed of logs.

Thorp has his doubts, but tries it. He finds that the stone can be moved that way.

We no longer have to wait until the snow covers the earth to move the stones from the base of the mountain to the encampment.

To raise each stone upright takes many, many days. But on the day the snow flies the two are standing.

Thorp and his men begin to move the last stone from the base of the mountain that will complete the first structure. Though we can move it winter and summer, the work is often stopped by attacking marauders.

These blond men, who wear horns on their heads and cry "Odin!" when they fight, are without fear. There are many of them and seldom do many days pass without my hunters having met one of their bands. More of our men then theirs have given up their life spirits.

The last stone is finally brought into the encampment. It comes before the snows start.

To place it on top of the two uprights Thorp begins the long hard work of raising it to the height of the two uprights. Melted bear fat is rubbed over the top of the uprights and the logs closest to them. Some of the men push against the stone while others guide its movement. It is slow, difficult work. The stone begins to edge on to the two uprights. Then suddenly they begin to tilt.

Thorp stops the work and looks at the two uprights. "I think," he says, "they will back into place once the crosspiece is on them."

I nod.

Thorp tells his men to begin pushing again.

More and more of the stone slides on to the two uprights. When almost all of it lies across the tops, they begin to shift in the other direction. The crosspiece begins to shift. Those who are watching gasp.

"Lines!" Thorp shouts. "Get lines around it!"

Men scramble over it and lines are secured.

"Pull!" Thorp barks.

To stop the huge stone from slipping, the men pull the lines taut.

The movement is halted, and slowly the stone is eased back until it rests securely on the uprights.

The first structure is raised. It frames the marker that stands over Pratt's grave.

The people gather and look at what they have done. They are very quiet.

I look at Thorp and say, "This will stand long after our days."

"Yes," he answers. "It will stand that long!"

XLII

The wind howls. The leaves are gone. Dawn has not yet come. In the cold gray light of a new day, I look at the dark shape of the stone structure.

How many more will I see standing before my days end?

My eyes move toward the stone marker. I hunger for Pratt as I once hungered for food.

The sky becomes smeared with red and then turns gray. It will soon snow. The scent is in the air. I turn——

"Odin!"

The quiet of the encampment is ripped apart by that sudden cry. The marauders are on us. They come with the sudden swiftness of a kestrel dropping from the sky to sink its talons into the flesh of its prey.

I dart into my hut and grab the long knife.

The fight with marauders is very close. Spears are hurled.

The marauders fire some of the huts. Black smoke grows toward the gray clouds.

I slash and hack at the whirling, twisting bodies. Blood drips from my blade. Blood stains my hands and wets my beard.

Death is a storm that sweeps men, women, and children before its terrible wind. But my people do not run. They stand and fight!

The marauders give way. They try to burn our structure, but cannot. They fall back. We follow hard on their heels.

Suddenly I am face to face with one of them. His eyes are blue. His beard is blond.

Our long knives crash against each other. And each stays the other's blow.

I slash at him. The blade misses its mark.

His cut is true!

My hand drops to the ground. My fingers are still clenched to the hilt of the long knife. Blood gushes from the stump. I look down at my hand. The fingers open.

The man roars with laughter. He lunges at me.

I cannot move. I am still looking at my hand.

His blade opens my belly!

I stagger and drop to my knees.

I fight to keep my life spirit with me a while longer.

I look into the distance. I see deep into the days to come. A man from my people will drive the marauders from the plain and from the forest. I can see that.

And I can hear The Giver of Life call to me. That voice is my own. That voice comes from inside of me!

I am The Giver of Life and He is me. Neither of us is complete without the other.

"You are Ronstrom the builder," He tells me.

And I answer, "Yes, I am Ronstrom the builder. . . ."

"Ronstrom the builder," his voice calls.

"Ronstrom the builder," I answer.

The sound of my name is like the crash of summer thunder. I hear it over and over again in my skull: "Ronstrom the builder . . . Ronstrom the builder . . . Ronstrom the builder."

Even as I see Thorp bending over me, I free my life spirit. . . .

THE BIG BESTSELLERS
ARE AVON BOOKS!

I'm OK—You're OK
Thomas A. Harris, M.D.   14662 $1.95

Jonathan Livingston Seagull
Richard Bach   14316 $1.50

Open Marriage
Nena O'Neill and George
O'Neill   14084 $1.95

Don't Embarrass the Bureau
Bernard F. Conners   14852 $1.50

The Ancient of Days
Irving A. Greenfield   14860 $1.60

Ringolevio
Emmett Grogan   14449 $1.50

The Barracudas
Keefe Brasselle   14639 $1.50

Net Net
Isadore Barmash   14621 $1.50

The Stewardess
Julia Percivall   14456 $1.50

The Fatal Friendship
Stanley Loomis   14118 $1.50

Moorhaven
Daoma Winston   14126 $1.50

The Call
Oral Roberts   W364 $1.25

A Raging Talent
Jack Hoffenberg   14027 $1.50

The Flame And The Flower
Kathleen E. Woodiwiss   J122 $1.50

Where better paperbacks are sold, or directly from the publisher, include 15¢ per copy for mailing; allow three weeks for delivery.

Avon Books, Mail Order Dept.
250 West 55th Street, New York, N. Y. 10019

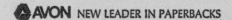